Relics of Life

DOROTHEA ANNA

Philotimo Press

Philotimo Press

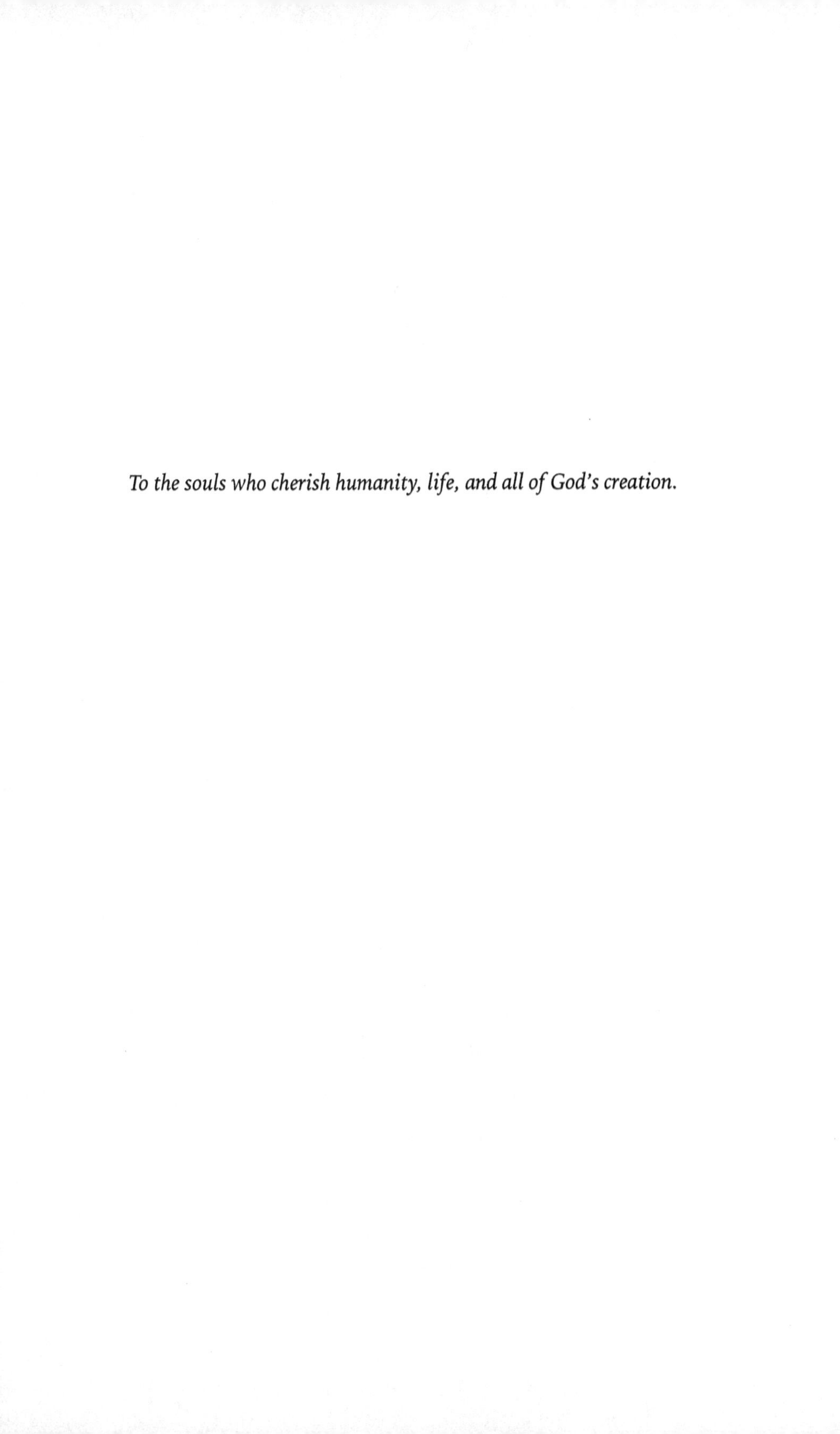

To the souls who cherish humanity, life, and all of God's creation.

One

APRIL 1935, RUSSIA

Alexei folded the wrinkled sheet around a small wooden box. Beside him, his elder lay reposed in a pine coffin he'd made per the priest's request. His heart burned and broke at the same time. Elder Dimitri had known when he would depart his earthly life. Alexei had bent close to the elder's twitching mouth when he'd whispered a prayer for his salvation before exhaling his final breath.

A hand touched Alexei's shoulder. He turned toward his fellow monk, Mikhail, who wore a grave expression. "Lock up the paper and the relic quickly. I saw the NKVD entering the monastery's main gate."

His brother scurried up the stairs.

Alexei hurried out of the chapel basement. Towering, snow-covered mountains flanked the sloping valley where the monastery's chapel stood. He ran down the weathered, dirt path toward the main building. Passing through the entrance, he raced down the small staircase to the library, the faint smell of dust and old parchment welcoming him. How he loved the place. He'd read nearly three-quarters of the tomes on the ancient wood shelves. Would it survive with the secret police's presence?

He rushed past the shelves and stopped in front of a large icon of Christ on the wall directly in front of him. Slipping the sheet-covered box into his cassock pocket, he removed the icon from its hook, revealing a twelve-by-twelve metal safe. He gripped the dial and concentrated on the combination. Lifting the latch, he opened the three-inch-thick door and set the paper and box in the alcove that held a container with Saint Innocent's relics and a mosaic of the Holy Trinity.

Screams outside the monastery shattered the silence surrounding Alexei. Dread threaded through his trembling body. Regaining his composure, he slammed the vault door shut, spun the dial, and picked up the icon.

Footsteps clattered down the stairs.

He fumbled for the icon, scraping it twice against the wall before it connected with the nail and hung off-balance.

Glancing behind him, his breath escalated and his body tensed. Two NKVD officers stood at the bottom of the steps with guns pointed at him.

"Let's go," one of them said with a sharp jerk of his head toward the door.

Alexei clasped his shaking hands together, hoping to quell the trembling and appear calm, praying to God repeatedly. *Lord, have mercy, Lord, have mercy, Lord, have mercy.* As he shuffled up the steps with the uniformed NKVD behind him, he spotted his brothers gathered at the fountain in the center of the monastery grounds. A dozen secret police stood in a line with guns aimed at them. He didn't dare look back. Everything would end up burned to ashes if he did.

Alexei joined his fellow monks. Closing his eyes, he focused all his mind and heart on God as he awaited the darkness before the Light.

~

PRESENT DAY, RUSSIA

Sergius worked alongside his fellow monks, stacking the library's ancient leather-bound and cloth-covered books onto four tables. A few of his brothers were putting together new bookshelves. The humming of table saws and the thump of stones hitting the earth echoed down the dilapidated staircase. The glare of the gray skies streamed down in a foggy shaft through the arched doorway to the library.

Sergius set down a book and strode to one of the monks hammering on a shelf. He touched the brother's shoulder. "I'm going to check on the progress above."

The monk grunted and returned to his work.

Sergius glanced at the bare wall across from him and frowned at the tarnished vault with its dented door cracked open, veiled in glistening cobwebs. Father Ilya, his spiritual father, had told him months ago that the precious religious items had been removed sometime after the Great Reign of Terror, never to be seen or heard of until the fall of the Soviet Union.

He ascended the stairs and walked across the dirt and concrete ground. Big blocks of stones littered the space. Black ash still covered most of the earth, remnants of the Monastery of Saint Innocent. Monks and laypeople wearing construction hats steered their bulldozers and shoveled out the charred debris in preparation for rebuilding the ancient monastery.

A forest encircled the area, veiling the holy place from the outer world. Sergius breathed in the fresh spring air, then nodded with his mouth in a firm line. That holy realm would settle there again when the monastery was rebuilt.

He walked over to the small cemetery with a huge cross in the center and stopped in front of Saint Dimitri's tomb. He'd learned from the bishop that the saint's grave had been unearthed during the last year of Stalin's reign, and portions of his uncorrupt body and clothes had been stolen. The few bones that remained in the plot had been reburied several years later.

He bent and touched the gravestone. That prophetic page from the vault belonged with Saint Dimitri.

The bishop, Father Ilya, and other clergy had discussed the safe before starting the rebuilding project. They'd reported it had contained a tiny, silver-plated bin of Saint Innocent's relics, a mosaic icon, a small wooden box with a piece of the original, true Cross of Christ, and a prophetic letter written by Saint Dimitri a year before his death.

Thank God Saint Innocent's relics and the mosaic icon had been found a few years later, nestled in another unmolested monastery in Voronezh. Such precious objects must be returned to share their blessings with the resident monks and visiting pilgrims.

The buzzing saws and creaking construction equipment fell silent. His Eminence, Nicolai, along with a deacon, their black robes swaying, approached the group of monks and Father Ilya standing by a partial stone wall. Sergius hurried over to them and stood next to his fellow monk, Father Herman. He bowed his head as the bishop and his deacon halted in front of them.

"Your Eminence," said Father Ilya.

Bishop Nicolai, holding his staff, nodded. "Good afternoon, Father." He observed the area. "You are making remarkable progress, working efficiently."

Father Ilya crossed himself and cupped his hands for the bishop to place his right hand. The priest kissed it. "Yes, Your Eminence. We are pleased with the work we've done thus far."

The bishop gestured toward his deacon, and the man slid his hand in his ebony robe, then pulled out a folded letter. His Eminence tipped his head for the deacon to proceed with opening the letter.

"We're close to discovering the location of the Cross of Christ relic and Saint Dimitri's letter."

Sergius raised his gaze to the pewter sky. *Glory to God!*

"Deacon Vasily, that is encouraging news." Father Ilya smiled.

"Yes," the deacon said. "In 1978, they were smuggled out of Russia and taken to the United States."

Sergius gaped. The relics had been moved to his home country. But where in America?

Father Ilya rubbed his bearded chin. "What has happened to them since then?"

"Reliable sources from Moscow's Patriarchate have stated that a small hermitage of Saint Andrew in California was the last place any of these holy objects were housed. Unfortunately, the abbot of Saint Andrew's reported last week that they were no longer in their possession but had been moved to Holy Trinity Monastery in Virginia, on the eastern coast of America."

"Virginia then?" Father Ilya asked.

"It appears so," the deacon replied.

"We must have them returned to this monastery," Father Ilya said. "Our monastery's treasured small piece of the Cross of Christ has healed many who have been ill. Both the Cross and Saint Dimitri's writings are vital to our parishes and fellow clergy, giving them strength and preparation for difficult events ahead."

The bishop twisted the bottom of his staff into the dirt. "Of course, Father. We are well aware of the urgency to retrieve our holy relics." He scanned the monks flanking Father Ilya. Sergius sucked in a breath as the bishop's eyes locked on his. "Although travel to America is a challenge due to the tensions between our two countries, God provides. We'll send a few monks to America to inquire about and collect the missing treasures."

Father Ilya turned toward Sergius and touched his arm. "Since we have two monks here from the United States, we will send them." He waved a hand in presentation toward Sergius and Herman. "Brothers Sergius and Herman." He held up his right hand in a blessing. "God be with you and keep you safe on your journey to America."

Struggling to remain stoic, Sergius stuck his fists into his cassock pockets and stayed the shaking of his body. "Thank you, Father, for this blessing to serve you and the bishop." He kissed Father Ilya's right hand, then straightened. "We'll find the Holy Cross and Saint Dimitri's writings and bring them back here where they belong." He shared a smile with Father Herman. "God has chosen us and is counting on us to return the miraculous relics."

Father Herman beamed. "Glory to God!"

Two

VIRGINIA, USA, PRESENT DAY

Stephanie placed a handful of peonies beside her father's tombstone jutting out of the soft, emerald grass. She wiped the tears from her cheeks. Her eighteen-year-old son, Jake, stood beside her, his hands clasped, head bowed.

A misty rain fell like a gentle shower as the warm April sun shed filtered light through the trees peppering National Imperial Cemetery—the weather suitable for the second anniversary of her father's death.

Stephanie breathed in the strong aroma of the pungent earth and vegetation permeating the air, a testimony to palpable life enduring around her, giving her a bit of solace. Rumbling distant car motors from the streets below the hilly cemetery drifted through the veil of drizzle to where they were, disturbing her peace.

"Two years already." She hugged herself.

"Feels longer." Jake folded his arms and frowned. "I miss talking to him."

Jake had only been two when Stephanie and her husband divorced. He'd run off with his mistress before she'd filed, never to be heard from since. She'd married too young at nineteen, naive and gullible. She sighed. Although she regretted her premature marriage, she'd never regret giving birth to and raising Jake. He was the most important person in her life.

Stephanie rubbed Jake's back. "I know how hard it was when Granddad died."

Jake lifted his stubbled chin, his gaze straight ahead. "Gran still thinks his death wasn't an accident."

Her body tensed. The memory of her mother fighting with the police over her father's death came back to her, and she slouched from the heaviness in her heart. Her mother's efforts had been fruitless, and it hurt too much to deal with today. "This isn't the time for that, Jake."

He turned to face her, his eyes misty. "When will it be?"

She shook her head, then focused on her father's grave. He had been a truly loving and supportive father to her and grandfather to Jake. He'd died too soon.

If only…

Stephanie sucked in her breath then blew it out. *Don't go there.*

Jake squatted in front of the tomb marker and laid a hand on the arched top. He'd been unmoored the past two years without his loving granddad.

She closed her eyes and sniffled. "He was the best man I ever knew."

A collective rumbling of noisy voices broke their silence. To their right, a group of around ten college-aged people marched across the wet, lumpy ground. Some of them held cans of spray paint while others held up their fists. They stopped no more than twenty feet away from Stephanie and Jake and stood in front of a few headstones. One of the larger men spray-painted a grave with the ugly words *Useful Idiots!* and *Murderers!*

Stephanie rose before Jake.

"No more wars!" they yelled in disjointed unison.

The man who'd sprayed the gravestone stomped over to Stephanie and her son. Fear ran through her like ice water as the man stared her down. His fellow rioters stood behind him with curled lips in disgust.

"You military?" the man said, his face hard as granite. He wore a wrinkled shirt and jeans, and his shoulder-length brown hair was as straggly as his beard.

Stephanie kept her gaze on her father's grave, wringing her hands and casting quick glances at her son. "No—"

Jake hissed a laugh with his hands on his hips. "Military? Are you for real?"

The man stepped closer to Jake. He towered over him with his beefy build, glaring eyes on his. Jake didn't as much as twitch. The mistaken belief youth had in invincibility.

"Yeah, we're for real." The man yanked on Jake's T-shirt, nearly lifting him off the ground. "So are these never-ending wars for profit."

Stephanie's heartbeat pounded in her ears, and she reached for her son. "Please—"

Jake folded his arms across his chest and jammed his hands under his armpits, pulling down and away from the man's hold on him. "You got that right."

The big man's stare lingered on Stephanie's obstinate son for a long minute before letting out a grunt and moving past them. The rest of the group followed as they kicked tombstones and spray-painted more of them, all the while continuing their angry, clamorous chants.

Stephanie let out a shaky sigh. "Thank God that's over." She laid a hand on her son's shoulder, squeezing it when she really wanted to shake it. "You've got to be more careful. People are crazy these days. You never know what they'll do."

"I didn't see any guns on them," Jake said.

"It doesn't mean they weren't carrying any. We were lucky this time."

Jake turned toward the bunch heading out of the cemetery. "It was all about destroying shit. Nothing new."

Stephanie glanced at the protestors before they disappeared over the hill. "*This time*, Jake. Random shootings aren't new either. Don't forget that."

She bent in front of her father's grave. "It's gotten so bad here, Dad. A part of me wishes you were still with us, but the other part thinks you're better off where you are."

Jake's hand gently gripped her arm. "Come on, Mom. Granddad can hear you at home too."

She nodded, then rose from the ground and locked elbows with Jake. Without looking behind her, she raised an arm in a farewell to her father. *Until next time, Daddy.*

ON THEIR DRIVE HOME, BOTH STEPHANIE'S AND JAKE'S phones shrilled annoying text alerts.

Stephanie glanced at her son as he pulled out his phone from his shirt pocket. "What is it this time?"

"Our corrupt clown president is gonna give another lame speech at seven tonight, courtesy of the shitty state TV channels."

Stephanie pursed her lips but didn't respond. She didn't disagree with her son's assessment of their president and the media. However, she worried what would come out of the president's mouth tonight. Too many terrible events had happened in the past couple of years. Their known way of life was changing before their eyes, with new laws, an economic depression, and continued bouts of war in the Middle East and constant threats from other powerful nations.

She wasn't sold on the latter being announced every hour, every day on the chaotic social media and news networks out there. Lust for power and greed were at the heart of her own country's decisions and moves about the globe. She was far from the only citizen who thought that. But their awareness didn't change the trajectory of the country's path.

They drove past boarded-up shops. Homeless people crowded the town's streets, lying in heaps on the concrete, the storefronts as their headboards.

A rectangular-shaped robot rolled out of one of the local supermarkets, its red eyes blinking like a broken taillight. It locked onto carts in their return metal slots and pulled them toward the supermarket entrance. Several soda cans, paper cups, and other garbage sprinkled the parking lot. If only the robot would pick up the litter instead of pushing carts. Nobody seemed to care about the growing mounds of trash on the streets, lots, and sidewalks.

They drove past the police department, where clusters of people were clashing with cops in riot gear. Colorful signs shot up from the throngs of people, with messages about police brutality and jobs for the ninety-nine percent.

As the hordes grew, the angry, jumbled voices echoed against the buildings sandwiching the road. Stephanie pressed harder on the accelerator, clipping ahead and out of the city.

"Bet Gran was there," Jake said, his head turned toward the commotion behind them.

Stephanie looked in the rearview mirror. Tanks and other armored vehicles rolled down the road in the opposite direction from their car, shooting off water cannons. People zigzagged across the streets and scrambled through open store doors.

She drove two more miles into their run-down neighborhood of older homes, the various scenes from the town barely registering in her mind or heart. Had she lost her ability to feel? She shook off the disturbing thought. Visiting her father's grave had done enough to her emotional state that morning.

Parking her silver sedan in their one-car garage, Stephanie cut the ignition and let out a sigh. Jake's comments finally came back to her. "Yes. Your grandmother was probably there."

Jake raised his hands, palms up. "Why didn't we stop and look for her?"

Stephanie opened her door. "Gran is doing her thing. We were doing ours."

Jake left the vehicle and looked at her across the hood. "Still. We could've helped."

"Not today, Jake."

Stephanie's body felt as if it weighed five hundred pounds. She dragged herself into the kitchen and set down her purse on the counter. Leaning her elbows on its surface, she cradled her head in her hands.

Their black mini schnauzer, Hobo, barked and bounced toward her. His body bumped against her legs, his tongue licking one of her shins. She bent and stroked his head and back while he smiled up at her with loving, chocolate-brown eyes.

"I've gotta check my channel," Jake muttered and ran up the stairs to his room.

The dog took off after him.

Sunday afternoons around her neighborhood were a mixture of dead silence with a haunting invisible presence of other humans tucked away in their homes. But she welcomed the quiet today, giving her space for the memories.

She crossed into the living room to her dad's plaid recliner. Running a hand over it, she could almost see him sitting there watching reruns of *Columbo*, his favorite old-time detective show. Her mother's reading glasses lay neatly on the end table between the recliner and the winged-back maroon chair draped with a multicolored afghan. A book about civil disobedience sat next to the lamp on the end table.

Coasters with two mugs from the morning rested on the coffee table. The missing third coffee cup hit her harder than yesterday. Her dad's favorite forty-inch TV screen hung on the wall above the gas fireplace. A sliding glass door, equipped with a doggie door, displayed the small patio and patch of grass in the backyard with a vegetable garden and a few blooming pots of geraniums.

She was grateful her father had left her mother financially secure because of his military and mail service retirement pensions that still existed then. After her divorce, she and Jake had moved in with her parents. With the current economic situation, she was grateful to be living with her mother for mutual comfort and to combine their wages for better survival. Her mother worked part-time at Jake's high school cafeteria, while Stephanie worked at Abby's Café.

Thank God her parents' home had been paid off ten years ago when the economy was better. Property was virtually impossible to own nowadays. They were numbered with the few families still in the middle class, made possible through living together. Stephanie believed the country was primarily populated by serfs in a world ruled by a small handful of lords.

She walked back to the kitchen and filled a glass with filtered water from the fridge. Dropping into one of the kitchen chairs, she took a sip, then opened her laptop, checking her email. Nothing important. She scanned Convo Central and found endless bickering between her friends over the state of their country before she clicked on WeVideo to search for any news stories that gave a clue about what the president would be saying tonight. No hints were given, but she figured it had something to do with the perpetual crummy economy, increasing violence, and wars.

Hobo came bounding down the stairs, barking just as the kitchen door opened. Her mother, Ava, entered the room, her shirt, pants, and disheveled salt-and-pepper braided hair damp.

Hobo greeted Ava with kisses and bounces. Her mother petted the dog's head.

Stephanie's eyes widened. "Did you get blasted with the water cannons?"

"Yep. But that didn't stop us. We got out our message before they started their tyrannical rubber bullets." Her mother put her hands on her hips.

Stephanie froze. "Rubber bullets?" She scanned her mother's body. "Were you hurt?"

"No. I didn't get hit." Her mother grabbed several paper towels in one hand and filled a glass with water from the fridge in the other. She then sat across from her.

Stephanie breathed a sigh of relief. "Thank God."

"Something's got to change," Ava said. "People can't last with dwindling jobs and living in this police state."

Stephanie closed her computer. "The president's supposed to speak tonight. Maybe he'll have something pos—"

"Don't count on it, honey." Ava used a paper towel to dab wet spots on her shirt. "Things aren't looking up." She shook her head. "There was another shooting before we drove home."

Stephanie pressed a hand to her chest, her heartbeat thudding. "Where?"

"Outside the cemetery."

"Oh my God." She swallowed. "Jake and I just came from there."

Ava grabbed her hand. "I thought you weren't going until later."

She shook her head. "This year, we decided to go earlier."

"That turned out to be a good idea."

"But we did run into a mob spray-painting graves."

Her mother squeezed her hand. "You and Jake are okay, aren't you?"

"Yes." Stephanie looked toward the stairs to the second floor. "But you know how Jake is. He snapped back at the group, but other than one of them grabbing his shirt, we were left alone."

Ava whistled. "Ah, to be young again. Thinking you can conquer the world."

Stephanie chuckled.

"Back when we could make a difference and change the world for the better," Ava muttered into her glass before taking a sip.

Stephanie's heart sank. Life was so different from her parents' world when they were growing up and even from the time she herself was a child. The invention of the internet, social media, twenty-four-seven news cycles, smartphones, smart homes, smart cars—all of it—had sped up time and events at a head-spinning rate. Nobody could think clearly anymore, living on a never-ending merry-go-around with no way to get off. Harrowing increases in disrespect toward others and disregard for life of any kind had spread like a disease over the world. It was so prevalent she could taste the bitterness of it everywhere she went.

"Tomorrow after work," Ava said, "I'm back at it. This time the gals and I will be passing out food for the homeless on Perry Street before we do our usual antiwar protesting." She pursed her lips. "They keep this up, we'll be in World War III."

Stephanie froze. "I hope not."

"Me too." Ava took a sip of water and gave Stephanie a sober stare. "The weapons are much more advanced since the last World War."

Hobo jumped onto Stephanie's lap, and she stroked him, trying to forget what her mother had said. She brought the conversation back to tomorrow's activities. "Jake and I'll be there to help hand out the food."

"Good. The more support the better." Ava left her seat and hugged Stephanie. "How are you holding up on Dad's anniversary?"

Stephanie patted her mother's back. "I'm doing the best I can."

"Me too, hon." Ava touched Stephanie's cheek. "He never should've died then. It wasn't—"

"Please, Mom. I just can't right now."

Ava ran a hand over Stephanie's hair and sighed. "It's not easy for any of us."

Stephanie could only nod as tears welled in her eyes.

"But he's never far from us." Ava kissed the top of her head like she used to do when Stephanie was a child. She moved to the living room, picked up the paperback, and sat on the wing-backed chair.

In a few hours, the president would speak about the state of the country. Stephanie couldn't imagine any of what he'd say would be encouraging.

Three

In the living room, Stephanie settled into her father's chair near her mother and turned on the TV. Hobo hopped onto Stephanie's lap and nestled into a ball. She rubbed his soft ears, just as the screen displayed the president coming into the press room.

Jake sauntered into the den with a soda and scowled at the TV. "He's probably gonna say the same shit again. No jobs and boatloads of wars." Popping the top on the can, he lifted it in a toast. "Here's to our worthless government."

Ava picked up her knitting needles and skein of yarn. "My smart grandson. Always on the ball."

Stephanie nodded. "I'm a proud mama."

Ava pointed the blunt end of one of her knitting needles toward her chest and grinned. "Proud grandma here."

Stephanie focused on President Harden approaching the podium. The constant clicking of press camera shutters echoed through the conference room.

"It's showtime." Jake set his soda on the coffee table, then flopped on the couch, leaning his head against the fat armrest.

"My fellow Americans," the president said. "My heart is heavy this evening." He grimaced, and his gaze traveled a few feet to the right.

"The shooting at the National Imperial Cemetery has now claimed twenty lives, including three children. This is the second mass shooting this week. The last one at the Flamingo Theater resulted in fifty-two lives lost."

Stephanie covered her mouth. *We could've been one of those twenty.* No matter how many times these horrific stories were reported, she never got used to the shocking reality of it or the loss of lives. She crossed herself.

The president's attention slid slightly to the left. "Because of these perpetual tragic events, we must take stricter measures for our safety."

Stephanie tensed, both hands on Hobo. Ava leaned forward in her chair, and Jake sat up.

"Starting tomorrow morning, we'll be implementing a new gun regulation." He paused, then raised his steely gaze to the camera. "In collaboration with the nation's city governments, we've created a voluntary gun-buy-back plan."

Murmurs floated through the press room.

"Yeah, right, prez. Like that's gonna work." Jake rolled his eyes and played with the tab on his soda can.

Ava huffed and looked at Stephanic. "Your father would be screaming bloody murder over this if he were still alive. The fact that it's voluntary right now doesn't mean it won't be mandatory later."

"Can they do that? Buy back all the guns?" Stephanie asked. "Not that I'm for all those military-style assault weapons out there, but this may border on violating Second Amendment rights."

"If it becomes mandatory, yes. But really, when has our loss of liberties bothered our government in the past fifty or so years?" Ava's face colored in irritation.

"I don't know and don't care," Jake said, folding his arms across his chest. He jutted his chin toward Stephanie. "And why should you, Mom? We aren't gonna give up Granddad's guns."

"That's not the point," Stephanie said. "It seems like a slippery slope."

"You know how I feel about guns." Ava wiggled her hand side to side in the familiar so-so gesture.

Jake took a swig of his soda, then set it down. "This isn't gonna turn into some type of civil war, is it?"

Stephanie opened her mouth to answer but shut it as the president held up a hand on the screen.

"In the Middle East, we continue to aid our allies in fighting the Al Ichbar terrorist group that's spread throughout Syria and Lebanon," the president said. "We're on standby to help with humanitarian supplies for both Greece and Turkey. Their heated conflicts have spilled over into the waters of the Aegean. We continue to send arms to Lithuania in its fight against Russia. And of course, we are monitoring China's ships." Harden narrowed his eyes. "We are on high alert and will respond if they move in closer to our positions in the South China Sea."

Ava grumbled, "Why are our ships off the coast of China?"

A chill slid down Stephanie's spine. "I hope those conflicts don't turn into a world war."

Ava set her knitting aside. "Heaven forbid." She crossed herself.

"Yeah, but when haven't there been wars?" Jake asked. He took another drink of his soda. "Ever since I was a little kid, I've heard the same shit about our troops in a bunch of countries."

"Well, there was a time when we weren't permanently over there." Stephanie glanced at Ava. "Mom's generation." She pursed her lips and eyed the TV. "And he's talking about going against two nuclear powers. Something he and previous presidents haven't toyed with before. It's dangerous and stupid."

The president held out his arms in a gesture of bringing people together. "My fellow Americans, we are fighting for the freedom and democracy of Lithuania and for all countries. In a time of war, solidarity is a must."

"So he admits we're really at war." Her mother picked up her knitting needles again. "A proxy war, grant you, but there's no guarantee that won't change into a full-scale world war."

President Harden cleared his throat, bringing Stephanie's attention back to the TV. "Chinese cyberattacks continue to be a security threat. Today two million accounts at Bank of the US have been hacked."

"Nothing's protected anymore," Ava said, her needles clicking together as she knitted.

"This is the fourth time in, like, the past month this type of shit's happened," Jake said.

Stephanie sighed. "If it isn't the banks, it's the online stores."

"Our cyberattack task force is working on preventing these attacks from continuing," the president said. "This will be a full community effort that will take a little sacrifice from everyone to keep us all safe and secure. We will keep you informed when we have unfolded our new program."

Another round of whispers and grumblings filled the room.

"That doesn't sound good," Stephanie mumbled as she stroked Hobo's head.

President Harden wrapped up his announcement with the usual ridiculous statements about being a good American and may God bless America.

Stephanie gritted her teeth. "I'm sick of hearing *God bless America* from politicians. Why would God bless a country that constantly instigates wars, topples other countries' leaders, and invades foreign lands for their resources? And at the same time does nothing for its own citizens. Greed has never been a virtue."

Her son shot up from the couch. "What's he really saying about those cyberattacks? Is he gonna shut down my channel? Social media?"

"You and your friends play video games in real time on your channel. You're not a threat," Stephanie said.

"Censoring our voices isn't anything new even though it goes against what this country has always stood for," Ava said. "They've been doing it little by lit—"

"Are they gonna throw us in jail if we say something against these shitty wars?" Jake asked.

"I wouldn't put it past them," Ava said. "Our government doesn't like antiwar activists. Never has."

Stephanie bit her lip. "I hope it doesn't get worse."

"It sure doesn't look like it's getting better," her mother said. "It's easy to get tossed in jail without any real cause these days." Ava's knitting needles clattered. "My experiences are proof of that. And I'd do it all again. Screw those tyrannical monsters."

Stephanie's heartbeat escalated. She clutched the chair's armrests. "Mom, you aren't still going out tomorrow to protest the wars, are you?"

"Of course I am. They're not going to stop me."

She swallowed hard. "But, Mom, things have reached dangerous levels now."

Her mother locked eyes with hers. "Giving in to tyranny only leads to more tyranny. No change happens that way."

"I'll go with you tomorrow, Gran. I'm not scared," Jake said, leaning forward, his elbows on his knees, his hands fists.

Stephanie's maternal instincts kicked in. "Jake, I know you're technically an adult now, but please stay home. You too, Mom."

"Nope," Ava said. "I've never backed down from what I believe in, and I'm not starting now."

"That's right." Jake pointed at Ava. "See, Mom? Gran rocks."

Ava chuckled, but Stephanie didn't. What if the government went off the rails and shut down the cell phone carriers and the internet in some way? How would her family and friends communicate?

Hold on. She rolled her eyes. Jake's panic over the Chinese cyberattacks had made her paranoid.

A knock came at their front door. Hobo sprang off her lap, trotting toward the noise, barking incessantly. Jake answered it. Stephanie's friend and neighbor Pam strode into the den, her face flushed. She glanced up at the TV screen and pointed toward it.

"Did you watch the president's speech?"

"Yes, we did," Stephanie said.

Pam chewed on her fingernail while planting herself on the couch. "He said a lot of crazy things, you know? I'm scared."

"It's expected." Ava took a sip of hot tea from her cup on the end table. "All of this was coming. The writing was on the wall years ago."

Hobo sniffed Pam's stocky, short legs. She reached down and petted him. He then spun back to Stephanie and jumped on her lap again. The dog smiled up at her, his tongue hanging out of his mouth. She stroked his soft head.

"Ava, you're used to fighting the government over these things. How do you deal with this?" Pam asked.

"You go out and protest. Make a stand. Make your voice heard."

"Do you think we can still speak out?" Pam continued chewing on her fingernail, her stare darting from Stephanie to Ava.

"We sure as hell do. We won't be silenced." Ava pointed at Stephanie, Pam, and Jake. "Don't ever allow that."

Stephanie wasn't sure how it could be stopped. She petted Hobo over and over, working to comfort herself.

"I'm not gonna make it easy for the a-holes." Jake sprang from the sofa. "I'm gonna stash my computer." He stomped out of the room and ran up the stairs.

Ava rose from her chair. "Well, I'm off to bed."

Stephanie stood, and Hobo hopped off her lap. Pam hurried to the front door with Stephanie behind her. She opened it, and Pam slipped out, then turned to look at her. "Keep me posted, okay?"

"Of course. You do the same." Stephanie hugged her friend. "Be careful out there."

Pam ran across Stephanie's driveway to the steel blue home next to hers.

Stephanie shut the door and locked it. She exhaled a ragged breath. *God, the world's going insane.* She'd need to remain alert and vigilant. A visit to her church tomorrow was in order. Maybe she'd find answers there.

Four

Sergius and his fellow monk walked toward the monastery grounds dwarfed by the Blue Ridge Mountains a short distance away.

He'd barely slept since flying into Virginia yesterday. The familiarity of his home country comforted him even though the home he remembered just a few years ago seemed unrecognizable. How could a place change so drastically in such a short time? *Ah, but time would speed up, as the Saints have said. It will continue to do so until His Second Coming.*

He crossed himself, then pointed ahead. Father Herman nodded. They headed toward the main building. A church with blue onion domes sat behind it, nestled between a copse of trees.

Sergius rapped on the door. A sense of anticipation bubbled inside him as he thought of coming face-to-face with the Holy Cross and Saint Dimitri's prophetic letter. He cast a hopeful look at Father Herman. "Let's hope this visit goes as well as our trip here, as unexpected as that may have been."

Father Herman smoothed down his cassock. "God willing."

The front door creaked open, and a young monk with a unibrow, full beard, and long hair pulled back in a ponytail stood in the doorway. He nodded at them. "Welcome, brothers. We are pleased to have you visit." He pushed the door all the way open. "I'm Monk John. Please come in."

"Thank you." Father Herman stepped inside.

Sergius followed him into the large foyer of the monastery. On either side of the space were alcoves with icons and a table with a basket for donations. He dug in his pocket, pulled out a five-dollar bill, and set it in the woven bowl.

Ahead of them, a large room held floor-to-ceiling bookcases on either side. Two small sofas, four chairs, and a coffee table sitting on a brilliant blue oriental rug stood in the center. The faint scent of books and furniture polish drifted through the space.

Monk John waved an arm. "This way." He headed toward an open door off the hallway past the living area.

Sergius followed the monk, with Father Herman behind him. They entered a room where the abbot sat at an old wooden desk. He appeared to be in his seventies, with a snow-white beard. Black-rimmed glasses surrounded gentle brown eyes. He scrawled something in a notebook before raising his eyes to them.

"Ah. Good morning, Fathers."

Sergius bowed and cupped his hands for the abbot to bless him, then kissed the abbot's hand. Father Herman followed suit.

"It's a blessing to meet you, Abbot Nicholas," Sergius said.

"Indeed, a great blessing," Father Herman added.

The elder rose from behind the desk and came alongside the monks. "I am sorry that I don't know too much about the missing relic and letter other than they aren't here." He gave them a sympathetic frown. "Only a few holy elders know the whereabouts of the sacred items."

Sergius's heart sank. He'd allowed his desire to quickly retrieve the relics to overcome his sober state of mind.

The abbot gestured for them to follow him as he stepped out of the room. They trailed behind him, heading down the end of the hallway to a back door.

"We have an elder here who is a hermit, and we consider him a saintly man. He lives in the forest in a hut. He knows about these holy relics. We've been blessed to have him here with us for twelve years." The abbot opened the door and ambled down the dirt path toward the forest.

They walked amid the smell of pine in the air.

Sergius gave a sideways glance at Father Herman and raised his brows.

"Do you think he will be able to help us?" Father Herman asked.

"I'm praying so." Sergius slid his hand into his pocket and grasped his prayer rope. *Lord, please help us.*

They entered the shaded woods, and coolness descended upon them. The abbot traipsed down the small trail between the trees, and the monks followed him.

About a quarter of a mile from where they'd started, they stepped into a modest clearing where a tiny wooden hut stood near a trickling stream. The gurgling water calmed Sergius's eagerness to talk with the hermit.

The abbot knocked on the door, and it opened slowly, revealing a hunched-back elderly man with shoulder-length hair and a flowing beard that reached to the middle of his chest. He wore a ragged blue cassock and tattered black shoes.

"Hello, Father." The abbot gestured toward them. "We have visitors."

The old man nodded. He reached for something behind the door, his hand returning with a cane.

Sergius and his fellow monk moved to the side for the hermit to hobble out of his home.

"Come sit on the log here by the stream." The elder pointed with a shaky finger toward the water.

Sergius sat next to his brother on the long log under the shade of a maple tree.

The abbot clasped his hands and bowed. "I'm returning to my office. It was a blessing having you visit us."

"Thank you. We are grateful for the valuable time you've given us, Abbot Nicholas," Sergius said.

As the abbot walked off, the hermit stood in front of them, pressing a wrinkly hand to his gaunt chest. "I am Father Hector."

"Father Sergius, and this is Father Herman." Sergius rose from his spot on the log. "Please sit, Father."

The elder shook his head. "I am fine." He raised a hand and turned it halfway. "Please tell me what it is you came to ask."

Sitting again, Sergius held his prayer rope in his hands and rested them on his lap. "We were sent here to find the prophetic letter of Saint Dimitri and the small holy relic of the Cross of Christ that went missing in Russia when the country was under communist rule."

The elder leaned on his cane, his bright eyes focused on him.

"We were told these holy objects were likely here," Father Herman said.

The elder raised his eyes and chin toward the sky. He closed his eyes as if taking in the filtering sunlight peeking between the tree's leaves.

Sergius recited the Jesus Prayer in his head while waiting for the elder to speak.

The hermit raised a finger. "I am aware of the relic of the Holy Cross, as well as the writings of Saint Dimitri. They were, indeed, here."

Were here. Sergius frowned and glanced at his brother, who seemed to share his feelings by the expression on his face. "When were they last here?"

"A couple of weeks ago."

We've just missed them. How did the bishop back home in Russia not know of this event? Sergius clutched his prayer rope and asked, "Where were they taken?"

"I do not know the details of where they have been stored, only that they are somewhere in one of our churches in the neighboring towns."

At least the sacred relics were still in the state. Sergius nodded, but he still had questions. "Why were they moved?"

"I was not told the reason, but I suspect to keep them safe due to the heightened dangers from our government and the impending world war."

"But isn't a monastery safer than a church?" Father Herman asked.

The elder shrugged. "It would seem so, since most of our monasteries are tucked away in the mountains or woods, where the average citizen is unaware of their existence."

Sergius stood, along with his brother.

"So we should begin by looking up the churches in the nearby towns and go from there," Sergius said.

The elder gave him a slow nod. "It is a reasonable plan."

"Thank you, Father."

He and his brother bent toward the elder, and he blessed them.

"God bless you and guide you on your search." Father Hector hobbled back to his hut.

Sergius stopped in the abbot's office and received a list of the five Orthodox Churches nearby, then headed to his rental car, where his brother was waiting for him. They'd start out their visits in the afternoon. Sergius sensed they were getting closer to two of God's treasures. One of the churches had to have the holy relics.

Five

That same morning, Stephanie led Hobo down the sidewalk. Across the street, her neighbor Ed and his family were in front of their driveway. They held handguns, and the sounds of their voices carried in the slight breeze.

Stephanie raised her brows. They hadn't wasted any time participating in the president's gun-buy-back program.

Two houses down, her neighbor Don and his family filed out their front door. Don shouted at Ed and his family, who had moved into the street.

As she and Hobo drew nearer, he barked, jerking against the leash pulling on his collar.

"Hobo, calm down." She bent and petted his head. "You're always so high strung."

Her friend Pam came out onto her porch, spotted Stephanie, and scrambled over to her.

"Stephanie, what's going on?"

"I don't know."

Hobo barked and pulled on the leash again.

Don stood a few feet away at the end of his driveway, cupping his mouth and yelling, "Dumbasses! Giving up your only protection against the surveillance state bastards!"

Ed fisted his hands at his sides. "We don't want our guns in the hands of criminals, Don!" He pressed an index finger to his temple. "Think! You're giving the criminals easier access!"

"Ed, you idiot. That's not how it works," Don yelled back with a scowl.

As if the police had heard him, a drone about thirty feet above them swept toward the group gathered in the road.

"Break it up, folks. A squad car will be by shortly to collect your freely offered weapons, and you will receive your compensation," the voice from the drone said.

Goose bumps ran over Stephanie's arms. Every time drones appeared in the skies, it reminded her of her father's death. She swallowed hard and held on tightly to Hobo's leash while he continued to thrust himself toward the people. They'd stopped yelling and gazed up at the hovering drone with its sleek black design, looking like a spider with two blinking, small red lights.

Hobo's voice grew hoarse. He sat and panted.

"It's okay, buddy." Stephanie squatted next to the dog and stroked behind his ears. But only for a second. She didn't want to lose track of where the drone was.

Pam rocked back and forth, hugging herself. "Those things are creepy."

Stephanie could only nod while watching the machine hover in a small circle above them.

A police car came around the corner and rolled down the street. It halted at the curb by the neighbor's driveway on Stephanie's side of the road. Two police officers exited the vehicle and approached Ed and his family.

The drone sped off like a black streak across the sky.

Stephanie let out a relieved breath.

"I'm out of here," Don grumbled and stomped back into his house with his wife and teenaged kids behind him.

"They sure got volunteers quickly, didn't they?" Pam asked.

"Yes. I'm kind of surprised."

"Maybe it's not really that big of a surprise, you know, with all the horrible shootings almost every day." Pam frowned.

"Good point." Stephanie focused on the people in the street.

The police officers took the three guns from Ed's family, gave them checks, then got in their vehicle and drove off.

The neighbors waved goodbye, their faces beaming.

"I think they feel like they've done a good deed," Stephanie muttered.

"Looks like it." Pam bent and petted Hobo's back.

Images of the homeless people on the sidewalks downtown filled Stephanie's head. "Or maybe they needed the money. So many people do these days."

"Yeah. When you're trying to feed your family, you'd probably give away your guns for food."

Stephanie patted Hobo's head. "Clever way to disarm the public."

"Do you think this means everyone will follow what Ed's family did?"

"I doubt it. There are always a few resisters out there. Look at Don." Stephanie led Hobo ahead with Pam walking next to her.

"I don't have any guns, you know, so it doesn't really affect me," Pam said.

"Me neither." Although her father's guns were somewhere in the house. She hadn't ever thought of them until now.

"At least it'll cut down on the shootings if less people have guns."

"Maybe."

"Maybe? You don't believe it'll help?"

Stephanie sighed. She didn't want to continue the gun conversation. Walking Hobo needed to be done so she could get ready for work. "I don't know, Pam. I've got to finish walking Hobo."

"Take care." Pam rubbed her arms as if she was cold and headed back to her porch.

Waving at her friend, Stephanie led Hobo down the sidewalk, keeping vigilant of her surroundings. Her neighborhood wasn't as safe as it had been even just a few years ago.

D RESSED FOR WORK AND WITH FIFTEEN MINUTES TO SPARE, Stephanie settled in a chair at the kitchen table. She opened her laptop and logged into Convo Central. She browsed the newest comments by her friends. On her newsfeed, suggested friends popped up, and a familiar name caught her attention. She rolled her eyes. *I'm sure there are plenty of men named Logan Wyatt out there.* A profile picture attached to the name showed the man standing in front of the local science museum.

She caught her breath. *It can't be.*

Stephanie clicked on the photo and moved closer to get a better look at this Logan Wyatt—the same name as her old boyfriend and first love before she'd met Jake's father, Sean. They'd been so young then, finishing up the last year of high school. Her heart fluttered, gazing into those soothing brown eyes. She covered her open mouth. *My God, it is him.*

Logan's sandy-brown hair curled just below his earlobes. His physique hadn't changed much. It was evident by the toned arm muscles peeking below his short-sleeved Polo shirt. He had no beer belly or tire around his waist. She smiled and pressed a hand to her chest, her heart racing. Life had been good to him.

Curiosity prodded her to click on his profile. His page came up, and she checked his location and personal information on the left side of the screen. He lived in town as of a year ago and was working as a museum technician. Under the Relationship box, it read *Single.* Strong emotions from the past came flooding back, making her lightheaded.

Stephanie leaned back in her chair. Why had his profile appeared this morning? She hadn't been actively looking for him; although, if she were honest with herself, he'd never completely vanished from her thoughts. In the past several months, memories from her earlier relationships had begun to surface. One regarding her and Logan's favorite show of affection after they'd kiss—touching and rubbing noses. She smiled. The silly but comforting recollection reminded her of the life she'd had before marrying Sean the snake. Maybe it was only natural after having been a single mother for the past fifteen years.

She tilted her head to the side and brushed hair behind her ear. The woman she'd been in high school didn't really exist today. Everybody changed over the years, maturing, growing, being impacted by life's good and bad experiences. Logan was no exception.

What type of man had Logan become? Had he always been single, or was he possibly divorced? When she'd known him, he'd avoided anything serious. After all, he had only been eighteen, same as her, and he had college to attend out of state. She laughed, remembering her unrealistic thoughts at eighteen. Why couldn't they get married in a few years? Surely he'd want that too. She shook her head. The naivete of young people, especially her.

She still recalled his sad, soft expression when she'd hinted toward marrying young and discovering the experiences of the world together. He couldn't give her what she'd wanted then, and he'd gently broken off their two-year relationship and left town.

At the time, his actions seemed so cruel, unfair. Didn't he care for her? Now a mother in her late thirties, she understood his past behavior and considered it smart. Years of living did make one wiser.

Curiosity continued to nip at her, so she clicked the Connect Request button by his name. Her stomach somersaulted, and her heart raced again.

She pursed her lips, then mumbled, "You're not a teenager anymore. Get a grip."

Her mouse pointer hovered over the connection request and clicked it again, reversing it. It was stupid to bother him after all these years. He'd likely forgotten all about her.

She shut her computer. *Enough playing around. Time to get to work.*

LATE THAT AFTERNOON, STEPHANIE DROVE WITH JAKE toward Main Street and parked in a store's lot.

Jake gripped the door handle. "Let's go find Gran."

She locked the car and headed up the pavement to the sidewalk. Shouts, whistles, and thumping came from the left of Main Street. Similar noises from the right of the road echoed and meshed with the chanting on the left.

When they reached the sidewalk, Stephanie glanced to the right. Demonstrators with signs for protecting the Second Amendment were marching north on Hanover Road intersecting with Main Street. Around two hundred people, moving in a colorful mosaic of American flags and signs that read OUR PRIVACY AND FREEDOM BELONG TO US and AGAINST THE SURVEILLANCE STATE, shouted and stormed south on the same road.

To her left, a large group of people crowded the street with antiwar signs, bouncing them up and down and yelling, "No more wars!"

The din from all the voices echoed throughout the town in a chorus of pain and rage. The partly cloudy sky shed shadows against storefronts, and its gray shafts slashed portions of the antiwar demonstrators. The smell of body odor, pungent perfume, cigarettes, and weed drifted in the tepid breeze.

Homeless people sat and lay in their usual spots in front of shops, some sleeping, some watching the commotion.

Another mass of people turned down Main Street toward Stephanie and the antiwar protestors. These marchers had signs that read WE ARE THE NINETY-NINE PERCENT! PEOPLE BEFORE PROFITS! They converged with the antiwar crowd, and the chants grew stronger and louder. They gathered near city hall, stomping their feet and poking their signs in the air.

A minute later, three police vehicles with their lights flashing rumbled down the road, parking sideways, blocking the hordes from going farther down the thoroughfare.

Two silver drones zipped across the pewter sky, their red lights winking at Stephanie and the people around her, as if playing games with them. She recoiled.

Jake put an arm around her shoulders. "Mom, you okay?"

She steadied her breath and nodded.

One of the cops left his car and held a megaphone to his mouth.

"Everyone, go home." His gaze traveled over the hundreds of people. "You've disrupted the town's streets long enough, and you'll be arrested if you don't clear out."

"You can't arrest us for peacefully protesting! We've got permits!" a man yelled.

"We have a right to have our voices heard! No more of these wasteful wars!" a woman's voice resembling Ava's shouted above the grumblings floating through the crowd.

"You've had your time." The policeman put a hand on his hip and spoke into the megaphone. "Last warning."

"The wars haven't stopped! So we won't!" another man bellowed.

Two more squad cars showed up with police in their militarized uniforms and helmets, and they descended upon the crowd, with handcuffs at the ready. The mob of people moved about like ants on a mound, shrieking and shouting obscenities.

Ava appeared between two groups of people, her shoes stomping the cement and her arms in the air. Stephanie made her way toward her mother, squeezing between bodies, with Jake behind her. Just before she reached her mother, a police officer cuffed Ava.

"Mom!" Stephanie rushed toward her mother.

Two cops flanked Ava and walked her toward a paddy wagon that had shown up a few minutes ago. She held her head up as the two bulky men opened the vehicle's back doors.

Stephanie reached her mother and grasped her mother's shoulder. "Mom, what are they going to do to you?"

Ava jerked her head around and wore a sneer. "Don't worry, hon. I've been through this rigamarole more than a few times." She yanked away from one of the cop's holding her and gave Stephanie an encouraging smile. "Come visit me at the county jail tonight if you want."

"Come on," the other policeman holding her arm said. He and his partner pushed her into the wagon.

Ava sat on the bench and faced Stephanie. She held her head up and jutted her chin out, her eyes narrowed in that familiar look of righteous determination. "See you on the flip side."

Stephanie wrung her hands. What could she do? Nothing but

stand there and watch. Watch her mother's courageous actions she'd witnessed since she was a child.

"Later, Gran!" Jake yelled, waving at Ava, just before five other protestors were herded into the van.

The doors closed on the truck, and the vehicle rumbled down the street, turning right toward the county jail.

Jake pumped a fist. "Gran's awesome."

"She sure has gumption." Stephanie dug through the large tote hanging from her shoulder. She pulled out a couple of quart-sized zip-lock bags of sandwiches and two bottled waters and gave them to Jake. "Don't forget we're also here to help the homeless."

"Yep. I didn't forget." Jake took the two bags and moved toward the people sitting against storefronts.

Several police not busy with arresting the protestors gathered on the sidewalk in front of the vagabonds.

"Move along," one of the cops said, making a shooing motion with his hands. His dark eyes burned, and his bulbous nose flared. "You can't keep lying here disrupting foot traffic."

Stephanie frowned. "But they have nowhere to go, Officer." She handed a couple of bags to a man and woman huddled together between shops.

The policeman snatched the bundles from the couple. "It's now illegal to feed or give money to the homeless."

"How the hell are they supposed to survive?" Jake snapped.

Stephanie put a hand on Jake's puffed-out chest as he glared at the cop.

"There are shelters around," the cop hissed.

"The last one shut down a week ago, and you know it," Jake said, pointing at the police officer.

With panic seizing her, Stephanie pulled Jake away from the policeman and whispered in his ear, "I don't want you arrested too."

"Why not? It would be a badge of honor." Jake had spoken loud enough for the cop to hear, but thankfully, the policeman had moved down the street to help break up a scuffle between a dozen people and his fellow law enforcement comrades.

Jake shoved his hands in her large bag as he huffed, his face coloring. He pulled out two more bags and gave them to the couple. "Hide 'em in your coats."

The man and woman did as he said, their faces pale with fear.

Stephanie tucked three bags into people's laps and echoed what Jake had said, before she led him back to her car.

They got in, and Jake sighed loudly. "What a crock of shit."

"I know, son, but let's just concentrate on Gran and getting her out of jail."

"She said she'd be out soon."

"It may not be until the morning. It's happened before."

Jake smacked his palm on the dashboard. "Sucks I didn't get to go with her."

Stephanie grabbed Jake's forearm. "Stop thinking that way."

"Why? What's wrong with standing up for what's right, like Gran?"

"I don't want to discuss—"

A gaggle of young adults ran past their car, carrying tire irons and baseball bats.

Stephanie gripped the steering wheel. "Oh my God. What are they going to do?"

Jake leaned forward with both his hands on the dashboard. "Looks like they're gonna stir up some shit."

Screams split the air. A loud thud reverberated through the street and lot. A plume of tear gas flooded the road. People scurried away from the smoke, down toward the right side of the street.

Her heart beat like the hooves of a derby horse. "It's time to go." Thankful their windows were up and blocking any residual putrid gas from seeping into their car, Stephanie pressed the ignition button with a shaky finger, then pulled out of the store lot. She turned right, having no other choice.

They passed the people running down Main Street toward Hanover, where the anti-surveillance protestors moved north in the gun supporters' wake.

She waited for the large mass to march past the intersection before zipping across the road and heading toward home.

Hobo greeted them with jumps and licks. Stephanie hugged him and kissed his head, working to lessen the leftover tremors moving through her. When would her mother be out of jail? Would the authorities keep her locked up this time? What could she do about it? Anything? She felt very small in an ever-increasingly insane world, and at this rate, nothing seemed out of the realm of possibilities.

Around five thirty in the evening, Stephanie followed a guard down the short, dimly lit hall to a door on their right. The guard opened it and stepped aside for her to enter. The twelve-by-twelve-foot stark room held three six-foot-long tables. A musty odor wafted through the space. Farthest from the door, a young man and a middle-aged woman sat across from each other, quietly conversing. She pictured her and Jake sitting there, and she shuddered at the thought.

"Wait here," the guard said and left the doorway.

Stephanie sat at one of the empty tables, leaned her forearms on the surface, and laced her fingers together. She kept her eyes on her hands, the cool space with its fluorescent lights giving her the chills.

Her mother and the guard appeared at the doorway.

"You have ten minutes. Visiting hours are ending soon." The guard stood near the door, facing them with a grimace.

Stephanie rose and went to her mother, embracing her. She sat back down, and Ava took the bench on the other side of the table.

"How are you holding up?"

Ava shrugged. "Oh fine. No sweat."

"I know jail for you isn't new, but it still must feel horrible."

"Exactly. It's not new. It's familiar, and because of that, it's not so horrible. Knowing what happens in here for a simple demonstrator isn't scary. You know you get out within twenty-four hours and are back home in your own bed the next night."

Stephanie sighed. Everything rolled off her mom as if it were nothing but a fleeting breeze. "I wish you weren't so used to this."

Ava leaned her forearms on the table. "Well, it is what is it. You do what you have to do."

Stephanie tensed. "You aren't going to keep doing this, are you?"

"Depends on what our government does next." Ava winked.

Her faced warmed. "Mom, this isn't a game."

"Of course it isn't."

"Could have fooled me."

"Honey, stop worrying." Ava smiled. "I'm glad you came by to visit. You're such a good daughter." She frowned. "But you need to work on getting a tougher backbone. Times aren't getting easier."

"I know. You don't need to tell me." Stephanie glanced at the other people in the room. Her gaze traveled back to her mother, who sat calmly in her chair, her back straight, shoulders relaxed, as if she were at the park or at a coffee shop, sans the coffee.

"How's my grandson?"

"He's at home on his computer."

"The usual. Good. That means he's doing well."

Stephanie nodded, tapping her fingers on the table. "Did the warden or whoever runs this place tell you when you're getting out of here?"

"Not yet."

"Not yet? You've been here at least three hours. Don't they let you know after they've assigned you a cell?"

"Yes. I usually know within the first few hours, but this jail is packed with fellow protestors, along with low-grade criminals." She wiggled her brows. "Busy day, it seems."

"So you may have to stay the night?"

"Probably."

Stephanie frowned. "And I guess I'll have to wait for you to call me when you can be picked up?"

"Most likely."

"Okay." Stephanie bit her lip. "I hate leaving you here."

"You don't have a choice, hon."

The guard approached their table. "Time to get back to your cell, Jenkins."

Ava nodded and stood. The guard took hold of her arm.

Stephanie rose and embraced her mother. "I love you."

"Love you too."

The guard guided her mother out of the room and down the hall opposite the reception area. Stephanie headed toward the latter. Her mother had been so calm. Why couldn't she?

Stephanie sighed as she left the building and went to her car. She needed to find some peace. *Time to go to church.*

SAINT JOHN ORTHODOX CHURCH SAT AT THE CORNER OF Hanover and Main Streets.

As Stephanie climbed the stairs to the double doors, a disheveled man and young girl sat on one of the steps by the entrance. They had become fixtures of the church building for the past few months, so much so that Stephanie and the parish knew the father and daughter by name—Brody and Lindy. Another person who had lost his job through the folding of the company he worked for and, as a result, lost his home a month ago.

She dug in her wallet, pulled out a lone five-dollar bill, and handed it to Brody. "God be with you."

"Thank you." Brody gave her a small, appreciative smile.

She headed into the church. The narthex and nave glistened from the prayer candles in the rectangular box of sand and the vigil lamps hanging in front of the icons on the marble iconostasis.

She lit a taper and entered the quiet nave, the faint fragrance of incense wafting in the warm space. Modest golden chandeliers hung from the twenty-foot ceiling. The Pantocrator painted in the dome portion of the ceiling gazed down at her, blessing her with His right hand.

The several rows of pews were empty except for the front one, where a well-known elderly woman, Olga, stood prostrating and crossing herself. She'd lived in Fairview all her life and was considered a pious woman who some people believed was suffering from dementia. Being a widow for five years, she wore her usual modest black dress and a transparent ebony scarf over her head. A prayer rope hung from her wrist, swaying side to side as she proceeded through her prayers.

Deacon Michael emerged from one of two doors in the icon wall that shielded the sanctuary. He began the Vespers service, and Stephanie slid into the second-to-last row of pews, remaining standing.

As the psalms were being read, the blare of sirens from police cars and ambulances sped by the church, their lights flashing through the clear windows in hues of red and blue before becoming colorless again.

Stephanie held her prayer rope in her hands, closing her eyes, working to focus on the service. She needed to be in God's realm for this one hour. It seemed so hard to reach that point of peace in her soul with all the chaos going on in the world outside those hallowed walls.

But she was thankful the church remained open. Due to the shortage of priests, the local bishop had given his blessing for Deacon Michael to fulfill the duties of the priest. This wasn't too much of a strain on the deacon, as no more than ten people attended any of the services at the church. Attendance at any place of worship in Fairview and the state, as well as the rest of the country, had decreased in the past ten years.

With all the violence, death, and despair infecting Fairview and the nation, Stephanie had always been puzzled by this downturn in seeking His comfort and guidance. She had decided years ago she wouldn't allow herself to disconnect from the person who was peace in her life.

The remainder of Vespers was chanted and read without outside interruption, and Stephanie sighed, solace warming her heart.

Deacon Michael disappeared behind the iconostasis.

She slipped out of the pew and approached Olga, who was now sitting facing the altar, her hands in her lap.

Stephanie laid a hand on Olga's shoulder. "Hello, Olga. How are you doing?"

The woman gazed up at her. "God and His angels came to this beautiful place tonight, as they do every service. I felt one of the angel's wings on my shoulder, just like I did your hand. He went by me when Psalm 50 was read." Olga held up her arthritic hands and looked up at Christ above them. "How glorious are God, His angels, and His saints."

Considering Olga regularly talked in such a manner, Stephanie was not surprised by what she'd heard. Still, her heart swelled, imagining the angels who'd wandered the church. Although this happened in every service, she wasn't anywhere close to the spiritual level that Olga was, having not experienced any of what the elderly woman had.

"Amen." She took a seat next to the old woman.

Olga placed a hand on Stephanie's leg. "We are blessed to have Him here with the angels to protect us and this church."

"Yes, we are."

Olga's mouth drooped. "We don't deserve it."

Stephanie bowed her head.

The elderly woman held up a wrinkly finger. "But the cat perpetually climbs the gutters, and my sister wears too many pants."

Stephanie froze. *What's she saying?*

"Tonight the orange will be peeled, and the cow will sleep soundly in the barn."

The rumors of Olga's mental capacity came back to her. She'd nearly forgotten since hearing Olga speak so lucidly about God and His angels.

"What do you mean, Olga?"

The woman shook her head. "Never mind." She pressed a palm to her furrowed forehead. "Things are getting worse."

Stephanie put an arm around Olga's soft, slouched shoulders. "Are you feeling okay?"

Olga swatted the air. "It's not that. The world is not well."

"It sure isn't." Her mother sitting in a cell in the county jail filled Stephanie's head. She hoped her mother would be out of that place no later than tomorrow morning. The thought of Ava sleeping on a flimsy mattress in a cold, empty room ate at her.

Deacon Michael in his black cassock approached her and Olga. "Hello, ladies. Thanks for coming to Vespers so it's not just me doing these prayers and readings." He chuckled.

Stephanie smiled. "I needed to be here." She squeezed Olga against her. "Needed peace."

The deacon reached out a hand, concern glowing in his brown eyes. "Are you doing all right? How's your son and mother?"

"Mom's in the county jail." Stephanie released Olga and clasped her hands in her lap.

"Time to do the laundry," Olga said, wagging a finger at her.

"What happened?" Deacon Michael asked.

"She was out protesting the wars."

The deacon smiled. "Ah, I should've known. When will she be getting out of jail? Maybe I should go visit her."

"Visiting hours are over right now, and she should be out tomorrow morning."

"I'm glad to hear that. Tell her to be careful and come to church." He winked and held up a key in his hand. "It's time to close up."

"Olga, is your daughter picking you up?" Stephanie stood.

Olga's face pinched, her eyes flashing with recognition. "My daughter Lily?"

"Yes."

"She hasn't put away her tricycle in the garage." She shook her head. "No car rides until she gets her chores done."

Stephanie folded in her lips and glanced at Deacon Michael.

He gave her a sympathetic smile, then looked at Olga. "Do you need me to drive you home?"

Olga raised her head. "Hmm?"

"I can drive her home, Deacon."

"It was a beautiful service, Deacon," Olga said, grabbing the cane next to her and trembling as she labored to stand.

Stephanie helped her by holding on to one of her arms. The deacon took the other one, and she stood leaning on her cane.

"Thank you." She grinned.

"Olga, do you need a ride home?" Stephanie asked.

Confusion swept across the old woman's face. "I think my daughter Lily is coming to get me."

"Oh good." Stephanie and the deacon flanked Olga as she moved slowly toward the narthex.

Olga jerked to a stop near the icon of Saint John and crossed herself. "Lord, have mercy. It is a sign."

Stephanie let go of Olga and approached the icon.

Under the dim light of the candles still burning in the sea of sand, a wet, dark red substance streaked the saint's cheeks and flowed down his robes in two vertical streams. Pulling her phone from her purse and turning on its flashlight, Stephanie aimed the beam at the glass-covered icon. Her breath hitched, and she fell back a step.

Blood.

"It is a sign from our Lord, Deacon," Olga said. "The world has gone mad."

Stephanie pressed a hand to her chest and took another step back. Her heart pattered against her palm.

Deacon Michael came alongside Stephanie and leaned over for a closer look. He straightened and crossed himself. "You are right, Olga." He clasped the cross hanging on the necklace around his neck and nodded. "This is the third time this icon has streamed blood."

"Why had it cried blood before?" Stephanie asked.

Olga placed a shaky, wrinkled finger on the glass covering the icon. "Don't cry, dear one."

Deacon Michael opened the front doors just as a red Volkswagen bug parked in front of the church entrance.

"Let's get Olga to the car, then I will answer your question," the deacon said, taking hold of Olga's elbow.

Olga's mouth pinched; her eyes narrowed. "The dishes need to be washed."

"Yes. I'm sure Lily will help you," the deacon said.

Stephanie placed an arm around Olga's waist and pointed with her other hand. "Lily's here."

She and the deacon helped Olga to the car.

Lily, with her wavy auburn hair bouncing, opened the passenger-side door. "Thanks for the help."

"Sure." Stephanie waved at Olga and Lily as the car rolled out of the church parking lot.

In the darkening sky, three drones flitted across, yellow beams of light scanning the lot in front of them.

Stephanie flinched, her body tensing.

A fire engine's horn and siren wailed in the distance.

Deacon Michael touched Stephanie's arm. "Come back inside for a moment. Afterward, I'll walk you to your car."

They entered the narthex and stood next to the icon.

Deacon Michael held up three fingers. "All three times had to do with a catastrophic event in our history." He gazed at the saint. "Those catastrophic events were two world wars. But icons have streamed tears and blood for other terrible events such as natural disasters."

Stephanie's mouth dried up, and she swallowed hard. "Either way, something worse will happen sometime in the future?"

"I'll send a message to the bishop. He can discern these signs better than me."

Stephanie nodded.

The deacon gestured her toward the doors, and once they were outside the church, he locked them and guided her toward her car.

Inside her vehicle, she bid the clergyman a good night and drove out of the parking lot.

She gazed at the small icon of Christ hanging from her rearview mirror. "Please, Lord, take away whatever terrible event lies ahead."

Stephanie crossed herself, then focused on the road for home.

Seven

In the county jail that evening, Ava sat on the lumpy, thin mattress. The acrid odor of urine and ammonia drifted through the stagnant air.

A tall, bulky female guard with a tattoo of a skull on the side of her neck approached Ava's cell with a tray of slop. Her name tag read BLAINE. She unlocked the barred door and entered the small space. "Dinner is served." She smirked.

Ava returned the smirk with an added curled lip. "You can keep it. I'm not swallowing what you call food in this dump."

Blaine shrugged, set the tray on her cot, then slipped out the door. Locking it, she sashayed down the dimly lit hall.

Ava put the tray on the cement floor, then glanced at her watch. Nearly eight forty-five. They weren't letting her out tonight. Something told her this jail stay would be eerily different.

"Lights out. Mandatory bedtime in fifteen minutes," a voice echoed through the cells.

All the lights shut off at once. Ava lay on the uncomfortable mattress in the darkness, folding her arms behind her head. Her mind spun with possibilities to free her from the stinky place. The book about civil disobedience sitting on the end table in her living room surfaced in her head. Historical references to Tolstoy, Gandhi, and King, Jr. filled many of the pages of the book. Gandhi's approach pulsed in her mind. *Yes, this is the route to go. Besides, I'd be better off in the long run avoiding the junk they have the gall to feed human beings here.* She smiled, staring at the water-stained, pocked ceiling. *I've already started tonight. Let's see what they do now.*

AVA WOKE IN THE MORNING WITH HER STOMACH grumbling. She ignored her roiling belly and sat up, just as Blaine appeared at her cell door.

She gave Ava a toothy grin that lacked empathy. "Morning, Sleeping Beauty. Breakfast kibbles." She unlocked the door, came into the cell, and set the tray on the mattress.

Ava grimaced at the watery bowl with colored loops floating in it. "Keep it."

Blaine raised her brows. "Skipping breakfast too, eh?"

"That doesn't pass for breakfast." Ava picked up the tray and thrust it toward the guard.

Blaine shrugged and replaced the untouched old tray sitting on the floor with the new one before leaving the cell.

Ava folded her arms across her chest. *She'll get the word out to her fellow jail tyrants, and soon they'll have to release me. Otherwise, they'll be responsible for my starvation, and that's not something they'll want on their hands no matter how monstrous they are.*

She pulled out a crossword puzzle from under her mattress. Even though she wasn't permitted a pen, she could visualize the answers. Turning one of the pages, she concentrated on the clue for the first word across: Patrick Henry was quoted saying, "Give me ______ or give me death." Ava used her finger to write out *liberty* in the boxes. She grinned. *How appropriate.*

THAT SAME MORNING, STEPHANIE HELD HER CELL PHONE while she sat in her dad's recliner. She hadn't slept well, rolling around in her bed most of the night. Her mother wasn't a young woman anymore. Ava suffered from arthritis in one of her hips and left shoulder, and she was borderline hypoglycemic.

What garbage were they feeding her in jail? Stephanie scrunched up her nose. Her mother was probably forced to eat food suited for dogs. The family had been eating organic produce and meat since she was a child. Years ago, her mother had told her they'd ditched the processed, chemically toxic food pushed on consumers when her mother was a teenager. Their little garden in the backyard had provided them with most of their vegetables.

She pressed the first two numbers to the jail on her phone just as an alert beeped. *Now what?* She stopped dialing the jail's number and read the message. *Special announcement by the president at seven thirty this morning.* Numerous scenarios filled her head, but the incident with the icon of Saint John dominated her thoughts. Would the president's speech have something to do with that sign of an unknown horror to come? She groaned and set the phone on the end table.

Hobo trotted into the living room, placing his front paws on her thighs and smiling up at her.

"Okay, okay. A quick one." Stephanie left the chair and went to the coat closet for Hobo's leash. He barked, jumping up and down, his whole butt wagging with his bobtail.

She hooked on the lead and guided him out the front door. Storm clouds veiled the sun, and the smell of rain permeated the dense air. Through the gray puffs, a silver drone glided across the sky, heading toward town. She tensed. That machine added irritation to her already jittery state over her mother's predicament and the president's upcoming announcement.

Pam's front door opened, and she ran down her driveway. "Steph, did you get the alert?"

"How could I not?" Stephanie stopped in front of Pam, who was now on the sidewalk.

Pam nibbled on her stubby fingernails and walked next to Stephanie. "I hope there wasn't another shooting."

Stephanie could only nod. Her mother sitting in the jail cell wouldn't leave her thoughts. She needed to get her mother out as soon as possible.

Hobo stopped near a fire hydrant and peed while she and Pam waited.

"Can I watch the news report with you?" Pam asked.

"Sure." Stephanie led Hobo back to her home.

Pam gestured toward Hobo. "You done walking already?"

"I'm worried about my mom. She's in jail."

"Oh no."

"Yes, and she should've been out by now."

Pam's face blanched. "You don't think they're going to keep her locked up in there, do you?"

Stephanie shook her head. There had to be some logical reason for the delay. "No, of course not. It's regular practice for Mom to spend a night in prison for protesting."

"I hope you're right." Pam frowned as her stare darted around. "Everything's so crazy these days. I don't know what to expect."

Pam's words sent icy shivers down Stephanie's spine, but she pushed any terrible thoughts aside and strode up her driveway.

She opened the front door, then removed Hobo's leash. He ran through the living room and out the doggie door.

They settled in the den, and Stephanie turned on the TV.

Jake thumped down the stairs and plopped on the couch. "I don't know why I keep coming down to watch this shit."

Stephanie shrugged. "We don't have much choice if we want to stay informed."

Pam leaned forward in Ava's chair, her eyes glued to the muted TV screen.

The president stood at the press room podium, dressed in a crisp navy-blue suit and red tie. He stared at the camera, his mouth tight and his eyes conveying what looked like a glint of regret.

Stephanie bit her lip. *Oh Lord. He's more tense than usual.*

"Geez." Pam turned toward Stephanie. "What's that look for?"

"He always looks like that," Jake grumbled, playing with his cell phone.

"Good morning, my fellow Americans," the president said. "Early this morning, I was notified that Russian, Chinese, and Iranian fighter jets and soldiers have crossed into the northern portion of Turkey. This invasion is in response to Turkey's offensive against Syria, as well as our military and our European allies' armies' involvement in Syria and Lithuania. There are reports of the Russians and Chinese using nuclear and biological weapons on par with our own. We'd sent in eighty thousand of our troops, joining the fifty thousand UK, thirty thousand German, sixteen thousand French, and seven thousand Canadian soldiers. In the past nine hours, we've lost over twenty-eight thousand of our brave troops, and approximately forty-two thousand have been wounded. We do not have the numbers yet for our allies or our enemies, but we are quite certain their casualties are much higher."

Murmurs filled the press room.

Stephanie froze, gripping the arms of the chair. "Oh my God." She couldn't shake the images of the icon of Saint John streaming blood. Could this be what had made Saint John cry blood?

"What a freaking waste." Jake scowled at the TV.

"This is unbelievable," Pam said.

"So many lives lost in such a short period of time." Stephanie closed her eyes, the shock still rocking her.

"Cannon fodder for the global oligarchs, as Gran would say," Jake snapped, his face coloring.

Stephanie pressed a hand to her chest. "Nuclear and bioweapons we have today are so much more powerful and deadly than the last world war."

"Yeah. They're, like, ten times more powerful, Mom, and that means a shitload more death and destruction." Jake set his phone down and crossed his arms. "It's gross."

"Terribly gross." Stephanie rubbed her queasy stomach, thinking about the hundreds of thousands killed on the other side of the planet.

"What's President Harden going to do about this?" Pam asked.

Before Stephanie could answer, the president cleared his throat, and she returned her attention to the screen.

Dead silence blanketed the room, as if everyone collectively held their breath, waiting for the president to continue.

Stephanie leaned forward in her chair and clasped her hands together. Her friend and son did the same.

"Because of the large losses in the past few weeks, we have reinstated the draft."

Blood drained from every part of Stephanie's body, her muscles tight as cable cords. She swallowed hard. *This can't be happening.* The draft hadn't been used in over half a century.

President Harden's jaw twitched as his stare went around the room. "All eligible men and women between the ages of eighteen and thirty must sign up at your local armed forces recruitment centers or online within five days of this announcement." He sniffed, lifting his chin, as if he had nothing to do with these new orders. "Our military recruitment centers will contact you shortly afterward to follow up." A tight smile slid across his face. "You will be contributing to your country's effort toward freedom, peace, and democracy for all."

Tears stung Stephanie's eyes. She rose from her chair, stepping toward her son.

Jake sprang from the couch and pointed at the TV. "This is BS! I'm not gonna fight for a bunch of psychopaths!"

Pam's jaw hung open. Her eyes glazed over. "I can't believe this is really happening."

Stephanie wrapped her arms around her son, his body stiff and unbending against hers. "You can sign up as a conscientious objector."

Jake huffed hot air against her hair. "I sure as shit will."

He pushed away from her and stomped from the room, taking the stairs two at a time.

"I've got to check on my daughter." Pam gave Stephanie a clipped wave and ran out the front door. It slammed shut behind her.

Pam's daughter attended college in a town adjacent to theirs, and she was a couple of years older than Jake. Stephanie's heart hurt for her friend, who was in the same situation as she was.

The den had been deserted within seconds, and the president still stood there, a disgusting monster, having spurted words that no family wanted to hear, without showing an ounce of care or compassion.

Stephanie picked up the remote and pointed it at the screen just as the president said, "An update on the cybersecurity situation will be given Friday morning at seven thirty. Thank you."

She smashed the Off button and threw the remote on the chair.

As her mind worked to absorb everything that had been said by the president, Stephanie grabbed her purse and keys and headed to the garage. She needed to see her mother and tell her what was happening. The nagging worry of the real possibility her son would be sent off to fight in the horrendous wars left her body trembling as she opened the garage door. *Concentrate on Mom for now.* She got into her car and started it up as nausea rolled through her belly.

Eight

At the county jail, Stephanie entered the same room she'd been guided to yesterday. But this time it was empty.

The guard shut the door, leaving her alone.

She pulled back a chair, its metal legs screeching across the floor, echoing in the hollow, windowless space. She winced and sat down. A faint odor of paint hung in the air.

She checked her watch. It was nearly eight. When she had arrived, the guard told her she'd find out her mother's status. But how would that status change after the president's speech this morning? The government would crack down on dissenters of the escalating wars, especially with the draft now enacted.

Queasiness rolled through her stomach. What would happen to Jake? She leaned her elbows on the table and face in her hands.

The door opened, and her mother came in, her face pale and eyes dull.

Stephanie rose and embraced Ava. "Mom, are you okay?" She pulled back to examine her mother. "You look exhausted."

Ava shook her head. "I'm tired of being cooped up in this lousy place."

"What's going on? Why haven't they released you yet?"

Ava rubbed her temple, then plopped into a chair across from Stephanie.

Stephanie sat back down and waited for her mother to speak.

Ava folded her arms on the table, her hands fisted. A flash of anger lit her eyes. "The warden said the organizers of the protests, especially those of us against the wars, aren't being let out of jail now. We've been slapped with disturbing the peace, jaywalking, loitering, disobeying the police, and any other random charge they can throw at us to keep us locked in this hole."

Panic knocked against Stephanie's chest. She leaned forward and clutched her mother's hands. "How long are they going to hold you? They can't detain you indefinitely, right?"

Ava gave her another weary look, as if pitying her. "Honey, remember years ago when President O'Hare was in office and signed the National Protection Defensive Act? It basically erased habeas corpus." She sighed and ran a hand over her hair that was pulled back in a ponytail. "People can be arrested and thrown in jail without a valid cause for however long the powerful in our corrupt prison system and government choose."

"But you've been through this many times since that act was passed into law, and you were released within a day."

Ava scanned the area, glancing at the security cameras on two sides of the room, mounted where the walls met the ceiling. "The winds have changed direction, Stephanie."

Stephanie's heartbeat escalated. "They can't make you stay in here to rot. You've done nothing wrong."

Ava made a slicing motion with her hand. "Shh. Calm down."

"No, I'm not going to calm down and neither should you."

"Getting worked up over this won't help the situation."

"Then what will?"

Ava rubbed her chin and said in a low voice, "I've implemented a plan, and I think it'll work."

"What is it?" Stephanie straightened in her seat.

Ava kept her eyes on Stephanie but made a slight jerk of her head toward one of the cameras. "Let's just say the food isn't worth eating here."

Earlier that morning, Stephanie had worried about what the guards were feeding Ava. She couldn't argue with her mother about the crummy food they served in the jail. Maybe she could help. She covered her mother's hand with hers and nodded. "I can bring you some food from home."

"No."

"No?"

Ava shook her head and whispered in a huff, "That's not allowed and not part of the plan."

Stumped, Stephanie furrowed her brow. "Then what is?"

"Read my book at home on civil disobedience. You should've read it years ago. It's got the answer."

"Mom, that's a thick book."

"Chapter forty-three." Her mother gave her a piercing stare. "In case things don't go as planned and something happens to me—"

"Mom, don't—"

"Shut up and listen."

Stephanie swallowed hard, her gaze darting around the room before focusing on her mother once more.

Ava peered at the cameras again, leaned toward Stephanie, then whispered, "Your father's guns."

"What?"

"You heard me."

Stephanie nodded as her hands clung to the sides of the table, bracing herself for whatever her mother was about to say.

"Do you know where they are in the house?"

Stephanie froze, not able to answer. Thoughts raced through her mind about where her father might have stashed the weapons.

"Crime has increased, especially break-ins and murders. One of your father's guns would come in handy for your protection."

The guard appeared at the doorway, her face pinched and beady black eyes on her mother. "Let's go, Jenkins." She approached them and grabbed Ava's arm, leading her out the doorway.

Stephanie rushed after them. "When will she be released? You can't keep her in here forever!" She came alongside the guard, working to keep up with the large woman's long strides.

The guard stopped and looked down at Stephanie as if she were a pesky fly. "When we get permission to release her, you'll be notified."

The woman turned to face the hallway to the cells, then pulled her mother along.

Holding back tears, Stephanie watched her mother walk with a ramrod-straight back and confidence she couldn't understand, then disappear behind the thick door at the end of the hall.

As her tears fell, Stephanie ran out of the building and got into her car. Letting go of the wave of emotions swirling inside her, she gripped the steering wheel and rested her forehead on it. Closing her eyes, she struggled not to be dragged down in the dark abyss of anxiety and hopelessness.

It's not that bad. She'll get out of jail. Jake will be fine. Don't go straight to the worst-case scenario. Think. Are there any lawyers left who still defend the public? She sniffled and opened her eyes, the dashboard a blur in front of her. There had to be some renegade lawyers in town somewhere. Undoubtedly hunkered down and formulating ways to help people like her mother. She'd find one.

Nine

Stephanie picked up a candle in the quiet, shadowed narthex. Thoughts of her mother's predicament sent Stephanie into a pleading prayer for her release as the tip of her taper ignited from the thick candle in the middle of the box of sand.

In one of the corners of the dimly lit space, Brody and Lindy were huddled together on the floor, both asleep.

She crept over to the icon of Saint John. Fresh blood streamed over the darker stained lines painting the saint's face and robes. Choking up, Stephanie reached toward the glass covering the icon and touched it with a shaking hand. *God, help us. What's happening?*

She closed her eyes and focused on her petition to the *Panagia* for her help.

The creak and whir of the door opening broke her concentration. She did the sign of the cross, then pivoted toward the entrance as two monks entered, crossing themselves.

Monks? They hardly ever visited Saint John's. Not when there was a monastery close by in the nearby mountains. Nevertheless, their presence gave her a sense of peace.

"Good evening," said one of them with shoulder-length, copper-colored hair and a straggly beard of the same hue. He was tall, around six foot three, and skinny as a twig in winter. His cassock flowed loosely off his body.

"Hello, Fathers." She gave a half bow.

The chubby monastic behind him waved at her and smiled through his thick black beard. His pink, bulbous nose shone like polished chinaware in the candlelight.

She returned a smile and placed a hand on her chest. "I'm Stephanie."

"Nice to meet you," the first monk said. "I'm Father Sergius, and this is Father Herman."

"Do you live at Holy Trinity Monastery?"

"No. We flew here a few days ago from Russia," Father Herman said in a deep, baritone voice that echoed through the narthex.

Stephanie widened her eyes. "That's quite a long way to travel to our humble little church. And you sound like you're from here."

"We are," Father Sergius said as he pulled out a dollar and set it in the woven basket next to the pile of candles. He took one and lit it, sinking it into the sand.

What were they doing here? And why were they in Russia? The more they spoke, the less she understood. Glancing back at the bleeding icon, she pointed toward it. "Look."

The monks approached the icon.

Stephanie came alongside them. "Do you know why the saint is bleeding tears?"

Father Sergius's brows knitted together. "Seems to be a warning of events to come."

Stephanie bit her lip.

Father Herman kissed the glass covering the icon. "There's a bleeding icon of the Theotokos and baby Jesus in Russia. It started streaming last month."

Stephanie gaped. "What events do you think are coming?"

"Can't say for sure. We aren't gifted with clairvoyance," Father Sergius said. "But we should always be in a prayerful state of repentance for our sins."

Father Herman nodded. "Repentance is always crucial."

Olga hobbled into the narthex from the nave. "Please turn the lights on, Stephanie, dear. It's dinnertime."

Stephanie shook her head, then faced Olga with an apologetic smile. "It's not time for dinner, Olga. It's nearly time for *Paraklesis*."

Olga's brows furrowed before her face brightened, noticing the monks for the first time. "Hello. You are a rarity these days."

"Good evening." Father Sergius introduced himself and his fellow monk. He pointed toward the nave. "Is your priest here?"

"We don't have one," Stephanie said, taking Olga's elbow and guiding her back into the nave.

"No priest?" Father Herman said. "How will the *Paraklesis* be led?"

"There aren't any priests available in town," Stephanie said. She settled Olga in her usual spot in the first pew, then turned toward the monks. "Deacon Michael does the services."

Father Sergius's face lit up. "Is the deacon here?"

"He should be," Stephanie said.

Olga lifted her cane with a trembling hand and pointed it a couple of inches off the floor. "Not quite yet. He will be here when the lights are on."

"Olga, the lights are always dimmed during this service," Stephanie said.

The elderly woman raised her eyes toward the lofty ceiling. The Pantocrator gazed down at them. "He's the source of the true Light."

"Yes, indeed." Father Sergius touched Olga's rounded shoulder. "May I call you Olga?"

"You may. It is my name after all." She winked and grinned, the lines in her face deepening.

Father Herman let out a hearty chuckle.

Deacon Michael came out of the altar area through the deacon's door on the left. His balding head shone from the dimly lit, sparkling chandeliers above him. His eyebrows rose as he spotted the monks.

"Hello. You are Deacon Michael?" Father Sergius asked.

"Yes, and welcome."

Father Sergius, once again, made his introductions.

"What brings you here to Saint John's?" Deacon Michael asked what Stephanie had wanted to since they first entered the church.

"We were sent here to retrieve a piece of the Holy Cross and the prophetic letter of Saint Dimitri," Father Sergius said. "They were brought over here in 1978 by pious laypeople fleeing the yoke of the Soviet Union."

Deacon Michael's mouth formed an *O*. "Your bishop sent you to this particular church for the relics?"

"Well, one of the churches in the area is supposed to be storing them, according to the hermit at Holy Trinity Monastery," Father Sergius said.

Deacon Michael frowned.

The Holy Cross relic and prophetic letter stuck in Stephanie's mind. How could the relics be at her church? She'd never seen them all the years she'd been attending.

Olga raised an arthritic, plump finger toward the ceiling. "My grandparents spoke of Saint Dimitri's prophecies."

Stephanie and the men turned their attention to the elderly woman in her usual black garb and headscarf.

Stephanie sat next to Olga. "You know about the saint's prophecies?"

Olga gave a slow nod, her gray eyes partially clouded with cataracts.

Father Sergius squatted in front of Olga. "Do you know if they are in your church?"

Olga stared off in the distance with her mouth ajar. "The candle has gone out, and only the wax remains."

Father Sergius frowned and looked at Deacon Michael. "What does she mean?"

The deacon moved his hands slightly up and down as if telling the monk to pipe down. He glanced at Olga, who was retying her headscarf. "She doesn't always remember things..." He folded his lips in as Olga finished with her scarf and gazed up at the deacon with a childlike expression.

Realization swept over the monks' faces.

Father Sergius got up. "We understand." He gestured toward the deacon. "Deacon, are you aware of these relics being in your church, if not now, perhaps at some point?"

Deacon Michael rubbed his thin beard. "I wasn't aware of those particular holy objects being stored here, but I've only been assigned to this church for two years." He pivoted toward a side door on their right. "But there is a room that holds relics and icons through there. However, I don't recall the Cross or saint's letter displayed in that place."

"Could they be in another more secure room?" Father Herman asked.

"The relics were kept in a safe in Russia," Father Sergius said. "They had to be hidden during Stalin's reign and under the communists since they'd destroyed so many of our churches and icons. They only allowed a few to remain for the facade of religious freedom."

Deacon Michael headed toward the door with the monks behind him.

Stephanie rose from the pew. "Deacon, may I come too?"

The clergyman turned to look at her after reaching the door. "You may."

Stephanie patted Olga's hands folded in her lap. "I'll be back in a little bit."

"Would you please turn on the lights?" Olga asked. She peered above her and squinted.

Not wanting to explain to the old woman again about the lights, Stephanie said, "Okay. I'll see to it," and hurried after the three men going through the door.

Deacon Michael unlocked the third door on the left of the long hallway. A paper icon of the Holy Trinity was taped to the wood.

Stephanie entered last. She'd been in this room a handful of times on special occasions when abbots or bishops would come through with holy icons and saints' relics, as well as when the church used to have its yearly festivals.

Beautiful old and newer icons hung on the walls and sat on

stands around the square space. Various sizes of wooden and silver-plated boxes holding relics lay on the two tables on either side of the room.

Deacon Michael directed the monks to the tables. She stood by the door, not wanting to be in their way but keeping her eyes on what they might find.

Father Sergius sighed. "Unfortunately, I don't see them."

Monk Herman's round face pinched. "There aren't any Orthodox churches left within a hundred-mile radius."

Deacon Michael headed to the door. Stephanie slipped out of the room and into the hallway before he reached the entrance. He locked the door behind the monks.

Olga shuffled down the corridor, her cane tapping the floor.

"Olga, why aren't you waiting in the pews?" Stephanie hurried over to the elderly woman, the clergyman and monastics flanking her.

"Stephanie's right," Deacon Michael said, taking hold of Olga's arm and leading her back to the door to the nave. He opened the door, and Olga hobbled to the front pew.

Olga turned to face Stephanie and the men. She raised a finger again. "I grew up in this church. Attended church school, got married here, my daughter's baptism." She pointed to the raised, rounded platform between the pews and the iconostasis. "My husband's funeral. His casket was sitting right there."

"This church has always been your home." Stephanie smiled and put an arm around Olga's shoulders.

Olga looked up at her. "I remember when you were just a little girl." She poked Stephanie in the ribs and chortled. "Such a cute thing you were."

Stephanie hugged her.

Deacon Michael shrugged at the monks. "I'm not sure where else the relics would be." He looked around. "I don't recall seeing any other hidden or special rooms. The rest are classrooms and the library."

Olga shook her head, the loose skin beneath her round chin jiggling. "That is not all." She pointed at the balcony and choir loft.

"Up the stairs from those pews." She tapped her temple and gave a nod. "I remember."

Stephanie folded in her lips. She didn't know what to make of what the elderly woman had said. For the past few minutes, she seemed to be talking with clarity. But there was no guarantee what she'd just said was part of that sense of intelligibility.

Deacon Michael peered at the loft. "What's up there?"

Olga beamed, her eyes nearly slits between the loose skin of her eyelids and bags under them. "I remember when I was a child."

"What do you remember, Olga?" Father Sergius asked.

"The cat would always get stuck in the attic. It would play in the gutters." Her hands trembling, leaning on her cane, Olga lowered herself onto the front pew. "Lily left her bicycle out in the rain again." She shook her head, then looked up at Stephanie. "We couldn't keep milking the cow because it had three legs, and my father wanted to shoot it. All because James broke the push mower." She tsked. "How do you break a push mower?"

Hoping to get Olga back on track regarding the room upstairs from the balcony, Stephanie sat beside her. "You were talking about the room above or next to the choir loft."

Olga scowled. "There is no choir loft in a barn, silly girl. Only the cow lives there. Weren't you listening to me?" She put a finger to her ear. "You have better hearing than me, so I don't see how you couldn't have heard me."

"Olga, you were first talking about a room by the choir loft when you said you grew up in this church." Deacon Michael bent toward the old woman as if she were a child.

Olga narrowed her eyes at Stephanie, as if inspecting her appearance. "I wore dresses to every church service, young lady." She wagged her finger at the deacon, then at Stephanie. "A lady didn't wear trousers in my day like they do now." She smoothed out her simple black frock. "My mother made all my dresses, and they were so beautiful. May her memory be eternal." She crossed herself.

"Memory eternal." Stephanie could feel the woman's grasp of the present slipping away.

"Well, it's time to start *Paraklesis*," the deacon announced and moved to the door on the iconostasis.

Father Sergius gestured toward the balcony, his mouth drooping in a deep frown. "Deacon, what about the room?"

Deacon Michael held up a hand. "The dear woman says a lot of things that are either from her imagination or from her childhood, the latter of which she remembers fondly. But what she says almost never coincides or correlates with anything in the present."

"But she was sounding well," Father Herman said.

"She was." Stephanie nodded. "It just doesn't seem to last very long."

"Stephanie, it's time to turn on the lights." Olga raised her gaze toward the ceiling.

She's back to the lights. Stephanie sighed. "I know, Olga."

Deacon Michael went through the door and into the altar.

The monks exchanged concerned stares as if unsure what to do.

Father Sergius clasped his hands together. "We will stay for *Paraklesis* and return Saturday afternoon before Vespers for a more thorough search of the church's many rooms. Your church gives us the most hope of finding the relics."

"Vespers is a lovely prayer service. It is wonderful it is done at sunset." Olga crossed herself. She closed her eyes as if imaging Vespers.

"Sounds good, Father. I hope you and Father Herman find the relics," Stephanie said. She glanced at Olga. Maybe Olga would remember some of Saint Dimitri's prophecies then. Her memories from childhood were so much more indelible than the present years. The empty balcony lay in shadows above them. And maybe the old woman would remember that secret room if there was one.

$$Ten$$

The next morning, Stephanie stood at the reception desk in the county jail. A plump woman dressed in a drab uniform wore the nametag HONEGGER. Her curly red hair framed her round face, icy blue eyes, and flaring nostrils, her expression that of a bull on the cusp of charging the matador's red cape. The smile she cracked looked painful as if it took immense effort to produce.

"Can I help you?"

"I'm here to see my mother, Ava Jenkins, and to inquire about her release."

The woman shook her head so violently one of her hoop earrings flew off her ear and landed on the countertop with a clatter. She sniffed, picked up the jewelry, and reattached it to her earlobe. "Nobody's being released at this time. And the weekly visiting hours are no longer eight to four but from twelve to two p.m."

Stephanie played with her purse strap. *What is she talking about?* "Why have they changed?"

"National security. The third Patriot Act. We're at war, and people protesting our efforts to protect our democracy and freedoms around the world are, as of last night, an illegal action."

Icy fear rained over Stephanie, leaving her frozen. She swallowed, then squeaked, "Illegal?"

"Yep."

"But my mother and the others had protested before it was illegal. They should be able to be released."

"Afraid not. Fairview City's President Greeley's in charge, and that's not permitted."

Stephanie shed the cold scales of fear as her face flushed. She leaned her palms on the desk and glared at the short woman shaped like a wine cork. "So they're supposed to flounder in this place?"

The woman scowled. "Of course not."

"Then you have a date when my mom can be released?"

Honegger glowered at her once more, and Stephanie got the impression she did this regularly. "I told you there is no information on any release dates, only that the prisoners—"

Stephanie straightened and took a step back. "Prisoners? Now they're prisoners?"

The woman huffed, resembling a bull again, and rose from her seat. "Only that the *detained* will be held indefinitely during this crucial time." She pointed to the entrance. "Call to schedule a visit between twelve and two before coming here next time. Otherwise, you'll be turned away."

Stephanie ground her teeth. What had her country become, holding its own for simply speaking and marching against an action they didn't agree with?

Honegger shuffled into a room next to the desk, and a coffeepot began to sputter, putting out a rancid and burnt odor.

Stephanie stomped out of the building, then jogged to her car. She'd forgotten to look up the remaining defense attorneys in town. Anxiety had fogged her thoughts.

As Stephanie drove home, she sucked in air, breathing in and out slowly, counting to ten to calm herself. Once she was home, she'd call a lawyer.

She turned in to her driveway.

Two military men stood on her porch, Jake in the doorway.

"God, now what?" She cut the engine, not bothering to put her car in the garage.

Stephanie hurried up the small walkway to the men.

"Mom, tell them I already filled out the form as a conscientious objector," Jake said, waving his hand as if wanting to pull the response from her.

The two men turned to look at her as she slid past them and stood next to her son, whose face was blotchy, his eyes on fire.

"That's correct," she said, lifting her chin. "Why are you here, gentlemen?"

The two men looked like twins with their harsh buzz cuts, smooth faces, and crisp olive-green uniforms. One had a name tag GRAVEN and the other STOCKTON.

"Good morning, ma'am. We're here to see your son regarding his signing up as a conscientious objector."

"Yeah, you saw me," Jake said, holding up two fingers on each hand, representing air quotes. He then made a shooing motion toward the men. "So you can leave now."

"When did you arrive?" Stephanie asked.

"Only minutes before you did, ma'am," Stockton said.

"I have the same question as my son. He did his duty signing the form. If there's nothing else you need to discuss with him…"

Graven's dark eyes locked on hers. "There is, ma'am." His stare fell on Jake. "Conscientious objector is no longer a valid reason for not serving in this war. All healthy men and women between the ages of eighteen and thirty must report for active duty."

"When'd that change? Two minutes ago?" Jake retorted.

"What do you mean conscientious objector isn't a valid exemption?" Stephanie folded her arms. "It's always been since the inception of our country."

Stockton straightened his posture. "It's invalid for this war. All able bodies are needed." He fisted his hands at his sides. "That's the order."

He gestured toward Jake but looked at Stephanie with a sober expression, his eyes void of any emotion. "Your son qualifies."

"This can't be right," Stephanie murmured, feeling sick to her stomach.

Graven jerked a nod. "We're here to transport your son to the recruitment office. He will report to basic training at Fort Benning."

Dizziness swept over Stephanie, and she took a wobbly step back, grabbing the doorframe. "Where is that?"

"Columbus, Georgia," the stone-faced Graven said.

Jake swayed side to side—a nervous movement he'd done since he was a child. He shook his head and flung his arms about. "This is bullshit!"

"No, it's real, Mr. Jenkins, so it's best to adapt to your new assignment as quickly as possible." Graven stepped toward her son as Jake backed up.

Hobo shot through the doggie door, crossed the living room, and came out on the porch, barking and jumping on the officers' legs.

Graven pushed Hobo off him. "Get ahold of your dog please."

Not knowing what they'd do to Hobo, Stephanie scooped him up, rushed up the stairs to her room, and set him on her bed. "Stay here and be quiet, Hobo. I'll be back soon."

He cocked his head to the side before she closed the door.

She ran down the stairs just as Jake thrust out his arms. "Stay out!"

The men stepped into the small foyer.

Heat crept up Stephanie's neck. She pointed to the porch. "You will stay on the porch."

The men retreated to outside the doorway. Stockton checked his watch. "You have ten minutes. We've got a tight schedule."

Jake blanched. "Ten minutes?"

"Yes."

"How am I supposed to grab all I need in that short of time?"

"We can help expedite the process," Graven said.

Jake huffed. "I don't need your help." He flicked a glance at Stephanie. "Mom?"

"I'm here, son." Still reeling from the unexpected appearance of the men, Stephanie grappled with the ache in her heart, seeing the panic in her son's eyes. Her own fear threatened to shake her to pieces. She swallowed, working to compose herself. "What can he take with him?"

"Mom!"

She rubbed his arm, trying to calm him. "We have no choice."

"Essential items. Soap, clothes, deodorant. You know," Graven said, clasping his hands behind his back.

Jake's stare darted from her to the men, then to her again, as he went back to swaying side to side.

Helplessness weighed her down, and she inhaled deeply to not feel as if she were suffocating. "I'll help him collect his belongings, but please can you answer one other question?"

"Yes, ma'am," Stockton said.

"How long will he be gone?" She wrung her hands, bracing herself for their answer.

"We don't have a permanent date of his return. However, after basic, he'll deploy with his unit overseas."

"Overseas? Shit!" Jake ran a hand through his shoulder-length, sandy-blond hair that he'd worked so hard to grow in the Orthodox Christian tradition.

Stephanie bit her quivering lip, knowing his hair would be shaved off soon.

Tears threatened to flood her cheeks, and the lump in her throat was so large she struggled to swallow. "Y-your answer does nothing to assure me he'll be okay."

"We know, ma'am, but we don't have any other information for you."

She sniffled, wiping the tears from her cheeks.

Graven checked his watch again. "Seven minutes. Best get moving, Mr. Jenkins."

Jake's eyes glistened with moisture.

Stephanie touched his arm. "I'll be up in a minute."

He nodded, then stomped up the stairs.

"Can you at least tell me how we'll be able to keep in contact?"

"At this point, writing letters will be the only communication."

"No emails? Texts?"

The men exchanged questionable looks.

Graven cleared his throat, lowering his chin. "No email or text, ma'am. Letters only."

They weren't telling her something. She chewed on the inside of her cheek as nausea swam in her belly. The whole encounter made her head spin. Before she lost her balance and let panic take over, she excused herself and climbed the stairs.

Stephanie found Jake stuffing underwear into his duffel bag in his room.

He looked up when she came in. "Mom, keep my computer safe. Oh…" He pulled out a sheet from his desk drawer and handed it to her. "These are my usernames and passwords." He pointed to the scribbled information on the left side of the page. His finger moved to the names on the right side. "Please go on my Accord server and contact my friends to let them know where I've gone."

Reality of his dire predicament sank in deeper than ever. Stephanie hesitated to tell him about his friends, but maybe he'd find a little comfort in knowing he wouldn't be alone. "Son, your friends will probably be in a similar situation as yours."

He paused and gazed at nothing. She held her breath as her throat closed.

"You're right." His voice was too calm. Was he in shock?

Stephanie came around his bed and folded him in her arms. She fought against letting herself go. *Later, when he's gone. Gone. Oh God.* Stephanie squeezed her eyes shut, pushing away tormenting thoughts.

Jake released her and went back to packing his clothes before going to the bathroom for other items.

Moving into the hallway, she spied Stockton stepping into the foyer once again. She fisted her hands at her sides. "Please wait on the porch as I'd asked you to. He'll be down in a minute."

"A minute is all he has." The officer backed out of the house.

Stephanie followed her son out the door and to the awaiting blue government sedan. As the officers got in, she embraced Jake. Running a hand over the side of his face, she memorized his blue eyes, flowing hair, and fuzzy, sparse beard. "You write me when you can."

Jake bit his bottom lip. "I will." He shook his head, looked over his shoulder, then faced her again. "Can you believe this shit?"

She could only squeeze his shoulder in response. He gave her a kiss on the cheek, locked eyes with hers. "Bye, Mom. I love you."

She wrapped him in one last quick hug, whispering through the thick tears clogging her throat, "I love you more than life, Jake. Take care of yourself."

"I will."

"Come on," Stockton said from the passenger-door's open window.

Jake got in the back seat with his bag.

The car rolled away from the curb, taking her heart with it.

Eleven

Brody sat on a bench in front of a Five-Dollar Store in downtown Fairview. He gave six-year-old Lindy the last half of his fast-food burger after she'd finished hers. "Eat up."

Lindy wasted no time biting into the sandwich.

Brody squinted down the street toward the shabby restaurant. "We were lucky somebody bought us a couple of burgers." *Don't know what we'll eat tonight.*

He glanced at his daughter, who was focused completely on the food in her hands. Each day the ability to get or find food dwindled. How would he feed his daughter? Himself?

The church they frequently visited used to provide bags of canned meats and vegetables. He wiped his mouth of residual crumbs. That no longer happened due to the newest rules pressed upon him and his homeless brethren.

He could tell that the police—and some of the people walking the streets in their fancy office clothes that he had once worn—hated him. They gave him looks of contempt every time they passed by. At times, they even had the audacity to glare at his daughter, who was in this predicament because he had lost his job, the company he worked for having gone under. No fault of her own. He put a hand on Lindy's head and smoothed down her stringy blond hair.

Brody peered down the road at the few small shops on either side. Clusters of people sat and lay on the sidewalk near the storefronts, as well as the alleys between the buildings. How long would those businesses stay open? If they shuttered, the few job opportunities left would be gone, never to return. He ran a hand down his face.

A woman with bronze skin, long raven hair, and a thin figure approached him. Her shirt and pants hung loosely on her. Behind her trailed a teenaged boy with the same coloring with a curly mop of hair on his head. He wore a stained T-shirt, torn jeans, and ratty sneakers.

"Brody, I'm glad I found you." The woman ran a hand through her hair. "You weren't by that church you like to hang around."

He lifted his chin toward her. "Hey, Mary."

Lindy waved at Mary, then looked up at Brody and pointed at the water fountain near the rusted swing set in a small patch of grass a few yards from them. "Daddy, can I get some water?"

"You bet. Go ahead."

Lindy ran toward the fountain.

He rose and gestured for Mary to take his seat on the bench.

Mary sat. "Thanks." She flapped her hand toward her son. "Noah, go see Lindy."

He frowned. "Why? She'll be back in a few seconds."

Mary's face pinched.

"What is it?" Brody asked.

She shooed Noah away again. He shrugged, then ambled toward Lindy.

Brody sat back down on the bench. "What's going on?"

"Did you hear the president's brought back the draft?"

"Yeah, I heard." He glanced at Noah. "He's not eighteen, is he?"

"Thankfully, no." She gave him a pitiful stare. "At least not for two more months."

Would that matter to the feds? If they got more desperate than they were now, he doubted it.

Mary rubbed her hands down her thighs several times.

He placed his hand on top of one of hers. He didn't say anything, not wanting to make her worry any more than she already was.

Two monks, a tall, thin one and a stout, shorter one, strolled down the sidewalk next to the park, stopping where Lindy and Noah stood by the fountain. The tall one bent and put out his hand for her to shake. Lindy gave him a shy smile. The other man patted Noah on the back. They asked Lindy something, and she pointed toward Brody. They nodded and headed his way.

He stood and approached the men. "Hey. I'm Brody."

The tall monk shook his hand. "I'm Father Sergius, and this is Father Herman. How are you doing?"

He shrugged. "I'm surviving so far."

The monastics frowned. The stocky one patted his back. "Brody, can we help you in any way?"

He gazed up at the sky. "Can you put in a good word for me?"

Father Sergius smiled. "Of course." He pulled out two granola bars and a ten-dollar bill. "You have our prayers as well as these."

Brody froze. He scanned the area for any nearby police officers, but they were congregating by the police station a couple of blocks down from them. "You may not know this, but giving food or money to a homeless person is against the law now."

Father Herman's thick brows knitted. "It's *not* a just law." He pulled out a five-dollar bill and put it in Brody's hand.

Father Sergius set his items in Brody's other hand. "Tuck them in your pockets."

Choking back tears, Brody nodded. "Thank you." *I have dinner for tonight.*

Each monk took a turn to embrace him.

He wiped under his eyes. "Are you going to Saint John's?"

"We are visiting the townspeople right now but will eventually go to the church." Father Sergius clasped his hands as if in prayer. "God be with you."

The two monks strolled toward the groups of homeless people down the street.

Lindy came alongside Brody. "Those guys said they're monks."

"Yeah, they are, sweetheart." He gathered her in his arms and kissed the top of her head.

Mary and Noah joined them.

"It's nice to see there are still some clergy around here," Mary said.

"Yeah." Brody watched the monks sit on the ground in front of a couple of homeless people and take their hands in theirs.

A blue government sedan parked next to the curb to the police department. Two army officers stepped out and joined the four policemen a few feet away.

One of the policemen nodded and raised a megaphone to his mouth. "Men and women between the ages of eighteen and thirty, line up here for mandatory service."

Grumblings and gasps came from the gaggle of homeless people on the sidewalks.

Brody rubbed his forehead, grimacing. *There it is. They've come to gather up the poor to sacrifice them to the War Machine.*

The same cop raised the megaphone again. "For the rest of you, I've got good news." He scanned the quiet audience.

Good news? I doubt it. Brody folded his arms across his chest.

"We're setting up a shelter for the remaining people who are not eligible for military service."

Murmuring floated through the crowd of tattered-clothed bodies.

"Be prepared to report in front of the police station Monday morning at eight o'clock to receive an assigned number."

Brody huffed. *What are they up to?*

His fellow homeless smiled and chattered as if they'd been given a free meal. He squinted at them. Desperation could muddle the brain.

Mary touched his arm. "That's only three days until we're signed up." She smiled. "This *is* good news. We'll finally have a safe place to sleep."

"Maybe."

She looked at him with a puzzled expression. "Maybe?"

"Let's see what happens on Monday."

Mary sighed and let go of his arm.

"I don't mean to get you down. I just don't trust our government."

She nodded with her lips pursed.

She doesn't agree, but that's okay. I'll be vigilant for all of us. His gaze traveled over his daughter, Noah, and Mary. He squeezed her shoulder.

A couple of young homeless men moved toward the police officers while most stayed where they were.

The army officers, along with a couple of the cops, descended upon the knots of penniless people and began questioning their ages. Knowing a few of his fellow vagrants, Brody heard some of them lie about their ages, even though they didn't look young enough to pass for sixteen-year-olds. The authorities gripped several of them and escorted the resistant men and women to the police station's entrance.

The monks followed closely behind two of the policemen, with gestures appearing to be questioning their actions. The cops ignored the brothers and continued up the stairs of the station.

Two cops marched toward Mary and Noah.

Brody tensed. *Shit.*

Mary's hand clamped onto his forearm. "Brody, what are they—?"

One of the policemen with a red nose and beefy chest pointed at Noah. "How old is he?"

Mary let go of Brody and put a protective arm around Noah's shoulders. "He's seventeen. Why?"

The officers exchanged looks, then nodded.

"Old enough," the stocky one said, grabbing Noah's arm.

"B-but I'm not eighteen," the boy cried.

Mary blanched, gripping her son's other arm. "Let him go!"

Brody stepped in front of Noah. "What are you doing, Officer?"

The cop glared at Brody. "The war effort requires all eligible young men and women to report for service." He grunted. "You heard."

"Mama, they can't do that, can they?" Noah whined.

Brody held up a hand. "He's not eighteen."

The other officer, who matched his comrade in heftiness, lifted his arm between Brody and Noah. "Step aside."

The officers patted Noah on the back.

"It's always an honor and privilege to serve your country, son," the first cop said.

"You'll be a hero one day," the other added.

Brody's jaw tightened. *They're as bad as the military recruiters.*

Mary burst out sobbing, clinging to Noah. Brody clutched Noah, trying to remove him from the claws of the policemen, whose expressions showed amusement, getting too much pleasure out of their task. Brody pushed one of the cops back from Noah.

The officer jumped forward and shoved a baton in Brody's face. "Unless you want to be arrested for interfering with War Department business, it would be wise to stay out of this."

The cops pulled Noah away from Mary's arms. "No!" she screamed.

Brody caught Mary before she crumpled to the ground. He embraced her, rubbing her back. Lindy clung to his waist. He wrapped an arm around his trembling daughter.

His anger singed inside him as he glowered at the cops marching frightened Noah to the station.

When will those bastards running our country get what they deserve? He kept his eyes on the thugs. *It better happen in my lifetime.*

Twelve

Stephanie woke at 7:16 the next morning with wet cheeks, crusty eyelids, and a stuffy nose.

The night had been long and saturated with sorrow. The utter silence and loneliness echoed in her head, her heart aching. She stared at the plain white ceiling.

What was Jake doing? Climbing ropes, scrambling over walls in basic training? Or was a drill instructor screaming in his face, chipping away Jake's very essence, his identity—the young man she'd raised and always known?

The cloudy sky poured gray glare through her bedroom window, which only intensified her melancholy.

She hadn't gotten the chance to look up lawyers for her mother. She clutched her hair. Everything was out of control. Governor Greeley, a wealthy corporate CEO of the huge video game company, Vordex Video Games, was in complete agreement with other governors and President Harden's administration. Nobody could talk negatively about the senseless wars.

Running a hand down her moist face, Stephanie sighed, then slid out of bed. She needed coffee... Something in her stomach. On the brink of despondency last night, she hadn't eaten.

In the kitchen, she started the coffeepot, made herself a scrambled egg, and set a cup of yogurt with fruit next to her plate.

The clock on the wall read 7:21. President Harden's press conference on cyber security would be airing at seven thirty.

Stephanie grabbed her laptop from the living room and set it on the table. Pouring herself a cup of coffee, she sat back down and clicked on the live press conference link.

While waiting, she made herself finish the egg. Before she dug a spoon into her yogurt, President Harden, dressed in a black suit, entered the press room flanked by two men from the National Protection Agency. Cameras clicked and flashed throughout the room.

The president displayed an artificial smile. "Good morning, my fellow Americans." He straightened his posture and jerked his head slightly to the left as if his tie was too tight. "General Kendrick has reported that enemy drones have been spotted over many important landmarks and cities in our nation. Our Defense Department has been tracking and destroying them."

Stephanie set down her mug. *How were they able to sneak through our defense systems?*

"The cyberattacks have increased since my last announcement. My fellow Americans, we are under direct assault."

A chill ran through her. *This is unreal.* She pressed a hand to her churning stomach, her appetite gone.

The president held up his hands. "Please do not panic. We are executing adequate measures to keep the citizenry safe." He raised a finger, silencing a reporter who'd stood to speak.

President Harden looked into the camera, lifting his chin as a creepy smile slid across his face. "I ask you all to participate in keeping yourselves and your neighbors safe. Watch out for each other. Report any suspicious activity."

Stephanie grimaced. *What* measures *have you and your administration concocted?*

"With regard to the thousands of hacks every day, we also are asking you..." He paused, casting a look that held doubt, toward the general, before his focus moved slightly to his left. He cleared his throat. "The internet is completely compromised, infiltrated by foreign enemies. It is not safe for anyone to be using the internet now. Banks, retailers, restaurants, schools—every institution is vulnerable and has been attacked by Chinese hackers." He swept an arm across the room. "You've seen this with the countless stories reported in the past few weeks. We are requesting everyone to stop accessing online sites until such a time when we feel it is safe to resume usage."

Grumblings echoed in the press room before several reporters shot up from their chairs, all yelling out questions at the same time.

President Harden held up a hand as if stopping traffic. "Questions can be asked after I've finished."

No internet? She ran a hand through her hair. Jake's worries about their computers being confiscated weren't far off. The federal government was just doing this in a more subtle way. How were people going to communicate without their phones? Texting? Reaching out to friends on Convo Central? And what about web pay for her bills? How was she going to keep up with important updates through the My Workplace app that she and her coworkers used daily for shift swaps, sick notices, and checking weekly schedules?

She blew out a breath that fluttered her bangs. Most of her shopping was done online. Was everyone going to be forced to go back to life before digital technology? Without these computerized conveniences, she would feel like a fish on dry land. She shook her head. They'd become too dependent on these machines. Two generations ago, people lived fine without them. Something told her she'd have to learn to as well.

"In addition, we've implemented an eight p.m. to five a.m. curfew due to the dangerous invasion of enemy drones penetrating our night skies. We've placed the National Guard at our borders with Mexico and Canada, and our intelligence agencies, along with the National Protection Agency, are utilizing the Stryker Force's system that has tracked every one of them and will continue to monitor and destroy them as necessary."

President Harden ran his palms over the lectern's surface and cast his gaze slightly to his right. "I know most companies depend on computer systems. Thankfully, through executive orders, my administration will compensate our workforce by providing thirty-five percent of your salary monthly for the duration of the war."

Thirty-five percent? Stephanie scowled while panic nudged at her rib cage. *Does he really think people can survive on that? We're barely surviving as it is.*

His beady eyes bored into Stephanie. "If we find mass cooperation is failing, we will take the necessary measures to ensure your safety and compliance."

A reporter shot from his seat. "Mr. President, sir, what does that mean exactly?"

Yes, what's the president talking about? She pressed her lips together. Was their idea of compliance what they did to Jake? Marching him off to a war zone? Stephanie swallowed hard and closed her eyes for a second, working to erase the worrisome thoughts threatening to take over her mind.

President Harden's mouth slid into a firm line, and he walked away from the podium toward the door, with the general and the two National Protection Agency officials filing out after him.

"So much for taking questions." Stephanie's stomach twisted into a knot as she shut her laptop. How she missed her son and mother. Trudging upstairs, helplessness pulled her down like an anvil, and her body seemed to weigh a thousand pounds.

Stephanie sat on the edge of her bed. Going to work seemed impossible. How could she stifle her pain?

Hobo trotted into the bedroom and hopped on her lap, smiling as always. What luck to be oblivious to everything terrible in the world. What a way to live. If only she had the capacity to do that.

Her belly roiled again. She rubbed it as her last conversation with her mother came to mind. Her father's guns. She hugged herself. With so much turmoil and hardship going on, her mother was probably right. She needed to protect herself. But two questions niggled at her.

Where had her father hidden his guns, and would she be able to use one if she had to?

The doorbell rang. Hobo jumped off her lap, barking. He ran down the stairs. She followed him and peeked out the peephole. Pam's pinched face filled the round space.

Stephanie opened the door.

Pam, with tears in her eyes, stepped inside and hugged her.

"Are you okay?" Stephanie asked.

Pam burst out crying. "They took my baby girl this morning."

Stephanie continued to embrace her until she was ready to let go.

"My brother called me a little while ago. He'd visited her at school just before they took her. The army sent her to boot camp," she said between sobs.

Stephanie settled Pam on the couch. "I'm so sorry. Do you know which camp?"

Pam plucked a tissue from the end table and mopped her soaked face. She blew her nose, then shook her head. "Can you believe it?"

Stephanie's throat closed.

Pam took Stephanie's hand. "Did they come by your house?"

Stephanie had been so gutted by what happened yesterday she hadn't had a chance to tell her friend. She'd barely been able to process it herself. She squeezed Pam's hand and nodded.

"Oh no. When?"

"Yesterday morning."

Pam hugged her and began crying again.

Hobo hopped on the couch and burrowed between them.

"I feel like there's nothing we can do." Pam sniffled and petted Hobo's head.

Stephanie sighed. "I feel the same."

Pops of gunfire outside shattered their mutual misery.

Pam dove onto the carpet while Hobo crawled under the couch, whining. Stephanie crept across the living room toward the front door. She turned the dead bolt before peering out the peephole. Nobody was on her porch or in the street. Where had the shots come from?

She ran upstairs and peeked out her bedroom window that faced the road. A crowd had gathered on the far-left side of the street, barely visible from her vantage point. A fire blazed from a dumpster.

Protestors? Of course. Who wouldn't be protesting all that had been pressed upon the public? But a portion of them were sitting in the county jail. She bit her lip as her mother's face surfaced in her mind.

Five young men in sweatsuits ran down the street past her house. Three older men chased them, shouting words she couldn't make out. One of the three men, who looked like her neighbor Don, held a gun and aimed it at the gang ahead of them.

"Oh God." Shaking, Stephanie sank onto the floor, squeezing her eyes closed. She covered her ears as more shots rang out.

Whining from downstairs drifted up to her room.

"Steph! What's going on?" Pam yelled.

With the lull in gunfire, Stephanie looked out the window.

"Stay outta our neighborhood, punks!" Don shouted and stood in the street next to her front yard. A strange sensation of relief mixed with horror poured into her chest. Maybe he and the two men with him were trying to protect the neighborhood. But where were the police? They usually showed up for disturbances like these. Had the police abandoned the citizens to defend their own homes and property?

The two other men joined Don, and they marched back down the street from which they'd come.

Stephanie fell on her bed, curled up. *My neighborhood has become a battle zone.*

LATER IN THE EVENING, STEPHANIE SAT ON HER DAD'S recliner and searched her phone for Fairview defense lawyers.

Pam lay on the couch, wrapped in a purple fuzzy blanket, sound asleep. She'd gone to her home, collected toiletries and pajamas, and returned to Stephanie's house to stay the night. The stress of her daughter taken away that morning had drained

Stephanie's friend, and she'd collapsed onto the couch after dinner.

Stephanie peeked on Convo Central. Panic from her friends filled half her newsfeed, sharing the same worries she'd been dealing with earlier. Others were eerily silent.

She had to put aside the alarming posts and track down a decent attorney for her mother. Fear gripped Stephanie at the thought of her phone and internet being traced. But how would she find a lawyer without at least one of them?

Her father's guns came back to her. After the earlier shooting incident, the desire to find at least one of the guns to protect herself and property grew inside her, outweighing her fear of firearms. Where could her father have hidden them?

She got up and headed toward the staircase when Hobo began growling behind her.

Spinning around, Stephanie spotted two middle-aged men at the sliding glass door, jiggling the door handle. Metal clattered against metal. Her heart sank into her stomach, her body rigid, frozen in fear.

Hobo ran toward the door and jumped up and down, barking and snarling.

Pam shot up from the couch and screamed.

One of the men pushed the door open, a gun in his hand. He kicked Hobo to the side. Her poor dog yelped and landed in a heap on the carpet a few feet away.

Stephanie snapped out of her paralyzed state, her heart thumping against her ribs. She rushed over to Hobo and folded him in her arms, his body trembling. Tears stung her eyes. "Hobo."

Anger streaked through her, and she glared at the men. "He's harmless. You didn't have to kick him!"

The man with the gun pointed it at her.

She sucked in a breath.

A tangled beard hung from his sallow face, his brown eyes dull and vacant. "All we want is some food. Haven't eaten in five days."

Pam came alongside her. She gave Stephanie a sideways look with knitted brows. Her lips quivered.

The second man, thin like his partner, stepped inside the living room. He followed the first man into the kitchen.

Pam squeezed Stephanie's arm. "Steph…"

She nodded and held Hobo close to her chest, his warm body a comfort. *If he's telling the truth, they'll leave in a few minutes.* She leaned her cheek against the top of Hobo's head. *God, I hope they just want food.*

The grungy man with the gun opened the pantry and snatched a jar of peanut butter, a bag of chips, and a loaf of bread, while the other man grabbed the remaining three sodas in a six-pack and two apples from the fridge. Opening a few drawers until he found what he'd wanted, the man with the gun took out a butter knife.

He turned and jutted his chin toward Stephanie. "Thanks."

He and his partner crept out the sliding glass door. Pam ran and closed it, locking it again. Stephanie clenched her teeth to stop them from chattering. That lock was worthless now. She'd have to get a new one to replace it. But they were safe, hadn't been harmed.

She sat on the couch with Hobo.

Pam settled next to them. "Is he okay?"

Stephanie stroked him over and over. He lay with his eyes half-open. His ribs and limbs felt all right. No bones broken that she could tell. She exhaled. "He's okay, just scared."

"I don't blame him. So was I." Pam rubbed Hobo's ear. "We could've been killed."

"They were starving, only wanting food."

Pam eyed her with a tight mouth. "This time, yeah."

Stephanie dialed the police and gave them the descriptions of the two men. With that done, she didn't want to think about the robbers anymore, allowing constant fear to rule over her. Jake surfaced in her mind. If he'd been there… The way he behaved toward antagonistic people, especially if they had threatened her in this instance, he might have overreacted and gotten shot or worse. She groaned, running a hand down her face.

Pam's arm rested on her shoulders. "We're okay. Hobo's okay. Sorry for scaring you."

She shook her head. "I was just thinking about Jake."

Pam whimpered, her face scrunching up. She squeezed Stephanie against her. "I'm always thinking about Laura too."

Stephanie could only nod, swallowing back the tears collecting in her eyes and throat. She embraced her friend. Too much had happened. But one flicker of light brightened the darkness running through her mind. Tomorrow evening was Vespers. She'd go for the service and talk with Deacon Michael and Olga. Being with them in the church, she could find some real peace.

Thirteen

Stephanie took a seat in the third pew from the altar and icon partition. The front doors creaked open, catching her attention. The monks that had visited a couple of days ago entered the narthex and gathered at the candle stand.

Her spirits lifted. They'd been able to return for Vespers, despite all the chaos in the city. Now only Olga was missing. She was usually early. Stephanie hoped the old woman hadn't fallen ill. As odd as Olga could be, she was a comfort to Stephanie—a constant fixture attached to the church throughout the years.

Deacon Michael and the monks approached her.

She stood and gave a nod to the monastics. "Welcome back."

"Thank you. It's nice to see you again." Father Sergius tilted his head toward the other monk. "We were blessed to make it here tonight."

Stephanie frowned. "Oh no. I was afraid you'd have trouble getting here."

"Our hotel is right outside the city limits. We had to have a reason for entering the city," Father Herman said, his deep voice intoning concern.

"They're in the process of constructing a cement wall," Father Sergius said.

She tensed, goose bumps running up her arms and legs. "Governor Greeley is closing off the city?"

"It looks that way," Father Sergius said.

"There's already about five miles of it up," Father Herman added.

Deacon Michael's brows pinched. "Not a good sign."

The front door squeaked, and Lily came into the narthex with Olga hobbling behind her. Lily waved at Stephanie, and the men then slipped out the door.

Stephanie hustled over to Olga and offered her arm to hold on to while the old woman lit a candle with a trembling hand. She then guided Olga to her usual spot in the first pew.

Deacon Michael went through the left door of the iconostasis and began Vespers.

During the chanting and reading of Old Testament scripture, Stephanie stole a glance at the choir loft behind her but quickly spun back around. *Focus on the readings.* She could inquire about that room after the service.

When Vespers ended, the monks joined Stephanie, Olga, and Deacon Michael.

Father Sergius knelt by Olga and smiled. "Dear Olga, are you willing to tell us more about the room you mentioned when we last visited?"

A deep crease settled between Olga's gray eyebrows, her stare reflecting a lost child's.

The deacon clasped his hands. "Father Sergius, that was a few days ago. Perhaps remind her what you're referring to in more detail."

The monk nodded and patted Olga's hand. "I'm sorry for the confusion."

Olga squeezed his hand. "Father, it's not confusing, really. It's only that I don't recall our conversation." She pointed to her head. "I can't remember what I ate for lunch, let alone what I'd said to you days ago." She leaned over, cupping her hand around her mouth. "If you haven't noticed, I'm very old."

Stephanie stifled a laugh. But Father Herman let out a deep, hearty one.

Father Sergius sat next to Olga. "Dear Olga, you aren't that old."

She let out a raspy chuckle. "Perhaps you need to purchase some glasses."

The monk held up his palms. "I have perfect eyesight."

Olga giggled, the sound light and childlike. "Very well."

Deacon Michael gestured toward Father Sergius. "Fathers, would you remind Olga why you've joined us here?"

"Yes, of course." Father Sergius straightened his posture. "You see, we are looking for a piece of the Cross of Christ and Saint Dimitri's prophetic letter."

Olga raised her index finger. "My grandparents told me many times about the saint's prophecies."

Stephanie leaned toward the elderly woman, as all the men's intense stares were on her. *Olga's in her right mind.* Hope was palpable in the hallowed space.

"Yes. You've told—" Father Herman began to say.

Father Sergius gave his brother a quick shake of his head, then looked earnestly at Olga. "Can you tell us about his prophecies or about where you think his letter may be now?"

Olga rested her hunched back against the pew and gazed at the domed ceiling with Christ in its center. A shy smile colored her cheeks pink. "I grew up in this church. It is my second home."

Father Sergius nodded.

Olga had repeated what she'd said the other day as she tended to do with anything she discussed. Stephanie grasped the top lip of the pew between her and Olga. These men were monastics. They had learned patience. She was still struggling with it, even after several past conversations with Olga. But none had been as important as this one.

Olga tapped Stephanie's arm, her filmy eyes narrowing as if trying to see her more clearly. "Please turn on the lights."

With Vespers over, brighter lighting was permitted. Stephanie rushed to the switches on the nave's walls near the narthex. The chandeliers gleamed with glowing incandescence.

Stephanie took her seat next to Olga.

Olga held up her hands. "Light. Wonderful, glorious light." She patted Stephanie's hand and grinned. "Now I can see."

Stephanie squeezed Olga's hand.

Father Sergius pointed at the balcony. "Olga, do you remember being up there?"

She followed his finger, and her face brightened. "Ah, yes. I was part of the children's choir."

While Father Herman sat on the pew across the aisle from them, Deacon Michael remained standing.

Olga laced her fingers together in her lap. "I enjoyed singing the hymns, especially for Holy Week and Pascha." She chanted a verse from the Holy Friday Lamentations service.

"One of my favorites." Father Sergius smiled, then gestured toward the balcony. "Olga, do you remember a room near the choir loft?"

Olga puckered her lips. "We kids played up in the loft, except James. He was scared of heights. Always was." She gazed at the ceiling, saying, "Memory eternal," and crossing herself.

Stephanie and the men did the same.

"Is there a secret room up there?" Father Herman asked.

Olga grinned. "Ha! Like the *Secret Garden*. Lily's favorite book."

Deacon Michael moved to the aisle. "We can go up and check."

"No," Olga said in a sharp tone, as if scolding the deacon.

He paused and looked at her with wide eyes.

"We must finish our homework before playtime, James. You know the rules." Olga tsked and shook her head.

Deacon Michael rubbed his chin and eyed Olga. "We don't have any homework, so we can go play."

Father Herman rose. "Saint Dimitri's letter could be up there."

Stephanie tensed. The monk was jumping ahead.

Olga put a finger to her lips. "Repentance. He spoke a great deal about this. The world was growing more and more cold, unbending, blind."

Stephanie's mouth fell open. She put an arm around Olga.

Deacon Michael and the monks surrounded Olga.

"That's right, Olga," the deacon said.

"What else did he say?" Father Sergius asked.

Olga's face paled. "Too much death."

Stephanie caught her breath and pressed a hand to her chest. Jake being driven off in the government vehicle filled her head. *Is he being sent to his death?* She squeezed her eyes shut. *Don't think such things.*

Olga's face drooped, which added to Stephanie's worries.

"*Babushka* and *Dedushka* witnessed so much death."

She'd gone back in time again. Was Olga's first remark about future deaths or her grandparents' generation?

Olga looked around the room. "Where's Lily? She's out too late. It's past her bedtime."

Stephanie slumped in the pew, Father Herman sat back down, and Father Sergius ran a hand down his face.

Deacon Michael sat on one of the three steps to the marble platform in front of the altar. "Fathers, would you like to go up to the loft?"

"Yes, Deacon. Maybe the room is up there?" Father Sergius asked.

"We can find out now." Deacon Michael strode down the aisle with the monks behind him.

Stephanie rushed after them, then stopped and looked over her shoulder. "We'll be back in a few minutes, Olga."

Olga's face scrunched up. "You're going to leave me here alone with so many of the enemy around, preying on the people?"

Stephanie tilted her head to the side, more confused than before. "Enemy? In church?"

"In the world…" Olga turned her head and faced the altar.

The words weren't registering in Stephanie's muddled mind, but she did understand Olga didn't want to be left alone. The little woman struggled to stand, leaning on her cane.

Stephanie hurried back to Olga and lifted her arm for the old woman to hold. She led her toward the narthex where the men had entered a few minutes ago. She and Olga reached the empty space.

The door on the right led to the stairs to the balcony. She took a step in its direction, but Olga didn't budge.

"What is it, Olga?"

"I cannot climb stairs."

She guided Olga to the elevator. They rode the slow machine to the second floor, then stepped into the small foyer next to the stairs and door to the loft. Stephanie opened it for Olga to hobble through, catching sight of the men standing near the balcony, looking down on the rows of pews and the iconostasis.

Deacon Michael turned toward them. "There you are."

Stephanie nodded. "Olga needed to take the elevator."

"Of course. I'm glad the church has one." The deacon headed toward the doorway to the flight of stairs, the monks behind him.

Stephanie bounced on the balls of her feet, ready to follow the men. She glanced at Olga. "You'll have to wait here. There's no elevator."

Olga lowered herself on the front pew and folded her hands in her lap. "The cat has safely gotten herself out of the attic."

Stephanie scrambled up the stairs. She reached the landing and found two doors on her left. Deacon Michael and the monks were crossing the threshold of the first door. She trailed behind them and stepped into the room with a dull light mounted on its ceiling. Stacks of old church schoolbooks, folded tables, a box of Christmas decorations, and one with a flashlight, hammer, duct tape, and other odds and ends occupied the space.

"Not in here," Deacon Michael said and pivoted toward the door.

Father Sergius nodded, and he and his fellow monk left the room.

Stephanie moved into the foyer, then entered the other room after the men. Pitch darkness met them.

"Where's the light switch?" Father Herman asked, his powerful voice filling the dark void.

"I don't feel one on the walls," Deacon Michael answered on her left.

Stephanie remembered the storage room. "There was a flashlight in the other room. I'll go get it." Stephanie walked into the light of the foyer.

"Mom? Where are you?" Lily's faint voice came from downstairs.

Stephanie bounded down the stairs and approached Olga dozing with her chin resting on her chest.

"Lily, we're up here!" Stephanie gently shook Olga awake.

Olga snorted, then opened her filmy eyes and shifted her disoriented gaze onto her. "Stephanie?"

"Yes. Lily is here to pick you up."

The echo of footsteps on the wooden stairs carried to the loft.

Stephanie helped Olga stand and handed her cane to her.

Lily appeared in the doorway with her mouth ajar. "What in the world are you two doing up here?"

Olga shuffled toward her daughter. "Why are you not in bed? It's a school night."

Lily took hold of Olga's free hand and placed it on her arm. "It's after Vespers. Time to go home."

Olga smiled. "Ah, Vespers. It was beautiful as always."

Before getting into the elevator, Olga turned slowly around, her cane tapping the floor. "Stephanie, the blood will not stop running without repentance. He will come to our aid only when our hearts soften and warm like the comforting blaze of a fire in the hearth and love expands as wide as the earth's firmament."

An incomprehensible peace overcame Stephanie as she watched the old woman and her middle-aged daughter enter the elevator, its doors creaking closed.

Had Olga remembered the saint's prophecy, or was it her own? Chuckling at the idea that Olga could be clairvoyant when she couldn't recall where she was most of the time, Stephanie shook her head, then froze. But Saint Dimitri's prophecy was told to Olga in her youth. She wouldn't dismiss the possibility that memory had stayed with Olga.

"Stephanie?" Deacon Michael called from upstairs.

She'd nearly forgotten about the flashlight. Racing up the stairs, she grabbed it from the storage room and clicked it on when stepping into the dark room. She ran the beam over the wall on her left.

The deacon shielded his eyes and chuckled. "Well, you found it."

"Sorry." She moved the light away from him and focused its beam on the walls on either side of the doorway. A light switch sat on the left side. She pushed it, but nothing happened. "The overhead light's out."

Stephanie directed the beam toward a long table resting against the wall. Nothing sat on its surface. On the left side of the room, an icon of Christ hung, and on the right side, two old wingback chairs pressed against its wall. One of them held a box of sewing items. The room wasn't familiar to her.

On the far side of the wall hung a painting of a monastery in the forest adjacent to a lake with mountains in the background. A carpet of pure white snow stretched over the land, dressing the pines and mountain peaks.

Stephanie squinted at the picture. Could that be somewhere in Russia? The onion-domed church likely confirmed her assumption. The serene scene drew her in as if she could transport to that spot and breathe in the cold, woodsy air and find comfort in that little building.

Sirens blared outside. Stephanie jumped, dropping the flashlight on the floor. It hit the floor with a thud, flicking off, as the sound of it rolled across the hardwood.

"Citizens, it's fifteen minutes until curfew. Return to your homes," an automated voice bellowed from the street.

Stephanie and the men hurried down the stairs to the narthex. The deacon and monks crossed the entryway with Stephanie behind them. Several drones with searchlights peppered the evening sky. A couple of cars rolled along the street next to the church, and groups of people jogged down roads toward their presumed residences.

"We must go to our hotel. We'll try to return for liturgy tomorrow, and perhaps we'll be able to see the room better," Father Sergius said. He bowed. "Thank you for accommodating us, Deacon."

"Of course," Deacon Michael said. "God willing, we'll see you tomorrow."

The monks hastened to a car in the lot—one of only three.

Deacon Michael laid a hand on Stephanie's shoulder. "I'll walk you to your car."

"Thank you."

Stephanie peered at the flashes of metal in the sky, the beams of light streaming across portions of the streets and buildings. A thundering blast of light ejected from one of the flying objects. A ball of fire erupted near a store on the street parallel to the church.

Screams flooded the smoky air.

"Enemy fire! Find shelter!" a robotic voice boomed from one of the metal birds in the gray-and-indigo sky.

Deacon Michael wrapped his arms around Stephanie and pulled her with him to the ground behind her car. Stephanie gasped, her heart pounding like a hammer against her chest and echoing in her ears. Was this how her father had felt the moment before he died? Dizziness assaulted her, and she sucked in the air, trying to catch her breath. *What happened?* She pushed herself off the concrete to stand, but her trembling body wouldn't cooperate.

"Stay down," the deacon said in a hoarse voice. He coughed as the splotches of smoke drifted past them.

Stephanie licked her dry lips, her mouth parched. She hacked on the remnants of the explosion even though it was at least two hundred yards from them.

Deacon Michael glanced at his watch and grimaced. "It's not even curfew yet."

More shrieks rang out as the people still on the streets dove into bushes and through opened doors.

Seconds later, dead silence blanketed the area, the skies cleared of drones, fires, and smoke.

Deacon Michael took Stephanie's hand and helped her get up with him. He put his hands on her shoulders and gave her a stern, fatherly look. "Get home now. You should make it before the curfew."

She hugged him. "Will you be okay?"

"Yes. I'll be right behind you."

Stephanie nodded, then climbed in her car. She sped out of the lot, wondering if her home would be any safer.

Fourteen

Hobo greeted Stephanie when she came in from the garage. Other than the sound of Hobo's panting, silence and darkness surrounded her. The emptiness reminded her that two of the most important people in her life were absent. She bit her quivering lip and swallowed back tears.

She switched on the overhead light, then picked up Hobo and hugged him. His wiggly body made her loosen her grip. He licked her cheek before she set him down, and he trotted to his empty food dish.

"Ah, I got the message, boy." She retrieved his food from the pantry and put some in his bowl.

While Hobo busied himself chomping on the morsels, she headed to the kitchen table and opened her laptop. Just a second on the net wouldn't hurt her. After all, it was three minutes until the curfew took effect.

Logan's profile on Convo Central flashed in her mind. What did he think of all the terrible events? She pursed her lips. How would she ever know? She'd deleted the friend request.

Hobo barked, interrupting her thoughts. He dashed out the doggie door.

She glanced at the sliding door's lock that hadn't been changed.

After the day she'd had, she'd forgotten to get a new one. Though she wouldn't have had time before the curfew. Racing to the coat closet, she grabbed a cane her father had used after his knee surgery and rushed over to the door. She shoved it in the gliding metal space between the door and the edge of the glass frame. It would have to do until she could get a lock tomorrow after work.

Back at the kitchen table, Stephanie stared at the computer monitor. The urge to reconnect with Logan nudged at her. She clicked the Convo Central icon. A loud buzzing permeated the quiet space before the computer screen went black. The lights shut off, and the refrigerator's humming stopped.

Crap. She closed her computer.

The flapping of the doggie door was followed by Hobo's panting and his paws padding around the den.

"Hobo, come here, boy." Stephanie bent and felt around for his solid, furry body. He bumped into her leg, and she rubbed his back.

As her eyes adjusted to the darkness, she felt her way around the kitchen counter, reaching the junk drawer. Taking out a box of matches, she made her way to the two thick candles on the mantel in the den and lit them. The flickering yellow flames brightened the room.

Rapping at the front door made her jump. Hobo took off, barking and bouncing.

She carried one of the candles with her and looked out the peephole. Pam held a large bag and swayed back and forth. Relieved to see her friend, she held Hobo's collar, then opened the door.

Pam hugged her. "My power is out. Is yours?"

"Yes."

"Can I stay with you tonight?"

"Sure." Stephanie moved aside, and Pam stepped inside.

"Thanks."

Stephanie plopped onto her father's recliner, setting the candle on the end table. Pam dropped her bag on the couch. Hobo sniffed Pam before jumping on Stephanie's lap and curling up.

Pam pulled out a pillow from her bag and set it on the arm of the couch. She stripped off her jeans and shirt and put on her shin-length cotton nightgown. "Before the electricity went off, I saw the news on my phone that there had been a drone strike from the Chinese right near your church." She squatted in front of Stephanie. "Were you there? Did you see what happened?"

The horrifying event flashed through Stephanie's mind. She closed her eyes for a moment to center herself. "Yes."

"You look okay, thank God." Pam patted Stephanie's arm.

"Yes, thank God." Stephanie shook her head. "But it was insane, terrifying seeing it happen right before my eyes."

Pam dug through her bag and pulled out her toothbrush and paste. "I would've felt the same way." Before leaving the couch, she frowned. "I haven't heard from Laura yet. I hope she's okay."

A lump formed in Stephanie's throat, and she swallowed hard. "I haven't heard from Jake either, but I'm hoping the same."

A distant siren outside blared for a solid minute, indicating that the eight-o'clock curfew was in effect.

Stephanie leaned back in the recliner. "I'm glad you're here."

Hobo jumped off Stephanie and settled on the couch.

"Me too. No power stinks. I can't watch or listen to anything," Pam said.

No power. An old memory of her father's battery-operated radio surfaced in her mind. She picked up the candle. "I think there may be something we can listen to."

Pam set her toothbrush and paste on the coffee table. "Really?"

Stephanie nodded and headed to the basement door. She peered down the dark steps into the abyss. She motioned Pam toward her. "Come with me."

Pam crept over and clasped Stephanie's arm as they carefully went down the stairs.

The musty cement space held a washer and dryer on the left-hand side and several boxes on the right. Straight ahead stood a wooden table. Tools and a couple of metal boxes lay on top of the table.

Stephanie stepped toward it with Pam still latched onto her arm. She held up the candle to the items on the table. A small silver radio sat next to a black box, both of which were draped in cobwebs.

"Wow. That's a really old radio. Was it your dad's?"

"Yes." Stephanie wiped off the cobwebs.

Pam fiddled with the knobs on the radio. She pulled up the ancient antenna, but nothing came to life.

"Crap. There may not be any batteries, or they're too old." Stephanie opened the back of the box and found corroded batteries.

Pam bent and examined the black box with a silver dial on the front of it. Attached was a curled cord with a handheld mouthpiece like the ones connected to megaphones. A separate two-foot antenna with a wide, round base stood next to the electrical device. "What is this?"

Memories of her at eight years old playing with Granddad Roger's CB surfaced in Stephanie's mind. She smiled and picked up the corded piece. "This was my grandfather's CB. My dad used to play with it when he was a kid."

"CB?" Pam's face scrunched. "Does it need batteries?"

"No. You can plug it into a wall socket if you're using it at home. But my grandfather and dad played around with them in their cars."

In the darkened stillness of the basement, possibilities of communication with that old CB floated in Stephanie's head. Holding the candle in front of her, she scanned the space. No electricity meant no plugging the CB into the wall. *My car. Maybe it will work in my car.* "Let's try something." She passed the candle to Pam and gathered up the items from the table.

"What? What are you going to try?" Pam asked.

Stephanie ascended the stairs with her friend in tow. "I want to try my car."

"Steph, you can't run your car in the garage. You'll die from carbon monoxide poisoning." Pam tapped Stephanie on the shoulder. "And you can't leave it in the driveway. You know after curfew our cars have to be inside our garages."

Stephanie reached the shadowed kitchen that began to lighten from the candle in Pam's hand. "Yes, yes, I know. But I've got another idea."

Pam screwed up her face, then shrugged.

Stephanie gestured for her to follow her into the garage. A flashlight sat on a shelf, and she nodded toward Pam. "Grab that and turn it on."

Pam switched on the flashlight. A round burst of light brightened the space in the garage and Stephanie's car.

Stephanie opened the driver's side door halfway, then set the antenna on the hood of her car. She smiled. *I remember how to set it up, Dad.* With her foot on the brake pedal, she pushed the ignition button. The dashboard lit up, and the radio came on as garbled static. Had the Chinese messed with their car radios too?

"Shoot." Pam frowned. "Even the car radio is out. Did the Chinese attacks do that?"

Stephanie held up a hand before sitting in the driver's seat and inserting an adapter into the holed slot on the lower portion of the dashboard.

Turning the dial on, static snapped. She set the CB channel to one. Nothing. She clicked through the next five channels. Nothing. On channel seven, several male voices chattered back and forth in traditional CB trucker language. The discussion revolved around the truckers' routes earlier in the day.

Pam bounced on the balls of her feet. "It's working!"

Stephanie flipped past it and the next several dead channels before reaching channel fifteen where a couple of female voices were speaking in Spanish. Sighing in frustration, she moved through the next several channels until voices came through on channel twenty-one. Two male voices barely audible were talking to each other. She turned up the volume.

"Ten-four, Logan's Run," one of the men said. "We'll continue our... poker game tomorrow. For now, we'll settle in for the night."

"Ten-four, Possum."

"What's your ten-twenty?"

"Homeport."

"Ten-four. Talk to you tomorrow. Over and out."

"Over and out."

Logan's Run? An old TV show when her mother was a child. And that voice. Deep with a tinge of a slight Southern drawl. It sounded so much like Logan's voice. Stephanie increased the volume, grasped the mouthpiece attached to the curly cord, and pressed in the side button. "Logan? Logan, is that you?"

Dead silence answered.

"Logan?" Pam's brows knitted.

Stephanie stared at the CB radio. She probably imagined it was his voice. *But he lives in town. Maybe…*

Gunshots went off outside.

Stephanie jumped in her seat.

"Oh no!" Pam's face paled.

Stephanie smashed the ignition button off. "Hurry! Back inside the house!" She leaped out, shut the driver's door, and ran inside with her friend on her heels.

Fifteen

Stephanie crept to the front window. Pam came alongside her with a candle and flashlight. The small flame of the taper reflected off the glass, making the houses and road harder to see.

Flapping her hand at Pam, Stephanie whispered, "Blow it out," before taking the flashlight from her friend.

Her friend extinguished the candle, and the room became completely black.

Hobo whined from under the couch.

Stephanie knelt so that only her head and neck were above the window. Her friend did the same.

Darkness blanketed the houses and street.

Loud gunshots thudded, with sparks flickering from the weapon. Someone in the street was firing up at the sky.

Stephanie quietly opened the front door. Staring through the outer screened door, she looked up into the ebony night. Two red blinking lights and a couple of solid yellow lights on a round machine hovered in the air.

A drone?

It was smaller than the ones she'd often see.

Pam appeared behind her shoulder. "Are you sure it's safe to open the door?"

Stephanie waved a hand for Pam to be quiet.

Outside, the person holding the gun paused to shout something toward the machine. He then let off a torrent of bullets. Flashes of light brightened the street and the person's face.

Plumes of gray smoke rose above the drone. Both the yellow lights and one of the machine's red lights went out. With the last red blinking light left to show where the drone was in the ink-splattered firmament, the machine moved haphazardly, dropping a few feet at a time, grinding and buzzing.

Stephanie squinted toward the man on the street. "Is that Don?" she asked more to herself than her friend.

Pam craned her neck, then shook her head. "I didn't get a good look."

"I think he damaged the drone," Stephanie said, her mouth open in awe.

More peppering of bullets from the man's weapon sprayed the drone.

A thundering boom came from the metal bird, and a yellow bolt struck the person in the road, knocking him to the ground.

"Oh my God!" Stephanie grabbed the flashlight and rushed down her driveway.

Pam stayed on the porch. "Be careful, Steph!"

The drone wobbled and veered toward the hedges on the side of her house, crashing into them. A plume of smoke spit from the bush. A burnt metallic smell drifted in the still air.

Ed and his wife, carrying flashlights, ran from their house toward the street, along with her neighbor three doors down—Dr. Alban, an athletic man in his forties. He carried a flashlight and his medical bag.

The collective beams from the four flashlights converged on the person in the road. Dr. Alban knelt in front of the tattered, bloody body and pressed his fingers on the man's splotched neck.

Stephanie gasped at the man's face. Don's eyes were glassy, and his mouth hung open.

Dr. Alban frowned. "He's gone."

Dear God. Feeling numb, Stephanie couldn't respond. She wiped her nose and peeked at Don's body again. *Poor Don.*

Ed pointed at Don. "See what happens when you go shooting off your guns?" His face pinched. "Who's the dumbass now?"

His wife put an arm around his waist and patted his chest. "He's dead, Ed. Let it go."

Stephanie hugged herself, suddenly cold.

A police car with flashing lights and an unmarked gray SUV rolled down the street, stopping ten feet from Stephanie and her neighbors. The SUV's lights shut off while the cruiser's headlamps stayed on, casting a wide white beam over the road.

Stephanie squinted through the brightness, tenting her eyes with her hand. Two cops with flashlights jumped out of their vehicles, and a man wearing wire-rimmed eyeglasses and a black suit exited the SUV.

They strode over to Stephanie and her neighbors. The man in the suit glanced at Don's body, then at the sky.

"Officer... er, I'm so glad you're here," Ed said.

The police officer jutted his chin toward Dr. Alban. "What happened?"

"I came out after I heard a loud boom and found Don here."

I saw the whole thing. Stephanie shook her head.

Ed pointed again at Don. "That idiot shot a Chinese drone! Got himself killed!"

The man in the suit waved a hand for Ed to calm down. He reached inside his blazer and pulled out an ID. "Agent Withers, IIA."

A chill trickled down Stephanie's spine. *Intrepid Intelligence Agency.* Their history of existence was dark and brutal. She shook off the chill and hugged herself again.

He shoved his badge back into his blazer pocket. "Where's the drone?"

Ed shrugged. "How should I know?"

The agent turned toward Stephanie. Her muscles tensed.

"Did you see anything?"

Calm down. His questions are expected. Straightening her back, Stephanie nodded. "It was as Ed explained."

"Where's the drone?" Withers gestured toward the policemen. "Go look for it."

One of the policemen walked through Ed's front yard while the other one jogged toward the house kitty-corner to Stephanie's and traipsed toward the grass space between homes. The first cop aimed his flashlight's beam on the first home's front yard.

Ed scrambled after him. "It wasn't over there!"

"Then where was it?" Agent Withers asked. His voice held impatience, and he scowled at Ed.

"I don't know, but it wasn't by my house." Ed lifted his head toward the sky. "It's dark. No electricity, you know?"

The agent's jaw twitched. He sighed, stepped in front of Ed, and glared at him. "We're in the middle of a war and attacks on our own country. This was an enemy weapon. We need to retrieve it. *Now.*" He drew out the last word in a threatening tone, his teeth clenched.

A Humvee turned down the road and rumbled to a stop before the other vehicles. Two army soldiers climbed out, then jogged over to Withers. One of them, who had a baby face, jerked a thumb behind him while focused on the agent. "We're securing the city's perimeter, especially the last five miles where the wall hasn't been completed yet."

Agent Withers gave a nod. "Let Officers Braden and Drake know."

The soldiers ran to the cops searching the yards.

The agent folded his arms across his chest and faced Ed, who shrugged.

Agent Withers spun on his heel toward Stephanie. "You saw what happened. Where did the drone go?"

The drone landing in the hedges against her house flashed in her mind, but something told her to keep her mouth shut. "Don destroyed it."

Withers narrowed his icy blue eyes at her. "He destroyed it."

She slid her hands in her pockets to hide their trembling. "Yes."

"She's right," Ed's wife said.

The agent aimed his glower back at Stephanie. "So where did it land?"

She borrowed Ed's response. "How could we see that in the dark?"

"Yeah." Ed nodded. "Like I said, no lights."

The agent sneered. "Of course."

Two explosions went off south of the neighborhood.

Withers looked in that direction, then glanced back at them. "After you give your accounts to the police, go back in your homes. It's still curfew." He gestured to the policemen in the yards.

The cops ran back to him.

"Get a coroner here and fill out a report." Agent Withers jogged to his car.

The man gave Stephanie the creeps. She breathed easier after he'd driven away.

STEPHANIE RETURNED TO HER HOUSE, NEVER SO HAPPY AS to be inside and away from the horror. Her hands still trembled, and nausea swam in her belly as the images of Don's shredded, dead body invaded her mind. *Poor Don.*

Hobo ran to her. She picked him up and sat with him on her dad's recliner, rocking him and herself for comfort.

The front door shut, and Pam crossed to the den. "That was terrible." She collapsed on the couch. "I'm glad I didn't see Don close-up."

"I did. Not easy to forget, but I'm going to try." Stephanie pushed away the image of Don's body and kissed Hobo's soft head.

"I can't believe a Chinese drone was flying around our neighborhood," Pam said.

"Very strange. And what's the point of them killing random Americans?" Stephanie set Hobo on the floor. He trotted to the kitchen.

Pam shrugged. "We're the enemy."

"But we're civilians, not soldiers." Thoughts of the many wars her country had participated in came to her mind. "Maybe it's a taste of our own medicine? Revenge?"

Pam didn't have an answer.

The destroyed Chinese drone was still out there. The police didn't find it, but they probably would if they returned in the morning, and they most likely would. Either they or Agent Withers and maybe a couple of his creepy comrades.

Pam frowned. "Poor Don's family. They were woken from sleep to find out their husband and dad is dead."

Stephanie laid a finger on her temple that had started to throb.

"I'm going to bed." Pam lay down on the couch and threw a blanket over her. "This terrible night has crushed my nerves."

"Why don't you sleep in my parents' bed? It's empty." *While my mother sleeps another night in jail.* Stephanie bit back the stinging in her eyes and nose.

Pam sat up. "That would be great. Thanks."

When her friend had gone upstairs, Stephanie crept to the garage. She'd try again to reach Logan no matter if it was nearly ten. He was the only person left who could possibly help her. Maybe, just maybe he'd be near the radio, waiting to talk to someone while the town slept.

Sixteen

S itting in her car, Stephanie turned on the car's dashboard, then switched on the CB. Still on channel twenty-one, she picked up the mouthpiece and pressed the side button.

"Logan's Run, are you there?" She let go of the button.

A faint sound of static broke through the silence. No one responded.

She slumped in the seat and blew out a breath. Turning up the volume, she straightened. *One more try.* "Logan's Run, do you hear me?" She released the button.

"Who's asking?" The unmistakable voice of her first love came through clearly.

"This is Server Steph..." She paused. What should she tell him on a radio that wasn't private? She had to say something to let him know who she was. Maybe there were other channels that were more private. He would know.

"Server Steph? Sorry, I don't know you. Over and out."

"No! Don't leave!" Stephanie pressed the button on the mouthpiece again. "Wait, please! This is your girlfriend from high school." She let go of the button and hung up the mouthpiece on the side of the radio. She buried her face in her hands.

Slight distant static rolled through the radio, followed by dead silence.

She shook her head. *This was a bad idea. He's not going to believe me, popping on a CB radio out of the blue after two decades of no contact with him.* She smacked a palm against her forehead.

"If you're who I think you are, go to channel fifty-six."

Startled by his response, it took her a moment to reply. "Okay."

"That would be ten-four," he said, a hint of amusement in his voice.

"Ten-four." She clicked over to the channel he had said. "Are you there?"

"Go to channel sixty-eight."

Is this a game to him? What's he doing? She didn't answer him and turned to channel sixty-eight. The radio was silent. Had he sent her on some false trail to drop her?

"You there, Server Steph?" he asked.

He's still on. She pressed the button on the mouthpiece. "Y-yes." Letting go, she smiled.

"This channel tends to be quiet and relatively private. Doesn't get interruptions from truckers or random people messing around on the radio." He paused, then said, "It's been a long time. How'd you find me here, and how did you know I was on?"

"Your CB handle has your name in it."

"Like yours?"

She chuckled under her breath. "Yeah."

He didn't respond for a full minute. Perhaps he needed more of an explanation.

"I heard you on channel twenty-one earlier, not long after curfew started. You were talking to a man called Possum."

"What'd you hear?"

"Just that you and he were in for the night. Then you both signed off."

"What made you look for me?"

"I wasn't." *That's a lie.* She squeezed her eyes shut, then gripped the mouthpiece. *Go with the safe truth.* "I tested the radio. It was my grandfather's, and I wanted to see if it still worked."

Don's killing and the destroyed drone surfaced in her mind.

They could talk about the past later. She needed to focus on Logan possibly helping her reach Jake and releasing her mother from jail.

The drone.

Something prodded her to get to it before the police or IIA agent did. "Listen, one of my neighbors was murdered by a Chinese drone tonight. It was horrible."

"A Chinese drone?"

"Yes."

"I'm sorry. My condolences to his family. But what does that have to do with me?"

She thought about his question. "I'm not sure."

"What happened to the drone?" he asked in a curious tone.

"My neighbor shot it down, and it crashed in a bush."

"Did the feds show up?"

"Yes, and the police and two army men."

"Not surprised." He sighed. "I take it they collected the drone and told you to go back inside since it was after curfew."

"No." How could they gather up the drone when nobody had answered where it landed? Maybe she could slip out and search the hedges for it at dawn. But what would she do with a smashed drone?

"No? What did they do with the drone?" His voice reflected confusion.

"They didn't do anything with it. It was too dark to see exactly where it crashed."

"You said it crashed into a bush."

I did say that. She rubbed her temple as a sense of mistrust swirled in her chest. *Can I trust him?*

He murmured something she couldn't make out.

"What?"

"Do you know what bush it might have landed in?"

He seemed as interested in the drone as the IIA agent. *I hope he isn't one of them.* She stomped her foot on the floor of the car. *Why did you search for him on the CB if you didn't have any trust in him?*

"You still there?"

"Oh, yes, I'm here. Sorry." She cleared her throat and straightened her back. "I'm planning to try to find it early in the morning."

"Where do you live?"

She tensed. *Why am I suddenly so jittery? It's Logan. Yeah, it's been a couple of decades since you and he were together, but he's never given you any reason to feel uneasy.* She shook her head. All those feelings must have been from those creepy guys that had broken into her house and that equally menacing IIA agent. Anyone would have been scared and unsure about giving her home address to someone she didn't really know. At least anymore. Her stomach unknotted, and she exhaled in relief.

"I'm in the Cedar Corner neighborhood. Lilac Road, number two three seven."

"Mind if I stop by around six in the morning?"

He obviously picked up on something she'd said, but she didn't know what it was. What did he know that she didn't? "That's fine."

Logan was coming to see her in a few hours. Her heart unexpectedly swelled in response.

"Ten-four. Take care and see you then. Over and out."

"You too. Over and out." Stephanie replaced the mouthpiece on the hook and shut off the radio. Her stomach fluttered and churned. She placed a hand on her abdomen. Her body didn't know how to react. This would be a strange reunion.

Seventeen

Stephanie stood at a rocky precipice. Below her, a wide, deep canyon spread the length of a football field, with a similar ledge on the other side. Flat land spanned far out into the milky slate-blue horizon. The dry heat baked her skin, the breeze brushing against her like the cough of a fiery furnace. She licked her lips, her mouth as dry as the environment.

In the hazy waves of heat rising from the ground, a Humvee materialized on the plateau across from her. A young man whose features mirrored Jake's appeared in fatigues, running toward the vehicle.

Stephanie's heart sank. She took a step closer to the ledge. "Jake?"

The military jeep took off, dust kicking up from its back tires.

A small missile came out of nowhere, white-hot and whistling. It pierced the machine, slicing through it as if it were made of cheese.

A loud boom vibrated through Stephanie's body and shattered her eardrums. She screamed and covered her ears.

The vehicle catapulted two feet off the ground, transforming into a fireball with angry orange flames and black plumes of smoke.

"Jake! Jake!" Stephanie reached for her son, her foot slipping on the loose gravel at the ledge. She stepped back and fell to her knees, tears pouring down her cheeks.

She covered her face, her heart aching as if it were cracking into pieces. Collapsing onto her side, Stephanie sobbed, her parched mouth gulping for air.

Knocking pounded against her head. The sound of a doorbell pierced her skull. She winced, cradling her head.

Incessant barking echoed through her already aching body.

She stared into blackness, the scene before her whisked away in a large gray balloon that deflated and fizzled into nothing.

More knocking came with yipping from Hobo.

She sat up in bed, her face wet, nose stuffed, and head hurting. The faint pink of dawn glimmered through her bedroom window. She rubbed her arms, then hugged herself, the trembling of her body and her escalated heartbeat dissipating.

Jake's all right. He has to be...

The doorbell rang again. Hobo yipped once more.

Stephanie glanced at the clock on her nightstand. Nearly six a.m.

Logan!

Hobo scurried into her room, yapping.

She scrambled out of bed. The nightmare still lingered, making her mind soupy. Entering the bathroom, she squinted at herself in the mirror. Swatting at her disheveled image, she splashed cool water on her face. The troubling nightmare finally recessed from her mind. Throwing off her pajamas, she replaced them with a T-shirt and jeans before leaving her room and scurrying down the stairs. Hobo beat her to the front door.

Peeking through the peephole, she spied Logan on her porch, looking around.

Stephanie smoothed down her shirt, ran a hand through her tangled hair, then opened the door.

Hobo started barking again, and before he could jump all over Logan, Stephanie grabbed his collar and pulled him over to her. She wagged a finger at him. "Quiet and stay."

Hobo obediently sat and panted.

Logan turned toward her. "Hey." His soft gaze ran over her ragged appearance. "Did I wake you? Forgot I was coming by?"

Heat crept into her cheeks. "I kind of did."

"Sorry."

"I didn't sleep well… nightmare about my son." The fear she'd felt during the dream slid through her. She hadn't meant to share that with him, but it was as if the twenty years away from him had never happened. *Astounding.* She tightened her grip on Hobo's collar and stroked his back.

"Your son?" His tone reflected curiousness.

She forced herself to look up at him. "Yes. He was drafted and sent off to a war zone somewhere." Her own words stabbed her heart and echoed in her ears.

"Sorry again." He grimaced. "Must be hard."

"It is."

"How old is he?"

"Eighteen." She pushed aside the nightmare and tried to focus on why he'd come. "I apologize. You're here about the drone, not to listen to me lamenting over my son."

He looked past her to the foyer as if searching for someone. "Where's your husband?"

"I don't have one and haven't for years."

Logan nodded and stared at the floor.

He's uncomfortable. I don't blame him. She needed to get to the drone issue. She led Hobo into the house.

He jerked a thumb toward the side of the house. "Is the drone over there?"

She waved him inside, then closed the door. "It's best we go through the garage to the side of the house instead of walking across the front yard."

"Good call."

He stepped inside, and the piney scent of him washed over Stephanie. Reflexively, she pushed away the memories. Ever since her divorce, she'd avoided any romantic relationship that might have had a chance to blossom. The automatic response to Logan troubled her, but she didn't have time to mull it over. She strode toward the door to the garage, with Logan behind her.

Inside the garage, she pushed a button on the wall, and the door squeaked open.

They quietly moved to the side of the house where the bushes were.

Stephanie pointed to the hedge. "I saw it fall somewhere around there."

Logan nodded and squatted in front of the greenery. He pushed aside branches and peeked inside. "Nothing."

She studied the hedge farther down where portions of it were damaged—charred and missing branches. Logan had discovered it at the same moment and moved with her toward it.

He knelt and pushed some of the gnarled branches aside. She bent and peered into the hedge. Several small pieces of the destroyed drone littered the bottom of the bush. Tiny red letters were on a few of the pieces.

Chinese? She couldn't tell and reached for those remnants.

The faint sound of squealing tires startled Stephanie. Logan shot up and headed toward her garage. She scurried after him. They both peeked around the side of her house. A gray SUV rolled slowly down the street.

"It's Agent Withers," Stephanie whispered, as if the man could hear her.

Logan spun around and took her hand. "I'll grab what I can of the drone. You keep watch."

"Please get those parts with the red letters."

A full smile finally spread across Logan's handsome face. "You and I still think alike."

She shyly grinned back, then focused on the approaching vehicle.

Logan came alongside her and jerked his head toward the garage. The SUV was two houses down from hers when they slipped into her garage. She pressed the button, and the garage door came down. They ran into the house.

Hobo barked and bounced toward Logan. He said, "Shh," and looked around. "Where is a safe place for these?"

Stephanie pointed toward the basement door. "Down here."

They raced down the stairs with Hobo on their heels. She grabbed a box of Christmas decorations and opened it. "Put them in here for now."

Logan dumped the pieces into the container. She closed it, and they headed back upstairs just as the doorbell rang.

Eighteen

Nausea and a hollow emptiness in the pit of Ava's stomach woke her from a night of troubling sleep. A sheen of clammy perspiration coated her skin. She attempted to sit up, but her body was too weak. Shaking, she lay back down on the damp mattress.

Ava rubbed her stomach. The urges to simultaneously throw up and eat something, anything, gnawed at her. *Damn. I haven't had a hypoglycemic attack in years.* Since switching to organic and nonprocessed food in her teens, the attacks had been few and far between. She'd nearly forgotten she'd had low blood sugar. Her weak, trembling body, constant sickness in her stomach, and desperate need to eat something with protein reminded her.

I can't do a hunger strike with this. She smacked her forehead with the palm of her hand. Closing her eyes, she groaned and rolled onto her side, curling into the fetal position.

The sound of barred doors opening followed by the shuffle of shoes on the floor grew louder.

Ava's eyes sprang open. *Is Blaine coming with breakfast?* She focused on the hallway ahead of her cell.

Blaine's bulky figure came around the corner and headed down the corridor toward Ava. The guard held a tray. Ava had never been so happy to see the woman with the crummy food in her hands.

The guard unlocked the barred door and came into the cell. She took the old tray and set the new one on the foot of the cot. "I'll be back to grab this uneaten one at lunch." Slipping out of the cell and locking the door, Blaine twisted to look back and gave Ava a creepy grin. "Continue to enjoy your starvation routine."

Ava scowled at the woman before the guard headed down the hall and disappeared around the corner.

Forcing herself to sit up, Ava examined the tray of food. Her belly screamed and twisted as nausea pressed upon her. She searched for something with protein. A small container of strawberry yogurt sat next to a crusty brown muffin.

Yogurt! With trembling fingers, she snatched the container, peeled off the cover, grabbed the plastic spoon, and dug into the creamy, cool delight with just a hint of sourness. The taste was sweeter than ever before. She scarfed down the muffin right after she'd finished the yogurt.

The nausea, shakiness, cold sweats, and weakness abated. Satiated, she sat leaning against the cinderblock wall.

With the hunger strike plan nixed, what would be her new scheme to break out? She glanced at the ceiling. *Got any ideas, God? I could use some. Yeah, I know it's been a while since I've talked to You. But I sure would rather be in Your church right now than here.* She lay back down, her eyes drooping. Maybe after some decent sleep, she could formulate plan B.

SERGIUS AND HIS BROTHER, FATHER HERMAN, ENTERED Saint John Orthodox Church and lit candles. Sergius prayed for them to discover the relics after liturgy. They'd have time to search.

In his heart, Sergius sensed this church was the one. It held something different and more profound. He nodded. The pious elderly woman had to be one of the keys to unlocking the prophetic mystery. God had led him and his brother to the right church.

Located overtly in the center of a small town, Saint John Orthodox Church's architecture was a smaller replica of the Greek Orthodox Cathedral in Istanbul—*Agia* Sophia—one of the greatest Orthodox Christian treasures in the world. Perhaps this church held extraordinary treasures only known by a few. If so, in a couple of hours, he and his brother would be added to the *few*.

He stepped inside the nave, then turned to look up at the loft. Yes. Olga had been in her right mind when she'd spoken about that area. Some special room or place.

Father Herman laid a hand on Sergius's shoulder. "Today, God willing, He will reveal to us the hidden place of the relics."

Sergius nodded. "I think the good Lord will."

Deacon Michael came out of the sanctuary, glanced at his watch, then approached them. "It's a pleasure to see you, brothers."

"It's a blessing to be back, Deacon," Sergius said.

"God is good." Father Herman gave the deacon a smile.

"Indeed, He is." The deacon gestured for them to move to the narthex, then pointed at his watch. "We've got twenty minutes until Orthros, or Matins, for you in the Slavic Church. Let's go up to that room behind the loft and look around."

God, you're leading us to Your gifts before we worship You this morning! Sergius dug in his pocket for his prayer rope, brought it out, and clasped it between his hands. He exchanged eager looks with his brother before following the deacon up the stairs to the loft.

They reached the storage room and the room they were in the other night before the curfew warning from the city's drones forced them to leave. The rooms were in the shadows, with no windows in the hallway to provide any light.

Deacon Michael headed into the storage room. "The flashlight."

Father Herman followed the deacon.

Sergius stepped into the adjacent room. His shoe tapped into a hard object on the floor. The item rolled on the wood. "Deacon, I think it's still in here." He felt around for the cylindrical base, grasped it, and pressed the button on its side.

The deacon and his brother filled the doorway as Sergius flooded their chests with light.

"Thank God." Deacon Michael took the flashlight from Sergius and ran the beam over the room, stopping on a recessed vertical crown molding traveling up the wall straight ahead of them. The indent ran up to a foot below the ceiling and continued across, then headed back down to the floor—the width the size of double doors.

The picture Sergius remembered of the Russian Orthodox Church in the Caucuses hung in the middle of that space. He clasped his prayer rope. "Do you think there's something on the other side of that wall, Deacon?"

"I don't know. To be honest, until the other night, I'd never been in this room."

Father Herman stepped toward the panel and moved the palm of his hand over the wall to the left of the first vertical groove.

Sergius and the deacon approached.

While Father Herman moved to the right side of the crown molding, Sergius eyed the wall where his fellow monk had just been. Deacon Michael kept the flashlight on where Sergius was running his index finger along the wall.

The clergyman focused the light on the painting. He stepped toward the picture and removed it from its hook. Nothing was behind it.

Deacon Michael jutted his chin toward Sergius. "Here, take this painting. Look on the back of it."

Sergius held the painting with the back of it facing him and the flashlight's beam on it. Father Herman came alongside him.

A paper smaller than the painting and frame was taped to the brown poster backing. The sheet displayed a sketch of Saint Innocent Monastery in Russia. The date of the drawing was scrawled in the right-hand corner—1933.

Sergius's jaw fell. He pointed to the picture and nudged Father Herman. "The monastery as it originally was!"

Father Herman grinned and nodded. He laid a chubby hand on Sergius's shoulder. "We're on the right path."

"Glory to God." Sergius gazed at the picture once more.

Deacon Michael studied the drawing. "Amazing work."

Sergius placed a finger on the middle of the sketch. The paper wasn't flat against the tan backing but, instead, bulged a bit. *God, are you showing us something here?* He pressed on the bloated spot again. It was soft, as if more paper backing or similar was inside that area. "I think there's something behind this."

Father Herman poked the puffy paper. "I agree."

Deacon Michael bent to examine it more closely. "We could just remove the tape and put it back. That shouldn't ruin the painting or the sketch."

Sergius smiled, anticipating what could be sandwiched between the brown paper and the drawing. He set the framed painting on a nearby table, with the deacon keeping the flashlight on the artwork. Father Herman held down the frame and backing while Sergius peeled off the four pieces of masking tape, then lifted the sketch sheet. The paper was more solid, akin to thin poster board.

Turning it over, Sergius gasped. A small brown envelope the size of a chalkboard eraser was taped to the paper.

Carefully removing the two strips of yellow tape, Sergius picked up the pouch, opened the flap, and peeked inside. Two index cards sat in the envelope. He pulled them out and set them on the table.

They focused on the cards.

Each sheet had a set of numbers written on them. The first had four numbers listed vertically: 1, 3, 7, 9. The second sheet displayed: 25R, 16L, 3R.

Father Herman rubbed his thickly bearded chin. "Codes for something?"

Eyes wide, the deacon nodded. "I think they could be. But to what?" He held the beam of the flashlight on the recessed sections of the wall again.

Nothing stood out to Sergius.

Father Herman glided his hands across the adjacent wall next to a two-layered shelf where a few books sat. It hung on the wall level to Sergius's chin.

Shorter in stature, Father Herman pointed to the tomes. "Anything up there?"

The deacon kept the flashlight on the shelf. "Only books. I'm not seeing anything out of the ordinary."

Sergius shrugged. "It wouldn't hurt to take a look." He collected the books—all five of them—and set them on a chair. He thumbed through them but found nothing unusual.

"Brother," Father Herman said, as if he'd lost his breath.

Behind the wooden rack, a small metal box painted bronze like the walls protruded between the two shelves. Nine white numbers, like on an old push-button phone, took up the face of the box.

"Well, I'll be…" The deacon scratched his head. "What do you think that goes to?"

Sergius picked up the two index cards with the numbers on them. "Maybe one of these is for that."

Father Herman squinted at the second set of numbers. "I don't think it's for those. They've got letters in it and that box doesn't."

"True," the deacon said.

Sergius glanced at the shadowed recessed section of the wall, then turned his attention to Deacon Michael. "Shine the light on the wall for a second."

The clergyman did so.

"Okay. Now back to the metal number box please."

Sergius approached the combination of nine numbers, then consulted the list on the paper: 1, 3, 7, 9. He pressed each number button into the metal case in the order they were written. He then shoved the two cards into his cassock pocket.

A scraping noise came from the wall. The deacon shot the light toward the sound. The recessed area between the vertical crown molding slid to the right, disappearing into the wall, like a pocket door.

Sergius stood with the deacon and his brother, speechless. He exchanged his surprised expression with them before stepping toward the opening.

Deacon Michael aimed the flashlight's beam into the opening, brightening a dully lit hallway about twenty feet in length that led to an elevator.

Sergius's heart skipped a beat.

"Where do you suppose that leads to?" Father Herman asked.

Deacon Michael checked his watch. "We have about six minutes to find out, then we've got to head back to the nave for Orthros."

"Let's go." Sergius entered the corridor and headed toward the elevator, with the two men behind him.

Only a Down button was available. The deacon pushed it. The elevator door slid open, and Sergius stepped inside first. Father Herman and the deacon joined him. Deacon Michael pressed the lone button with a *G* on it, for the ground floor.

A minute later, the doors opened to another hallway, but this one stretched only about ten feet. Another pocket door stood at the end of the corridor.

I wonder where You're leading us, Lord. Sergius scrambled down the hall with the others.

Father Herman gestured toward him. "Try that code again."

Sergius nodded, pulled out the paper again, and punched in the numbers.

The door slid open, revealing a ten-by-ten room with one dull light fixture on the ceiling.

A metal safe stood in the center.

Sergius sucked in a breath. *Is this where the relics are?*

"Holy Mother of God," the deacon said.

Father Herman gaped and pointed at the safe. "Like at the monastery back in Russia."

Deacon Michael checked his watch. "We've got to get upstairs. Orthros is supposed to start in three minutes, and I must prepare for it."

Sergius bit his lip. *Patience. God reveals in His time.*

The deacon nodded. "We'll definitely come back after liturgy."

Sergius slid the paper back into his pocket, then clutched his prayer rope. *Thank you, Lord.*

At Fairview Park, Brody, a still-distraught Mary, and his daughter sat across from two men on a picnic bench. The shade of an oak tree kept the sun out of Brody's eyes. The third day of May held a white sun in the cloudless blue sky, shedding unusual heat for that time of year.

The two men with him were clad in shabby shirts, pants, and worn shoes. He'd encountered them at the previous shelter in town before it had been shut down two months ago. They'd become friends in no time.

Brody asked, "What did you think of the new shelter announcement?"

"What does it matter?" Mary grimaced, leaning her elbows on the table and resting her forehead against her palms. "I can't sleep with Noah gone anyway."

Brody rubbed Mary's back. No words could console her, so he kept silent and gathered her closer to him by draping an arm around her. He looked up at Russell, the younger of the two men. "What do you think?"

"I'll believe it when I see it," Russell said. At fifty-two years old, he was a couple of decades older than Brody.

Brody nodded. "Yeah, I get that." His gaze fell on the police station kitty-corner to the park. "But I'm not convinced the shelter is going to be anything state-of-the-art. They never cared about us. Why would they start now?"

"Always been treated like we're not human, as if we're not the same as they are," Walter said in his gravelly voice. He let out a smoker's cough.

Russell patted his father on the shoulder. "Do you want to get some water from the fountain?"

Walter shook his head. "I'm fine." He opened his mouth as if out of breath and wheezed. "It's too damn hot already, and it ain't even summer yet."

Russell pressed his mouth into a firm line and narrowed his eyes at the police station. "If only there was a real shelter to help us." He gestured toward Walter. "Help him. He needs a decent place to rest. Instead, we're living in the alleys, sleeping with one of our eyes open, watching so we don't get robbed or murdered. We've been lucky these past two years."

Walter spewed a garbled hack. He sniffled while running the back of his hand under his bulbous nose.

"The government never passed a socialized healthcare program that my parents and most their generation had filled the streets and screamed for," Russell said.

Brody folded his arms on the table. "Those in power don't care about the average American citizens. And us? Even less. We're nothing but a boil on their botoxed, collagen-filled faces that needs to be lanced and tossed out."

Lindy scrunched up her face, then tugged on Brody's sleeve. "What's a boil, Daddy?"

He flapped a hand toward her. "It doesn't matter, honey." He pointed at the swing set near them. "Why don't you go play for a while? Just stay close by."

She nodded, then headed toward the swings.

Walter snorted and wiped his nose again. "It's a shame your daughter's gotta live like this. So young."

Brody tightened his folded arms as shame burned his cheeks. *Is he blaming me for her situation?* He looked away and scratched his neck. *It's not like I wanted to live like this.* "It's been hard, but we're doing okay. Whenever any job opening comes up, I jump at it. But they've been sparse, and when they do pop up, I'm competing against dozens of other guys like me, except at least half of them aren't homeless."

"The city doesn't have good job programs anymore either," Russell added.

A lone police officer walked over to them. His platinum blond hair caught Brody's attention. *Holland.* His tense muscles relaxed.

"Hey, guys. Good to see you're doing okay." His stare fell on Mary, and he frowned. "As well as can be expected."

Mary only moaned in response, her face still in her hands. She folded her arms on the table and rested her head in the open space between them.

Holland looked away as if he couldn't cope with Mary's pain. He forced a smile. "It's a nice day to be in the park."

The man had to be around Brody's age. Holland had said in one of their earlier conversations that he'd been on the force for four years. Long enough to not be a rookie but short enough to not be totally disheartened and corrupt yet. This explained why Holland tended to be friendly to him and his fellow homeless brethren, talking to them as human beings. Studying the blond man's face, he wondered how long Holland would be able to survive in a militarized police force that had abandoned years ago what it meant to be a human being.

Russell shrugged. "As good a place as any, I guess."

Brody leaned his elbows on the table and laced his fingers together. "It would be even better if there were jobs so we could feed our families."

Holland nodded and pointed down the street. "There are some job flyers posted in the local supermarket as well as the library."

"Library's closed today and only open three days a week." Brody glanced at Lindy riding on the swing, pumping her legs to go higher. "I know because I take my daughter there every chance I get. She loves to read."

The officer smiled. "That's great. Feels like kids… nobody… really reads books these days."

"Yeah." Brody rubbed Mary's back again. She hadn't moved an inch. "Holland, can you tell us something about the new shelter? What's it like?"

Holland shook his head. "Sorry. I haven't seen it yet, but I'm assigned to help arrange the shuttling of you all to the building starting tomorrow morning. So I'll know soon enough."

Brody nodded. "Good. I'm counting on you to give us the 411 on my friends' new dwelling."

Holland patted Brody's shoulder. "I'll do what I can, what's permitted of me…"

Uh-oh. Brody cringed. That meant not much of anything. Nevertheless, he shook Holland's hand. "Thanks."

Russell eyed the cop. "Yeah, uh, thanks."

Walter coughed, then nodded. "That'll be good to know. I look forward to a decent place to lay my head. If only you had a free clinic for us." He wheezed out a laugh. "Our government never thinks of those things. Heaven forbid."

Holland chuckled, putting his thumbs through the belt loops of his pants. "I'm glad everyone will have a place to eat and sleep, out of the rain and dangerous streets."

The officer had politely skipped over the obvious elephant on the bench with them—medical care. He glanced at Russell and believed his friend hadn't missed that either.

Russell draped an arm around his seventy-five-year-old father's slouched shoulders. "Free clinics are a huge oversight in this town."

Holland's brow furrowed. "I think there may be a doctor on call at the shelter. I'll have to look into it."

"That would be great. Thanks." Russell patted his father's shoulder.

"Sure would be." Walter's forehead and neck were damp. He sniffled again before blotting his face with a stained handkerchief.

A cop came out of the police station and strode toward them. His bald head glistened in the sunshine.

Oh terrific. Brody sighed. *It's the bastard from the other day.*

The bald officer marched onto the grass and waved a hand. "Holland! Let's go."

Holland's jaw twitched. He headed toward the cop waiting with hands on hips, then walked with him back to the station.

Lindy ran over to Brody. "Daddy, I'm hungry. Can we get something to eat?"

Brody frowned. Maybe the church had some leftover bread they usually gave out after their services Sunday mornings. With the soup kitchens closed, where else would he find food for a day? He squeezed his eyes shut. *Concentrate on the present and not the what-ifs.* He stood and put out his hand for her to grasp. She slid her hand in his and beamed up at him.

"How about we go visit the church?"

Lindy nodded.

Brody touched Mary's back. "Come with us. You need to eat something."

Mary let out a long sigh but left the bench and took Brody's other hand.

"See you guys later." Brody jutted his chin toward Russell and Walter, then guided his daughter and Mary onto the sidewalk.

I hope that church doesn't close. It's the only one left in town. Brody kept his eyes on the road ahead.

Twenty

Sergius followed the deacon and his brother into the elevator once again and pressed the *G* button. The doors clattered shut, then the machine squeaked as it shuddered downward.

No one spoke as Sergius grasped his prayer rope in his cassock pocket. In a few moments, he and his brother would finally see the long-lost relics. He'd make sure to tuck them away in the small leather pouch stored in the inner pocket of his robe. Then they'd fly back to Russia in a couple of days as scheduled. What an honor it would be to return to the monastery with the relics. God had indeed abundantly blessed him and his brothers.

The door creaked open, and they advanced down the short corridor. Sergius pulled out the folded paper in his other pocket and punched the code into the numbered box next to the closed entryway.

The door rattled open. The metal safe still sat in the center of the room. Sergius didn't know what he thought might have happened to it during liturgy. Nonetheless, any concerns he had over the treasures somehow escaping the room vanished.

Deacon Michael bent in front of the face of the safe, then looked back toward Sergius. "That other code you found may work for this."

Sergius took out the second index card in his pocket. The deacon and Father Herman flanked the safe as Sergius squatted across from the combination lock. He studied the paper with its numbers and letters: 25R, 16L, 3R. He turned the dial to the appropriate numbers to the right, left, then to the right. Lifting the latch, he pulled the heavy door open. In the dim light, a partially blackened envelope encased in a glass container and a small wooden box sat in the hollowed space.

Sergius's heart sank in his chest. *Has the prophetic letter been burned?* He rested his knees on the floor, and Father Herman joined him.

Deacon Michael reached for the letter case. "Dear God, has it been damaged beyond repair?"

Father Herman tilted the case toward his face and frowned. "It looks bad."

Sergius took the case from the deacon. "Yet it's saved in this glass box." He shook his head. "If it were totally destroyed, would it be secured in this container for years?"

Deacon Michael rubbed his chin. "It's possible there are parts of the letter that are salvageable."

Father Herman stood. "Yes, that makes sense."

"I agree." Sergius removed the wooden box as well. "This looks in decent shape." He eyed the three small pieces of the Holy Cross inside. "Perfectly preserved."

Deacon Michael held out his hand, and Sergius set the container in it. "Indeed. Thank God."

"Glory to God," Father Herman said.

"Glory forever." Sergius studied the charred letter through the glass. He set the container on the metal safe and removed the glass top. His brother and the deacon approached on either side of him for a closer look.

Deacon Michael pointed to the fragile paper. "Be careful, Father."

Sergius nodded, then gingerly picked up the folded sheet and opened it. Burn damage blotted out three-quarters of the letter. Incredibly, the middle section of the paper was mostly free of harm.

Squinting to read the small, printed handwriting, Sergius said aloud, "The blood will not stop running without repentance. He will come to our aid only when our hearts soften and warm like the comforting blaze of a fire in the hearth and love expands as wide as the earth's firmament."

He stood with his brother and the deacon in total silence as if they all were working to digest the message. It made perfect sense to Sergius, and it was typical of the type of language used by the saints and holy elders.

Father Herman scratched his beard. "Saint Dimitri's words of wisdom are so needed right now. We're blessed to have found this."

"And the Holy Cross," Deacon Michael added.

"Yes," Father Herman said.

"Most certainly. What he said is so relevant to what's happening now with this terrible world war," Sergius said.

Father Herman placed his hand on the safe. "Should we take them now or leave them here for safekeeping until we fly out in a couple of days?"

Deacon Michael took the relics. "I suggest keeping them here." He bent and placed them in the safe and closed its door, spinning the dial before straightening. He jutted his chin toward Sergius. "Tuck away those papers somewhere safe. Perhaps back in the painting. All as was. We seem to be the only ones who have discovered them."

How did the deacon know they would stay unmolested or undiscovered? Perhaps the clergyman hadn't experienced closely what he and his brother had seen historically in Russia. Nothing guaranteed the relics would be permanently protected. He scanned the room and turned toward the pocket door. Where else could they stash the treasures? No other place in the city came to mind.

The realization prompted him to respond. "You're right. There is nowhere else to hide them at this point."

Deacon Michael headed out the door with Father Herman behind him. Sergius glanced one last time at the safe and the wall behind it. *The wall.* It, too, had a recessed crown molding vertical and horizontal section, but it was less wide, only spanning about two feet. The height of the door seemed made for children or small adults—around four feet.

He caught his breath, muttered, "Deacon, Father," then pointed to the wall.

Sergius's brows met. *What could be behind that possible opening?*

Father Herman reached the wall. "How is this supposed to open? There aren't any other code boxes in here."

Deacon Michael shook his head as he examined the recessed molding. "Good question."

Sergius let out a frustrated breath before facing the entryway to the room. A tiny metal box hung next to the doorframe like a doorbell. He approached. It only revealed four numbers. "Father, Deacon, there's a number box here."

The men flanked him.

"Yes, but no note for the code," Deacon Michael said.

Father Herman stroked his beard. "Did we miss any other papers in the upstairs room?"

Sergius shrugged. "The envelope behind the painting only held the two I have in my pocket. I don't know if there were other papers somewhere else in the room. I don't recall seeing any other paintings on the wall."

"There weren't any others. I do remember that," Deacon Michael said.

Father Herman held up his palms. "Then how are we going to find the code for this box?"

Sergius's heart fluttered, and he laid a hand on his chest. He smiled. "God will reveal it to us in His time."

"Indeed," the deacon said.

Father Herman nodded and drew near the number box.

"For now, we've found the most important items and will keep them safely hid," Deacon Michael said as he headed out the door.

Sergius stepped into the hallway behind his fellow monk. He glanced back at the room as the door slid shut. *Why is there another secret entryway? What would be the purpose of that when the relics were tucked away in that hidden room? There's something else there, but what?* He frowned as he got into the elevator with the others. *And how are we going to find out?*

Twenty-One

EARLIER IN THE MORNING

Agent Withers stood on Stephanie's porch, giving her a cold stare. She swallowed down her fear and held Hobo's collar, pulling him back from lunging at the man.

Logan stepped partially in front of her. "Can I see some identification?"

Withers whipped out his badge and flashed it at Logan. "Agent Withers, IIA."

Stephanie smoothed out her shirt and cleared her throat. She knew why he was there, but she'd play dumb. "Weren't you here last night?"

The man's jaw twitched as he shoved his ID back into his coat pocket. "Yes, I was. Now that it's daylight, I've come to retrieve the drone." He jerked a nod toward Stephanie. "I'm sure you remember what happened."

Stephanie cast a quick glance at Logan, whose gaze fell on her for a few seconds. His eyes gave no answers, but she doubted the agent would leave without discovering something. "I did find pieces of the drone on the side of the house this morning."

Logan's eyes met hers again, a flash of caution lightening them.

"Lead the way, ma'am," Agent Withers said.

Stephanie put Hobo back inside the house, then closed the door behind her. Clasping her shaking hands, she crossed the porch to the front yard. She hurried toward the bushes on the side of the house with Logan and the agent on her heels.

She pointed at the hedges. "The pieces left from the crash are in there."

Agent Withers stooped down and parted the branches. He leaned farther into the bush and came out with several metal pieces in his hands. He plucked out two small pieces with red lettering.

She covered her mouth to hide her gasp, as her wide stare fell on Logan. He gave her another cautious glance. Why hadn't he taken all the pieces with the red letters?

Agent Withers held up the remnants. "Is this all that was left of the drone?"

Stephanie opened her mouth, her throat dry.

Logan shoved his hands in his jean pockets. "Yep, those are it."

The intelligence officer eyed them with suspicion for a moment, then pulled out a two-gallon plastic bag from his jacket and dropped the pieces inside before sealing it shut.

Stephanie let out a quiet sigh of relief, then strode toward her front porch with Logan and the agent flanking her. They stopped on the porch.

She forced a smile and waved at the intelligence officer. "I'm late for church. Thanks for stopping by."

Agent Withers handed her his card. "If you find any other possible pieces to the drone, contact me." He turned to go, then pivoted back. "I may return at some point if I see the need to." He headed to his black SUV, slipped inside, and drove away.

Stephanie led Logan back inside her house, with Hobo jumping on their legs and yipping.

She pushed the dog off her shins, then patted his head. "Shh, boy. Calm down."

"I figured you'd have company from spooks like Withers." Logan pointed toward the basement door. "We going down to put the puzzle together?"

She scurried toward the basement stairs, with Hobo on her heels. "Yes, but I thought you'd grabbed all the pieces with the letters on them."

Trailing behind her, Logan said, "Best to leave a few crumbs. Less conspicuous that way."

"Ah." He was smart. She hadn't thought of that.

Flipping on the light switch at the top of the steps, she was interrupted by Hobo. He trotted down ahead of them. She hurried after him with Logan behind her. Hobo sniffed around the boxes. She retrieved the Christmas container and set it on the wooden table where her dad's old radio sat. Logan opened the top of the box and pulled out the pieces. He spread them across the dusty tabletop.

She studied the small red letters. Obviously, with Agent Withers possessing a few of them, the words wouldn't be complete. Nonetheless, Logan assembled them into possible words:

S-T-R-K F-O-R I-C.

"Strike For IC?" Stephanie scrunched up her nose. "Those missing letters would really be helpful right now."

"Maybe." Logan pulled out a pencil and small notebook from his shirt pocket. He tore a sheet from it and ripped the page into smaller pieces. He wrote letters on the papers and inserted them between some of the drone pieces:

STRYKER FORCE, INC.

A sick feeling roiled through her stomach. "One of our weapons manufacturing companies?"

"Yep." Logan leaned his rear on the edge of the table and folded his arms across his chest. "Not surprised." He raised his brows. "Are you?"

"Yes..." Her father's murder surfaced in her mind. "No... This is pretty strong proof of what really happened to my dad two years ago." She slumped against the table and pressed a hand to her forehead. "My mom had been right all along."

He laid a hand on her shoulder and lightly squeezed. "You okay?"

She sighed. "Yeah."

"If you don't mind my asking, what happened to your father?"

"Dad went with Mom to the March on the Pentagon to protest our proxy war with Russia at the time."

Logan nodded. "Right. I remember. Two years after I'd left the Fairview Police Department."

Stephanie paused and looked up at him, his penetrating gaze the same as she remembered in their teens. "You were a police officer?"

"Yeah. For seven years." He ran a hand through his hair, his mouth in a firm line. "I'd had enough of its militarization and abuse of power. I saw it wasn't getting any better. Could see where it was heading. Clear as day today."

The many fragments of their government's abuse of power and war machine came together into one solid block. It was clear as day to her too. Her father had been one of its victims.

"What happened to your father?"

He brought her back to that day again.

"Mom said there had been a few tussles with the DC police there. A few drones were flying around the area dropping tear gas canisters into the crowd. Mom said there were around two hundred protestors. Not a huge amount like you see in Europe, of course. But she'd been proud of the turnout." She paced the basement floor, the clenching of her stomach reminding her of how she felt that day when her mother had called her three hours after she and her father had left for the event.

Logan watched her, still leaning against the table, a frown on his face.

She stopped pacing and spun around. "Nobody in the group had weapons on them, despite the police's claims."

He nodded.

"It seems a couple of those drones had the ability to fire bullets, and they did." She looked away from his stare and focused on the floor, as the memory of her mother's ashen face came back to her. "Three people were killed… One of them was my dad." Tears stung her eyes.

Logan's arms were around her in seconds. Her face pressed against his chest as she lost the fight against releasing tears in front of him. He rubbed her back, his embrace filling her with a sense of comfort and safety.

He said nothing, just let her collect herself before she pulled away from him. She looked up at him and gave him a weak smile. "Thanks."

He stepped back. "Sure."

She pointed to the pieces. "What do we do about that?"

"Nothing."

"Nothing?"

"Not yet. It's too dangerous to say anything right now."

Dangerous. She absorbed his words. Yes, too many horrible things were going on to come forward, and who would believe them? And her mother was still in jail, her son stuck in a war zone. She wrung her hands. The need to call a lawyer rushed back to her mind like a splash of cold water on her face. She had to try to find one that held out against the State.

Logan poured the pieces of the drone back into the Christmas box.

Maybe he'd know someone, having worked in law enforcement. She touched his back. He turned his head to look at her.

"Logan, do you know of any lawyers that are willing to fight against the corrupt system to get my mom out of jail?"

His eyes widened. "Shit. Your mom's in jail?"

"Yes. She has been for weeks now."

"Why was she jailed?"

"Protesting the wars."

Realization lit his frowning face. "Just became illegal not long ago."

"It wasn't illegal when Mom and her friends demonstrated." Stephanie moved away from him and headed up the stairs. Hobo raced ahead of her while Logan lagged behind, just reaching the steps before she walked into the kitchen.

Stephanie pulled out an old yellow pages book from the small recipe desk across from the stove. With the internet companies turning off their services to the public due to the cyberattacks, she had to resort to old ways of gaining information. "Do you know of any decent lawyers that haven't bowed to corruption?"

He took the book from her. "Yeah. Her name is Deborah Stewart. Sharp, honorable, effective." He thumbed through until he found an ad with her name on it. "Hope this number is still good."

Stephanie returned to the desk and grabbed a pen and paper. "It's all we have." She jotted down the number.

An alert siren blared outside—the new way of communication from the government to the citizens.

She and Logan froze.

"My fellow Americans, this is your president. We have banned the use of any type of gun. It is illegal to own any from this time forward."

Stephanie bit her lip.

Logan's face hardened. "It was just a matter of time."

"In the midst of a war for our country's survival, we have enacted this law effective immediately. In addition, it is now treasonous to speak or act against this war. Anyone caught in this act will be incarcerated without bail. Subsequently, capital punishment will be carried out. Report with your guns to your town's city hall on Monday morning by nine a.m. This concludes my announcement. Stay safe and God bless America."

Treasonous? Capital punishment? Fear trickled down her spine. Her father's hidden guns somewhere in her house flashed in her mind. Would she dig them up and turn them in or just leave them hidden? Or would she venture the third most dangerous choice? Keep them for use when needed. The options blurred into a cloud of confusion taken over by panic. Grabbing the chair tucked under the desk, she used it to balance her swirling equilibrium.

Logan rubbed her arm. "You okay?"

She nodded and took out her phone from her purse on the kitchen counter. "Let's try this number."

Three rings went off before a woman's voice came on. "Deb Stewart."

Surprise stunted Stephanie's ability to answer quickly.

"Hello?"

"Uh, Ms. Stewart—"

"Deb, please."

"Deb, this is Stephanie Jenkins. I need your help."

"What can I do for you?"

"My mother has been in the county jail for several days now for protesting the war."

"Which is now illegal," Deb replied in a matter-of-fact tone.

Stephanie cast a wary glance at Logan. Was this woman a true fighter against the State? She gripped her phone and pressed forward. "Yes, I know, but my mother was put in jail before our government passed that law."

"Okay. Sounds like you may have a case."

Stephanie sighed in relief. A hint of hope made her smile. "Can we meet at the county jail tomorrow morning around eleven thirty? I can run over there during my lunch hour."

"Sure. I'll do some digging and see you then."

For the first time since all this horror had started, there was a light amid the darkness. A sense of real hope, at least for her mother. She clasped her hands together. "This is good news for once. I've got to go change for church."

Pam came down the stairs with her tote bag. "Hey, the siren woke me up. Guess I overslept."

When her friend went to bed for the night, she was out for hours. Nothing could wake her.

Pam knuckled one of her droopy eyes. "Who's he?"

"My..." Stephanie glanced at Logan, who portrayed a look of bewilderment. "My friend Logan. Logan, this is my friend and next-door neighbor, Pam."

Pam shuffled to the door. "I've got to get home. Nice meeting you." She slipped outside and shut the door.

Logan pointed toward the entryway. "I've gotta go also. Need to be at the museum in fifteen minutes."

Stephanie hurried over to him. "Wait, how can I keep in touch with you? Do you have a cell phone?"

He chuckled. "Don't we all?"

She dashed to the kitchen desk to get a piece of paper.

"But cell phones aren't safe to use for sensitive conversations."

Spinning around, Stephanie dropped the sheet on the desktop. "You're right. If the intelligence agencies of our government are involved with homeland security and the military industrial complex, why wouldn't they have been listening to our mobiles by now?"

"They have been. For years." Logan jutted out his chin. "You have a CB radio. We'll keep in touch that way."

She trailed behind him as he approached the front door. "But I don't know when you're on there or when to check in."

He pulled out his car keys, then gazed down at her. "Possum and I hop around on there, so those listening are less likely to catch our convos. For now, turn to channel forty-four. I'm on most every night. And you'll be notified whenever we change to another channel."

Scuttling back to the desk, she scribbled down the information. "Got it."

"See you later." He quietly shut the door.

Stephanie ran up the stairs to the bathroom to shower. She had something new and crucial to be thankful to God for and being in His house this morning would be an even bigger blessing.

Twenty-Two

Rushing toward the church steps, Stephanie glanced at her watch. By the time she got into the nave, the deacon would be passing out the antidoron. *Ugh!*

A group of about twenty people with agitated expressions passed her on the sidewalk.

One of the men in the cluster, who was heavyset with a pug nose, buzz cut, and a belligerent stare, roared, "Monday can't come fast enough."

The red-headed man next to him, who sported a casual work suit, nodded and pointed at the church. "Those deadbeats won't be able to hide in that place anymore."

"If they do," said the man with the buzz cut, "we'll find them and turn them in."

A short, stout woman with a pinched pink face and unruly brown hair bunched her fists and pulled her arms down. "We'll finally have our streets cleaned up."

Everyone cheered. They gave Stephanie one last collective contemptible stare and moved down the sidewalk in a constant murmur.

She shook her head. *Mean-spirited people.*

Entering the church, she found the monks, Deacon Michael, and Brody and Lindy in the narthex.

"Stephanie," Deacon Michael said. "I'm afraid the liturgy has already ended."

She sighed. "Yes, I know. So sorry I didn't make it. Something terrible happened last night."

"Lord, have mercy. What was it?" the deacon asked as he and the others stepped closer to her in a half circle.

She wrung her hands. "One of my neighbors was murdered by a drone."

Brody's face hardened, but he didn't say anything. Lindy clung to him, her gaze darting from one person to another.

Pain etched creases in Deacon Michael's face. "Holy Mother of God."

"Lord, have mercy," Father Sergius said, crossing himself.

Father Herman lowered his head. "How tragic."

"Makes me even more suspicious of what the new homeless shelter is all about," Brody said.

Stephanie hadn't heard of that, and it appeared by the looks on the other men's faces, they hadn't either.

"What new shelter?" asked Deacon Michael.

"Don't know all the details, just that we are supposed to be bused to it tomorrow." Brody shrugged. "But I'm not sure I'm going to go."

Stephanie raised her brows. "Why not?"

Brody gave her a sour expression. "'Cause I don't trust our government, state or federal."

"But where would you and Lindy go since all the other shelters in town have been closed?"

He looked away as if he didn't want to deal with her question.

Father Sergius held a prayer rope in his hands and fingered the knots. "We'll be here until Wednesday morning. Let us know if we can help in any way."

Brody glanced at the monk, then smoothed down Lindy's hair. He managed to nod.

A commotion outside prompted Stephanie to open the front doors.

The same group of people she'd seen before entering the church were walking past it again.

She spun and faced the men but focused on Brody. "It's the same crowd I saw earlier. They're not happy with the homeless people in town. They can't wait until you're moved to the shelter." She bit her lip. "I hope they won't do anything rash in their anger."

Brody came alongside her. The cluster was at the corner, before they wandered across the street, marching and chanting something inaudible. "They've always been around."

He didn't seem worried, and that concerned her. "Yes, but everything is more fraught and dangerous these days."

"I know." He glanced at his daughter standing by the monks. "I'll do whatever it takes to protect my daughter."

Tears welled in Stephanie's eyes as her own son came to her mind. He had to be okay. She couldn't handle anything happening to Jake. "I understand."

Brody lifted the plastic bag in his hand. "Thanks, Deacon. We'll be going now." He gestured toward Lindy, and she followed him out the entrance.

Stephanie clasped the cross pendant on the chain around her neck. *The government has killed its own people right in front of my eyes. God, please protect Brody and Lindy.*

AVA'S MIND WAS A BLANK. SHE COULDN'T COME UP WITH A plan B. Leaning against the cinderblock wall while sitting on her lumpy cot in her cell, Ava rubbed her stomach. Even though she'd gone back to eating, the food she was taking in didn't give her the good nourishment she'd gotten from her usual organic diet. Nonetheless, she had no choice.

Cell doors clanked in the near distance. The sounds seemed to be coming from down the hall. She sat up and cocked an ear.

Shuffling shoes on the floors drew nearer. Blaine came down the corridor with another guard.

Blaine held a baton and pointed at Ava. "Jenkins is last in the group."

The other female guard, who was tall and stocky, gave a jerky nod, with a grimace on her face. "Got it."

Blaine stood at a distance with her arms folded behind her back as she watched the other guard unlock Ava's cell.

Hope surged inside Ava. She was finally going to be set free. All the injustice of her situation was over. She stood and moved to the door.

The guard held out a hand. "Hold on, Jenkins. We've got some of your personal items to give you. Then you will follow me out."

Ava grinned. "Gladly."

The tall woman snorted but said nothing.

Blaine's mouth widened, flashing a large smile. "Jenkins, you're finally leaving us."

Ava smirked. "Don't miss me too much."

"Ha." Blaine sashayed down the hallway and around the corner.

Another guard who had bigger muscles than most men approached her and tossed a small bag into her arms. She snickered, then pivoted back down the hall.

Ava followed the tall guard down the same corridor. They turned in the opposite direction toward the front desk and entrance. They stopped by the counter as the guard signed a couple of papers. Two other guards showed up with Ava's three fellow protest organizers. She gasped, then smiled and reached for Mel, her friend of forty years. They embraced. All of them were being released together. What could be better?

Through the open doors at the entryway, a microbus rumbled up to the curb in front of the jailhouse.

Ava paused, letting go of her friend and gazing at the microbus. *Wait a minute. Where's Stephanie? And why aren't anybody else's relatives here to pick them up?*

The guard towered near the vehicle's door that she slid open. "Ladies, time to go."

Ava exchanged concerned looks with her best friend and the others.

Mel leaned toward Ava's ear. "What do we need this van for? I'd rather wait for Whitney to pick me up."

Ava squeezed her friend's hand. "I'd rather wait for Stephanie."

A couple of guards came from behind and gestured them toward the microbus. "You heard Raddick. Get in the vehicle."

One of the guards pushed Ava toward the van. She nearly stumbled into the two women ahead of her. Anger simmered in her, and she spun toward the guard. "Why are we taking that minibus?"

The guard behind her sneered. "Free transportation. You're welcome."

Ava and the other women were herded into the vehicle, with the two guards tramping down the short aisle, monitoring them. Everybody talked at once, looking around.

An unexpected chill ran through Ava. She looked up at the guard about to pass by. She grabbed the woman's hairy arm. "Where are we going?"

The woman gave her a toothy grin, her eyes cold as Antarctica. "Home."

Home? The deep, sinking feeling in her gut told Ava the guard's idea of *home* wasn't the same as hers.

The door slid shut, and the microbus left the curb to an unknown destination.

Twenty-Three

That afternoon, Sergius and his brother stepped into the room above the loft.

Deacon Michael came in after them with a flashlight in his hand. "Do you want to give the back of the painting another look?"

Sergius removed the picture from the wall and set it face down on the nearby table.

Deacon Michael approached with the light on the back of the painting.

Sergius slipped the small envelope out of the side of the brown paper backing and opened the top. Another paper folded several times sat at the bottom of the pouch. "I didn't see this before." Sliding his index finger and thumb into the narrow slot of the envelope, he pulled out the sheet. "The other notes hadn't been folded."

Father Herman bent toward the paper in Sergius's fingers. "Ah, another code?"

"Let's hope so," Deacon Michael said.

Opening the sheet, Sergius read out the numbers on it. "Seven, three, nine, seven." He held up the paper. "Gentlemen, I think we've got it."

Father Herman moved toward the doorway and waved for them to follow. "Let's go."

Sergius followed his brother out with the deacon behind him.

They rode the old elevator down to the secret room and entered. The faint aroma of sweet incense floated in the room from the safe.

The relics are still there. Sergius crossed himself. "Thank you, Lord, for keeping Your treasures safe."

The deacon laid a hand on the metal safe. "Indeed. Glory to God."

"Glory forever," Father Herman said.

Sergius turned toward the numbered code box by the door. Taking out the note he'd placed in his pocket, he punched in the numbers.

The space inside the recessed borders of the far wall moved to the side like the other pocket doors in the room and the one above the loft had done.

Sergius and the others hurried to the short entryway. He peered down the dark corridor. "Deacon, we're in need of your flashlight again."

The deacon clicked it on and aimed it down the hallway.

Sergius followed the deacon, with his brother behind him. They walked crouched over in the cramped space smelling of dirt and old septic water. In the pitch black, the flashlight's beam splashed the spider-veined walls a foot ahead of Sergius.

Father Herman's heavy breathing floated over his shoulder. His brother had always been uncomfortable in small, tight spaces. He said a prayer for his fellow monk and crossed himself.

They continued to walk slumped for the next forty feet when the cracked drywalled ceiling above them lifted to the point that his brother and Deacon Michael could straighten to their full heights. Being the tallest, Sergius had to lower his head.

A steel door shone ten feet ahead of them. Sergius rubbed the side of his cheek. *Where does this lead?*

They stopped in front of the door.

Deacon Michael gave them a frown. "Are we going to need another code for this one?"

Father Herman shrugged while Sergius studied the doorknob and the round lock above it. A dented metal box hung from the knob. He opened the top. A scroll filled the small container. Pulling it out, he unrolled it. A written sentence in all capital letters ran across the middle of the paper.

Having taken classes in biblical Greek, Sergius deciphered the note. "He is the Door, the Way, the Source of Life."

"Amen," Deacon Michael murmured.

They stood silent, and Sergius pondered the words of the Lord. Sergius rolled up the scroll, then gestured the deacon to aim the beam of light on the opening of the metal box. He peeked inside. A small silver key lay at the bottom. He poked his index and middle fingers into the small slot, clasped the key, and took it out. He held it up and smiled.

Father Herman grinned, his teeth flashing between his black, thick beard.

"A simple entry this time." The deacon crossed himself.

"Yes. No more codes." Sergius chuckled, slid the key into the lock, turned it, then twisted the knob.

The room ahead of them was circular with a built-in bench that jutted from the walls on either side. On the far wall, a hallway of about four feet split the room and led to a metal ladder attached to the wall. Sergius approached it and gazed toward the ceiling where a round metal plate like one on a street sewer with a latch sat three feet above his head.

The deacon and his brother flanked him.

"What's up there?" Father Herman asked.

"Well, there's one way to find out." Deacon Michael climbed the ladder and clasped the latch. He raised it toward him and pushed with some effort. Grunting, he pressed his shoulder against the lid. It gave way and fell to the side with a clunk. Sunshine poured through the hole and onto the deacon's balding head.

Sergius tented his eyes from the brightness. Where did the underground passageway lead? "Deacon, are you going to go up there? See where this ends up?"

The deacon shaded his face with his arm. "Yes. Come with me."

Sergius climbed the ladder after the deacon, and his brother came up behind him. They stepped onto the grassy area amid the church's backyard with its beautiful garden. A carpet of rich colors surrounded them. In the center stood a large marble cross and small fountain made from rocks. A border of hedges encircled the church's large backyard, hiding them and the garden from the street.

When Father Herman had crawled out of the hole and shut the lid that was covered in patches of grass, they headed to the closest bench near a trellis of wisteria.

Sitting next to his brother, Sergius pulled out his prayer rope, thanking God for their discovery.

The deacon approached him and jutted his chin toward the building. "It seems the church has had a type of secret passageway for decades for one reason or another. It certainly could come in handy now."

"Yes." Sergius nodded. "The timing is definitely divinely inspired."

Father Herman rubbed his beard. "I wonder if anybody knows about this besides us."

Olga came to Sergius's mind. She'd brought up her daughter's love of the children's story *The Secret Garden*. And she'd known about the room above the loft. "Perhaps Olga is aware."

Deacon Michael raised his brows. "It's possible."

Sergius fingered a pink petunia. "It seems she's lucid at the right times."

The deacon tilted his head in thought. "True. There are moments—"

A siren blared from downtown.

"Good afternoon, citizens. This is your president. My announcement is regarding air travel. As of five p.m. tonight, there will be no incoming or outgoing international flights to and from enemy countries for as long as this war lasts. Please make the appropriate changes to your travel plans. Stay safe and God bless America."

Sergius clutched his prayer rope. *We are trapped in our own country. But it truly feels more foreign than our present home in Russia.* "We'll have to call the monastery and let Father Ilya know."

Father Herman came alongside him. "Yes. When we return to our hotel this evening."

"I'm sorry that you're unable to go back to your homes," Deacon Michael said. "If you need any help with the cost for the extra days at the hotel, let me know, or you can stay at my house."

Sergius bowed. "Thank you, Deacon. That is very kind of you to offer. We will consider it."

The deacon nodded. "With all that's going on, it's good to stay close and keep in touch."

"I agree," Father Herman said.

Sergius pointed toward the church. "We should be going. Thank you for allowing us to go through the passageway with you."

Deacon Michael smiled and patted Sergius's back. "Of course. Come back soon."

"We will," Sergius said.

As they headed back to the church ahead of them, two surveillance drones slid across the sky toward downtown. Stephanie's words floated in Sergius's mind: *"One of my neighbors was murdered by a drone."* He crossed himself. *We must be careful.* As he glanced behind him at the grassy spot where the entrance to the underground passageway was, he felt a stirring in his heart. He closed his eyes. *That hidden place may be needed soon.*

Twenty-Four

Standing near the door to the Piccadilly Bar off Main Street, Brody laid a protective arm around his daughter. He checked his watch. The buses would be showing up any minute. Part of him wanted to take off, while the other part wanted to observe the event. Nevertheless, he hadn't changed his mind about going to the new shelter. Something inside him discouraged boarding the bus.

A group of about thirty homeless people hung around the steps to the police station across the street.

Mary came alongside him and wore a hint of a smile—something he hadn't seen on her face since her boy was taken away. "Today's the day."

"Yes, it is." If only he could convince Mary not to go to the shelter, even though she seemed so eager. He had to be careful with how he'd go about relaying his concerns. The last thing he wanted to do was cause her more worry and misery.

He held his daughter's hand, rubbing his thumb against the side of her wrist.

Leaning toward his ear, Mary said, "At least we'll have a place to sleep. Finally."

He tilted his head to loosen the tightness in his neck. "I know. You've said that before."

That ghost of a smile vanished, and a frown replaced it. "You still don't want to go, do you?"

"No." He put a hand on Mary's shoulder. "Listen, why don't you come with Lindy and me?"

Mary folded her arms. "And where would that be?"

"To the church."

"The church?" Mary shook her head and scowled. "There are no beds there."

Brody rubbed Mary's arm to calm her. "I feel it's a safe place for us."

Mary's gaze fell on Lindy. "I suppose I can understand. You still have your child with you." She looked away as if the sight of Lindy was a painful reminder that her son was gone.

He cupped the back of his neck. The conversation only seemed to be getting worse.

The police station's doors opened, and a handful of officers marched out. Holland was one of them. No doubt they were the ones in charge of loading people onto the bus, because Holland had mentioned it the other day at the park.

One of the cops raised a megaphone to his mouth. "Form a line, single file."

The officers stood near the curb.

Brody turned to scan the end of the street for the bus. The cluster of angry rioters that stomped past the church yesterday congregated in front of the barber shop two doors down from him. *What are they doing? Going to celebrate all the dirty, undesirables being banished from the streets?* Two of the burliest men from the group glared at him and his daughter. He wrapped his arms around Lindy, who stood in front of him.

Mary pointed toward the opposite end of the street. "Look! The bus is coming!"

The yellow vehicle chugged down the road.

The thugs moved toward him, passing the barber shop.

Brody clutched his daughter tighter.

Lindy gazed up at him. "Daddy, are we going on the bus?"

He bent and whispered in her ear, "No, honey. We're going to the church."

He held Mary's forearm. "Come on."

She looked up at him with surprise. "You changed your mind?"

He pulled her toward him. "No. We're getting out of here."

Just as Mary pulled away, the bus stopped at the curb by the police station. He reached for her but only got air. She stepped toward the road.

"Mary!" he yelled.

She didn't look back but got in line in front of the bus.

Holland stood by the door, holding a clipboard and pen. Another cop stood on the opposite side of the door with a stamp in his hand. Brody's eyes met Holland's. The officer's intense stare made his stomach churn. He took Lindy's hand and guided her quickly toward the street corner. Glancing over his shoulder, he spotted the rioters keeping him in their sight.

The group left the road and headed in his direction.

Brody picked up Lindy and turned down the street on his left. He ran with her in his arms, her body bouncing against his shoulders and chest, as his shoes beat the pavement.

"Daddy!" Lindy whimpered and buried her face in the groove between his neck and shoulder, her arms around him.

He dared another look behind him. Three of the guys from the mob were running down the sidewalk no more than thirty feet behind. Picking up the pace, he raced with all his strength, holding his daughter against him.

At the intersection two blocks away towered Saint John Orthodox Church, as if beckoning him. He bit down on his bottom lip and sprinted toward it, as yells and curses from behind him grew closer.

Come on! It's not much farther! Ignoring the ominous sounds trailing him, Brody lowered his head, focused on the ground, and ran for all he was worth.

❧

On her lunch hour, Stephanie drove past the crowds around the police station and headed to the county jail. She parked in the lot, then hurried up the steps and through the doors. Checking her watch, she expected the lawyer to arrive in a few minutes.

Honegger sat at the desk, staring at her computer screen.

Stephanie wasn't in the mood for the woman's attitude she'd dealt with twice before. "Hey, I'm here to see my mother, Ava Jenkins."

Honegger looked up at her as if she'd never seen her before, then glanced at the log in front of her. "Did you schedule an appointment?"

Stephanie's face warmed as she gripped the ends of the counter. "No. My mother is getting out of this place today."

Honegger laughed. "What makes you think that?"

Biting back anger, Stephanie leaned forward. "Her lawyer will be here soon to settle this."

The short, stout woman shrugged, then went back to looking at her computer screen.

The front doors opened, and a woman around five foot eight inches, wearing a navy pantsuit, marched toward Stephanie and Honegger. She reached them, pushed back her purse hanging from her shoulder, set her suitcase on the edge of the desk, then offered her hand to Stephanie. "Deb Stewart. And you must be Stephanie Jenkins." She flashed her a smile.

Relief showered Stephanie, and she shook the lawyer's hand. "Yes. It's great to meet you."

"Likewise." Deb turned her attention to Honegger, who was filing her nails. "And you would be?"

The woman lifted her chin and pointed to her name tag.

Deb bent forward and narrowed her eyes at the tag. "Honegger." She straightened, then placed her case on the floor. "Fantastic." She thrust out her hand again, but the woman behind the desk only gave it a disgusted look.

"I see someone lacks manners." Deb gave Honegger a tight smile. "Nevertheless, I am here to see my client."

Honegger's mouth pursed. "Your client?"

"Yes. Ava Jenkins."

"That's not possible."

Stephanie's eyes widened. *This woman is unbelievable.*

Deb pulled out papers from her case. "She is to be released—"

"I don't have that authority."

Deb threw up her hands. "Then get someone who does."

Honegger sighed, then pointed to the office door diagonally behind the counter. "Sheriff Rokes."

Deb grabbed her briefcase. "Very good." She approached the door and knocked.

Stephanie came alongside her. The confidence the lawyer showed gave Stephanie a good feeling. Hope surged inside her.

"Come in," a man's deep voice said from behind the door.

Deb opened the door and gestured for Stephanie to go ahead of her. Stephanie stepped inside the office, where a large man with olive skin, black hair and mustache, sat behind a behemoth rosewood desk, his fingers laced together.

"Can I help you?"

"Yes." Stephanie replied, but Deb patted her arm as if to say she'd handle this.

"Yes, sir." Deb shot out her hand. "Deb Stewart, attorney."

The sheriff shook her hand, then leaned back in his leather chair. "How can I help you?"

"I'm here to have my client, Ava Jenkins, released."

"Let me get her file from my assistant." The sheriff pressed an intercom on his phone. "Honegger, bring me Jenkins's file."

A minute later, Honegger strutted in and handed Rokes the file. Without looking at Stephanie or Deb, she stuck her nose in the air and walked out of the office.

Rokes opened the file, shuffled through the papers, his gaze scanning over the sheets. "Yes, she was being held here due to illegal protesting of the war."

Deb clutched papers in her hand. "Except the date she had been protesting was before the enactment of the law that prohibited demonstrating against this war." She set the papers on top of the folder.

She was *being held?* Stephanie froze. *What's he talking about?*

Sheriff Rokes looked over the documents and nodded. "So I see." He leaned back in his chair again.

Stephanie folded her arms tightly across her chest. *What's he waiting for?*

"So she must be released immediately." Deb tugged on the cuffs of her blazer. "And what did you mean by saying she *was* an inmate?"

Rokes stroked his mustache. "She was released yesterday."

Stephanie gaped. "What?"

Deb glanced at Stephanie. "Exactly. And where did she go?"

Stephanie moved toward the desk. "Nobody notified me. Where's my mother?"

The sheriff held up his palms toward Stephanie. "As was noted by you, counselor, she and the other protestors had not truly broken the law. However, their behavior warrants three months of community service."

"Community service?" Stephanie shook her head. "When did this come to pass?"

"Friday."

Deb leaned the heels of her hands on the desk. "Where was she sent for this community service?"

"The new shelter hotel for the town's homeless people."

Mom's at a homeless hotel? "What's she supposed to do there?"

"She's working one of the hotel positions."

Stephanie tapped her fingers against her jaw. That didn't sound too bad. At least she was out of jail.

Deb eyed the warden. "So the war protestors are now hotel employees, so to speak?"

The warden nodded. "You could say that."

Stephanie leaned toward the file, craning her neck. "Do you happen to have an address for the location and a phone number so I can call her and visit during the hours allowed?"

The sheriff's face hardened. "No one is to visit the shelter, except authorized personnel and those there to complete their community service."

Deb's eyes narrowed. "Why?"

Stephanie's heart sank. "What about a phone call? Can't people call their loved ones there?"

"The use of phones or cell phones is still not permitted in Fairview or nationwide for that matter. Sorry." He stood. "I must go. I have a meeting to attend."

"I'd still like to know why no one can visit people at this new hotel shelter," Deb said. "Is it a privately owned building?"

"Ladies, I don't have time to continue this conversation." Sheriff Rokes ushered them out of his office, then strode down the hallway.

Stephanie bit her lip as she followed Deb outside.

The lawyer spun around and faced her. "I need to investigate these ever-changing rules. It's ridiculous." She pulled out her phone and typed something in it. "I'll get back to you on this."

Stephanie could only nod while her head swam with images of the horrible events that had happened to her and her family in the past month. A chilly uneasiness trickled down her spine. Her trust in government and state officials was gone. How would Deb be able to help her?

Deb squeezed her hand. "Don't worry. You'll see your mother. I'll make sure of it." She handed her a business card. "You've got my number, and I have yours in my recent calls. We'll be in touch."

The lawyer headed to her car. Stephanie did the same, tucking Deb's card into her purse. *I hope she gets answers soon. I need to know that Mom is okay.*

<h1 style="text-align:center">Twenty-Five</h1>

Stephanie rolled up her driveway and pressed the remote. The garage door lifted slowly. She glanced toward Pam's house where her friend's car sat in the driveway. Why was Pam's car left outside, and why was she home from work? Was she sick?

Once inside the garage, she turned off the engine and jumped out of her car. She jogged over to Pam's house and knocked on her front door.

No one answered.

A sick feeling settled in her stomach.

Stephanie knocked again.

Still nothing.

She grabbed the knob and turned it. The door was unlocked.

A gasp escaped from her lips. Her anxiety-ridden friend never left her door unlocked, especially lately with the multiple break-ins in their neighborhood.

Stephanie opened the door and crept into the empty living room. "Pam?"

Silence answered. Worry ate at her as she went through the kitchen and downstairs bathroom.

No Pam.

Don't jump to any conclusions. Maybe she's upstairs in her bathroom. Stephanie swallowed hard while climbing the carpeted stairs and heading for Pam's bedroom.

The door was ajar.

Pressing a hand to her churning stomach, she pushed the door back.

Pam lay on her unmade bed, her eyes closed as if sleeping.

She ran over to her friend, grabbed her hand and squeezed. "Pam. Pam, wake up!"

Her friend remained unresponsive.

Dread streaked through Stephanie, causing her to shake. She glanced at the nightstand by the bed. Two empty prescription bottles lay on their sides. How many pills had been left? Fear paralyzed her for a second before she snatched the bottles. One was an antidepressant, the other for insomnia.

Dear Jesus. How many did she take? Her hand trembling, Stephanie dropped the plastic bottles on the nightstand. One rolled off and onto the floor. Ignoring them, she moved to Pam and patted her pale cheek. "Pam, can you hear me?"

Pam didn't respond.

Stephanie yanked her phone from her jacket pocket and called 911.

"We're experiencing a high volume of calls. Your wait time is approximately five minutes."

She gripped the phone, her heartbeat thudding. "Five minutes? This is an emergency!"

But what else can I do?

Dr. Alban came to mind.

She sprinted down the stairs and out the front door, racing to Dr. Alban's home. Still holding the phone, she banged on the door. "Dr. Alban!"

Checking her watch, it read 11:53. *What was I thinking? He's at his clinic, working!*

"Nine-one-one operator, what's your emergency?"

She leaned against the door and blew out an exasperated breath.

Thank God. "Yes, please help my friend. She took a bunch of pills. I can't wake her!"

"Okay, ma'am. Are you with her? What is her address?"

Her mind muddled. Pam's address wouldn't come to her. She pressed a palm to the side of her head. *Come on! You know this!*

"Ma'am, are you still with us?"

"I'm not with her right now." Stephanie propelled herself off the doctor's porch and dashed back to Pam's house, scrambling up the stairs to the bedroom. Finally the address came to her. "I'm back with her. Two three nine Lilac Road. Please hurry!"

"We're sending out an ambulance and patrol car. Can you check her wrist or neck for a pulse?"

Stephanie laid two shaky fingers against Pam's wrist. Her pulse was weak, barely present. "Oh God. It's weak."

"Sit tight. They'll be there soon."

Stephanie nodded, forgetting she was on the phone.

"Ma'am, do you need me to stay on the line with you?"

"Y-yes." Stephanie's throat closed. "I'm afraid she's going to die."

"They'll be there soon to take care of her."

"Hang on, Pam. They'll be here soon." Rubbing Pam's cool arm, Stephanie's eyes welled with tears, blurring her vision. *Please, God, let her be okay.*

Seven agonizing minutes later, sirens blared, then commotion downstairs became louder. Two paramedics came through the bedroom doorway with a stretcher and medical bag.

"They're here," Stephanie said to the operator and disconnected the call. She moved away from the bed and gestured toward the nightstand. "Those are the pills she took."

The first paramedic picked up the bottles. "Get the pump," he said to the other paramedic, who had been checking Pam's pulse.

One of the men sprayed some type of liquid in her mouth. He pulled out a tube, opened Pam's mouth again, and gently pushed the tube down her throat. They began suctioning Pam's stomach.

"Will she be okay?"

Too busy with their task, neither responded.

After they'd finished and put away their equipment, the first paramedic said, "We're taking her to Evans Hospital."

"Will Pam be okay?"

"We're doing all we can to help her," said the second paramedic.

The men placed Pam on the stretcher.

"Can I ride with her?" Stephanie asked, clasping her hands tightly.

The first paramedic nodded.

"I'll grab some of her things," Stephanie said.

As they carried her friend out of the room, Stephanie glanced at the dresser, where two bent photos of Pam's daughter, Laura, rested next to several balled-up tissues. Her heart sank into her stomach. With trembling hands, she picked up a torn sheet adjacent to the tissues. The short message was handwritten from Pam's brother, discussing funeral arrangements for Laura.

Oh no! Poor Pam!

The creaking of the front door's wooden threshold downstairs sounded miles away. Pain surged through Stephanie like a searing iron. Everything around her turned into streaked, abstract colors. The distant, faint voice calling her from below faded.

Laura's dead.

Stephanie fell to her knees and covered her wet face. *Pam's got to live!*

Her son's face flashed in her mind. *Jake! Oh God, please let him be okay!* Her sobs dragged her down into darkness. She curled on the floor and whispered, "Jake."

Ava stood next to her friend Mel outside the administrative building next to the new shelter hotel. It looked more like a two-story warehouse with a bunch of dirty, drab windows than an actual hotel. Not cozy at all, especially with the ten-foot chain-link fence surrounding the buildings.

Ava scrunched up her nose. "Looks like a prison, and we're stuck in this place for three months." *Damn.*

"Yeah. So much for a fancy new shelter."

"None of the jerks from the jail were straight with us when they forced us in the van."

"Of course not."

Ava scowled. "Right. It shouldn't be a surprise. When have our government officials ever been honest with us?"

"Never."

As two guards came out of the administrative building and headed toward her, Ava leaned into Mel. "These authorities are about the same." Stepping back in her spot, Ava said, "At least they gave us info on what we'd be doing at this stinking place."

Mel shrugged. "Working in the cafeteria ain't too bad."

"No. We're basically doing what we did on Main Street. Feeding the poor and homeless."

"Sure thing. We're experts."

"Yeah, but this assignment is new. Wonder why we were chosen."

Mel put a finger to her temple. "We're smart."

"Still… I don't see the need for the fencing around this place." Ava folded her arms as she surveyed the area. "Are they trying to keep people in or out?"

One of the guards with jet-black hair came alongside Ava and handed her a clipboard and pen. "You'll match the numbers on their wrists with the ones on this form, then you'll look at the room number that corresponds with them. You'll tell them their room number and check them off the list. Got it?"

Ava squinted at the guard with the name tag SCARBORO. "Why not just use their last names?"

The guard's jaw tightened, and he glared down at her. "Last names can be duplicates, and some homeless people won't divulge their names." He tapped the numbers in the column. "Numbers with no duplicates are the most efficient way to register and keep track of the people."

Keep track. She'd heard too much about tracking citizens' whereabouts for just about everything these days, but maybe this wasn't the same thing. She knocked her knuckles against the side of her head.

Come on, Jenkins. You know ninety-nine percent of the time it's not for anything good.

"Got it?" Scarboro asked in a louder voice.

She swatted at the air. "Yeah."

"After you've checked them off," Scarboro said, then pointed at Mel, "you'll show them around the hotel. Help them find their rooms, the cafeteria, and such."

Mel nodded.

The bus drew up to the curb to the hotel. Ava and Mel, along with the guards behind them, approached the vehicle and stood near the accordion door. As soon as the bus driver got out, Ava started checking numbers on the people's wrists with the numbers on the form. Many of the houseless people looked familiar to her, having seen them often in town.

A woman with light brown skin and long black hair stepped off the bus with a smile.

Ava studied the woman's features. *Is that Mary? The lady who used to hang around the park with her teenage son.* "Mary?"

Scarboro's stern voice came from behind her as he pointed to the paper on the clipboard. "Number nine."

Ava rolled her eyes. "Right."

Mary nodded, then tapped a finger to her chin. "Aren't you one of the ladies who gave out food downtown?"

Ava grinned. "Yes."

"It's nice to see a friendly face." Mary frowned at the shabby shelter. "It's not how I pictured it."

"Keep the line moving," Scarboro called.

Ava checked off Mary's number and pointed at Mel. "She'll show you around."

Mary clasped her hands together and moved toward Mel.

Ava hadn't gotten the chance to ask about Mary's son. And he wasn't with her. *How odd. Where could he be?* He was too young to be drafted into the military. She'd ask Mary when she saw her at the cafeteria later.

A man in his fifties stepped off the bus, followed by an elderly man, sniffling. The man in his fifties wore a frown, walked up to her, and showed his wrist. She recorded it and gestured for him to move toward Mel.

The elderly man wiped his nose with a handkerchief, then pointed at the man ahead of him. "That's my son, Russell. I'm Walter."

Scarboro came alongside Ava. "You're number eleven."

The old man's face went slack, his eyes reflecting sorrow. "Yeah, that's my number."

Ignoring the guard, Ava said, "Hi, Walter. Please follow her." She pointed to Mel.

Walter shuffled after his son.

A grunt came from Scarboro. She didn't care.

He pulled out a baton and tapped the clipboard. "Numbers, no names. I won't remind you again."

His threat caused a chill to trail down Ava's spine. She looked away from him. "Sure. I got it." After checking off Walter's number, Ava focused on the fence again. *This really does feel like a prison, and I'm not even a number.*

Twenty-Six

Brody stumbled on one of the steps to the church's front doors but managed to right himself. Holding Lindy tightly against him, he dashed through the entrance and into the narthex.

The shouts from the rioters invaded the quiet space, echoing through the marbled foyer.

The two monks he'd seen the other day emerged from the nave, along with the deacon and an elderly woman with a cane.

Out of breath, Brody set Lindy down, then leaned over with his hands on his knees.

Deacon Michael strode toward him. "Are you and Lindy all right?"

The commotion outside grew louder.

Panic knocked against Brody's ribs. *I can't risk the jerks busting in and trashing the church. This is the only safe place left.* He grabbed Lindy's hand. *After she's out of danger, I need to get back outside.* He rubbed his daughter's shoulder, pleading with the deacon, "Please hide my daughter. They're coming for us."

Tears dribbled down Lindy's cheeks as she gazed up at the clergyman.

Deacon Michael's eyes and mouth drooped. He waved at the tall, thin monk who approached him. "Father Sergius, you know where to hide the child."

The monk nodded and took Lindy's hand, guiding her toward the door that led to the choir loft.

Lindy wailed, "Daddy!" She reached for him.

His heart aching, Brody hurried over and squatted in front of her, gently laying a palm against the side of her face. "Go with Father Sergius, honey. I'll see you in a little bit." He gave her a quick hug, then stood.

His little girl disappeared behind the door.

Swallowing the lump in his throat, he whispered, "She'll be safe now."

The elderly woman hobbled toward the entrance. "Close the doors behind me."

The deacon scurried after her. "We won't let you go out there alone, Olga." He moved ahead of her.

Coming alongside the elderly woman, the stout monk lifted his arm for her to hold.

Brody rushed out the door. Four of the eight rioters he'd seen downtown stood at the bottom of the steps. The two main thugs glared up at him while the man and woman behind them frowned and stood with hands on hips.

Sweat gathered on Brody's forehead. He wiped his face. *It's me against them.* He grimaced. *What are my chances?*

"Hey, Deacon, you can't hide homeless people in your church anymore! The bus is here to take them away!" The tall, meaty man, who seemed to be the leader, scowled at the clergyman.

"Give 'em up, Deacon!" the leader's thuggish sidekick sporting a buzz cut shouted.

Olga tsked, shaking her head. "Is that any way to treat your fellow man?"

"Stay out of this, lady," the sidekick said.

"We're in a dark period, and our continued sinful actions are causing more darkness and suffering in the world." Olga tapped her cane on the concrete. "We must come together, repent, and love one another to warm our cold, hardened hearts."

Brody's jaw fell open. He had never heard anyone talk in such a way. Not an ounce of fear or hatred.

Deacon Michael sidled next to Olga, laying his hand on her frail shoulder. "She's right. We do need more love and compassion for others. And maybe some homeless people don't want to go to the new shelter."

"It's not a choice! The police said they all gotta go!" the leader said, his hands fisted at his sides.

Brody straightened his back and folded his arms. "I'm not going."

The leader yelled, "Like hell!" and marched up the stairs with the other thug until they were only three feet away from Brody, Olga, the monk, and the deacon.

Thrusting out his hands, the leader tried to grab Brody, but Brody dodged him by backing away.

Olga leaned on her cane and stared up at the reddening face of the first man. "The bloodshed won't stop until we change our hearts."

Beet-red blotches bloomed on the leader's face. In a snap move, he pulled out a handgun. "Shut up, you crazy old witch!"

The monk next to Olga put an arm around her while the deacon held up a hand.

"Hey, you didn't say anything about using guns!" yelled the woman with the thugs, pointing at the beefy man. "They're illegal! We could go to jail!"

The leader glowered at the woman. "Protectors of street trash gotta pay, Emily." He held up the gun, aiming it at the deacon and Olga partially behind him.

Brody tensed. *The guy's insane! I've got to do something!*

Before Brody could charge the gunman, the thug fired the weapon twice. The bullets tore into Deacon Michael's chest and shoulder.

The deacon fell to the ground. The monk knelt by him.

Brody gasped. *Shit. The bastard got him!*

Emily's screams pierced the air. She pulled out her phone. "You've gone crazy! I'm calling 911 and the cops!"

The leader waved his gun at the woman behind him. "You want a bullet in you too?"

With a shake of her head, Emily backed away, her mouth wide in horror. The man next to her put an arm around her shoulder.

Turning and pointing his gun at Brody, the gunman roared, "Look what you did." He snorted. "Killing you would be a public service."

While the gunman's back was turned, Emily and the man with her bolted down the street.

The thug kept his pistol aimed at Brody.

Just as the leader pulled the trigger, Brody dove to the ground, slamming onto the concrete. Searing pain pulsated from his side, knees, and palms. Pressing a hand below his ribs, he felt a small patch of sticky wetness. The bullet had grazed his skin. Behind him, he spotted the bullet lodged in the stone facade. He turned to face the leader and caught the thug looking away, talking to his sidekick.

Adrenaline coursing through him, Brody ran toward the leader like a battering ram. Tackling him to the ground, Brody yanked the gun from his hand and stood.

"Let's go!" The sidekick scrambled down the steps and raced down the street.

Before Brody could grab him, the leader jumped up and scampered after his sidekick. Setting the gun down, then kicking it aside, Brody joined the monk and knelt by the deacon.

Olga hobbled over to them and placed a hand on the side of her face, her mouth forming an *O*. "God help Deacon Michael."

"Lord, have mercy. Deacon, how can I help?" The monk's face was ashen. He stared at Brody with a furrowed brow. "I hope the woman got in touch with an ambulance," he said. "I don't have a cell phone."

Brody shook his head. "Me neither." He tore a strip of his shirt, bunched it up, and pressed it against the crimson splotch on the deacon's chest. Grimacing, he muttered, "He doesn't look good."

In seconds, the piece of shirt Brody had put over the deacon's wound was soaked in blood. Brody tore at his shirt for another strip. "The ambulance needs to be here *now*."

Deacon Michael's pale face glistened with sweat. He licked his lips and grasped the monk's robe. "Father, the keys to my home… and the church… in my pocket." His breath was shallow, his voice barely audible. "Take them."

The monk shook his head. "It's not important right now, Deacon."

The deacon coughed, then slid a shaking hand toward his pants pocket and pulled out the keys on a ring. He coughed again and held it out for the monk to take. "Please. Do as I say."

Taking the keys, the monk stuffed them inside a fold of his cassock.

Brody worked to ball up another strip of his shirt and press it against the wound on the deacon's shoulder. "The ambulance should come soon." *Why did I say that? There's no way to know if that woman ever called anyone.*

Deacon Michael rolled his eyes toward Brody, as if he couldn't focus on him. Dread threaded through Brody's gut, and he bit his lip hard. *Christ. I've got to believe she called an ambulance!*

Olga stooped over the deacon with tears welling in her eyes. "Deacon, I wish you hadn't done that. You're a courageous, selfless man." She gazed skyward. "He's not far from you."

Stunned by the old woman's words, Brody sucked in a breath. *No, he can't be dying!*

Deacon Michael flinched and gave a slow nod.

Olga's focus shifted to something ahead of her that Brody couldn't see. "Your guardian angel is ready to take you to Him."

The words "Lord, have mercy on me" were but a whisper from the deacon before his eyes closed. He let out a gurgled sigh and fell silent.

The monk pulled out a knotted rope and bent in prayer over the deacon.

"No!" Brody choked on the tears clogging his throat and blurring his vision.

Sirens blared in the distance. The sounds meant nothing to Brody. It was too late. *This is all my fault.* He covered his face and wept.

Twenty-Seven

Stephanie rushed to the ER counter where a patient care technician sat. She glanced at her watch. It had been nearly a half hour since she'd pulled herself together, grabbed Pam's stuff, and sped to the hospital. Gripping the counter, she said, "I'm here to see Pam Denson. Do you have her in a room?"

The lady looked up at her. "Are you a relative?"

"No. I'm her friend, Stephanie Jenkins."

As the technician focused on her computer screen, a hand touched Stephanie's shoulder. She turned.

A heavyset man wearing glasses, jeans, and a plaid shirt gave her a sorrowful stare.

Her heart sank.

"I heard you say you're Stephanie. Pam's friend."

She nodded. "Yes. The ambulance brought her here."

"I know." The man laid a hand on her arm. "I'm Gary. Pam's brother."

"I'm so glad you came! I know she's happy to have you here."

His face drooped even more. "She didn't get to see me."

"Are they not allowing visitors?"

He shook his head. "She was gone ten minutes before I arrived." He wiped his nose with the back of his hand and bowed his head.

"Oh no!" Without hesitation, Stephanie reached over and held him tightly. "I'm so, so sorry." Tears stung her eyes, and she swallowed the lump in her throat.

Still in her arms, Gary said, "Now I've got to bury my sister *and* my niece." He wept against her shoulder.

Tears rolled down Stephanie's cheeks. Words wouldn't come. She continued to hold him until their crying had subsided.

Gary let her go, then plucked a tissue from a box on the front desk. He blew his nose. "The hospital is making arrangements for her transfer to the funeral home." He shoved his hand in his jeans pocket and pulled out his phone. "Could I have your number to contact you with the date of the funeral?"

"Of course." Stephanie gave him her number, then held up a plastic bag with Pam's toiletries and pajamas.

He frowned at the bag, his eyes still wet.

What was I thinking? He's hurting enough! She sucked in her bottom lip to stop another crying jag. "I'll drop these off at her home."

He gave her a nod and plodded down a hallway next to the lobby.

Pulling out a tissue from the box as well, she dried her face, then headed out of the ER.

She drove home, her mind on the memories of the five years she'd known Pam and the fun times they'd had together. The terrible incident from earlier haunted her. She pushed the traumatic encounter from her thoughts even though she knew it would never completely go away.

Parking her car in the garage, she opened the door to the kitchen and strode in, then stopped.

Hobo's barking sounded blunted. He hadn't greeted her in the kitchen. She stepped into the living room. The doggie door was closed off by the panel she slid into place every night before she went to bed. Chills rained over her. Every morning, she removed that cover to let Hobo out. The doggie door had been open before she'd gone to the county jail in the morning.

Persistent barking continued, and she spotted Hobo at the sliding glass door.

Relief engulfed Stephanie. She hurried to the door, lifted the panel, and set it to the side.

Hobo barreled through the little entryway and bounced against her, licking her cheeks.

For the first time in hours, Stephanie grinned as she gathered him in her arms. "Okay, boy, okay. I missed you too."

An uneasiness overcame her once again when she studied the doggie door. *Who locked Hobo out?* Letting go of the dog, she stood, her mind whirling. She touched the sliding glass door's flimsy lock. *Crap.* She scolded herself for not getting the lock replaced days ago. Now somebody else had broken into her home.

Icy panic streaked through her as she ran to the basement stairs, switched on the light, then rushed down the steps. Hobo scrambled down after her.

Grabbing the Christmas box where she and Logan had dropped the pieces of the destroyed drone, she looked inside and gasped. "They're gone!"

After setting down the box on other containers, she chewed her lip as thoughts raced through her mind. She froze. The burglar had to have been Withers. He'd never believed she and Logan didn't have the pieces.

The realization shook her. Agent Withers was onto her. She was now a target of the State.

Her knees trembled, nearly buckling. She grabbed the railing on the stairs to anchor herself before racing up the steps.

Scouring the rooms for any listening devices or small cameras, she found none.

Fear tore through her as a nauseating sensation swam in her stomach. Her home had been violated by the feds!

With shaking fingers, she snatched her purse from the kitchen counter.

Hobo jumped on her legs.

"I'll be back a little later, boy." She kissed his head, then bolted out of the house.

In the car, she pressed the garage door opener. *I need to reach Logan. Tell him what happened to the remains of the drone.* The CB radio came to mind. *I'll have to contact him away from the house. Somewhere else that may be safer…*

Stephanie backed out of the garage and headed for the destination she believed was her best choice for reaching out to Logan.

STEPHANIE PARKED HER CAR NEAR THE CHURCH'S entrance. She ran up the steps and turned the doorknob. It was locked. She blew out a breath that fluttered the hair on her forehead as she gazed up. Above her, a silver drone slowly slid across the cloudless sky, its lights blinking.

Fear paralyzed her, making it hard for her legs to move. *I've got to get out of here!*

She raced back to her car and got in. "Plan B."

Parking in the first slot in front of her workplace, Abby's Café, Stephanie gripped the steering wheel and forced herself to take deep breaths. After peering at the sky empty of drones, she switched on the CB to channel forty-nine and grabbed the mouthpiece. "Logan's Run! Logan's Run, do you hear me?"

"Who's asking for Logan's Run?" a man's calm voice asked.

"Server Steph. I need to reach him."

"This is Possum. I can get a message to him."

How could she explain what happened on the radio? How truly safe was it? *Think!* She pressed the button again and let out a breath. "Please tell him the Christmas ornaments are gone and that I need his help."

"Roger that. Probably won't be able to help you with the ornaments until tonight. That okay?"

"Yes! Thanks so much."

"No problem. Over and out."

Stephanie hung up the mouthpiece, turned off the radio, then leaned back in her seat.

Two drones skidded across the sky above her.

Shuddering, she squeezed the wheel, then sped out of the lot toward the hardware store. After she replaced the lock on the back door, she'd feel a little less vulnerable. And Hobo would be with her, comforting her until Logan arrived in the next couple of hours.

After serving lunch in the cafeteria, Ava took a seat at a table across from Mary. She gave the dark-haired woman a smile. "Hi. It's me again. Ava."

"Hi, Ava," Mary said.

Ava waved an arm at their surroundings. "How do you like the accommodations?"

Mary shrugged, looking around the large room, the tables filled with the new residents. "It's not what I'd expected, but at least I've got a bed to sleep on and food to eat."

"It's rarely what the government says it's going to be." Ava leaned her elbow on the table and rested her chin on her hand. "Where's your son? Did he find a job?"

Mary's eyes welled with tears, and Ava immediately regretted asking her. "He was sent off to war."

"What? I didn't think he was of age."

"He's not. He's only seventeen." Mary's mouth turned down. "I miss him. Afraid for him." She covered her face and wept.

I'd feel the same way. If they'd done that to Jake, I'd have gone ballistic. She froze. *Jake is of age. Was he taken away? I've got to find out somehow!* Ava left her seat and hurried to the other side of the table. She hugged Mary. "I'm so sorry. That's more than wrong."

A middle-aged man and an elderly one approached their table. "Do you mind if we sit with you?" the younger of the two said.

"Not at all." Ava gestured to the two chairs next to hers.

They set their trays down and took their seats. "I'm Russell, and this is my father, Walter," the middle-aged man said.

Walter rubbed his wet nose with a filthy handkerchief.

"Nice to meet you." Ava grabbed a napkin from beside her plate. "Do you need this?"

Shaking his head, Walter said, "No. I'm fine with what I got."

Russell bit into the piece of chicken on his fork, then leaned back in his chair. "This isn't too bad for shelter food."

"I didn't care for it," Mary said. "But I don't have much of an appetite."

"Me neither," Walter said.

Ava sat in her seat. "Can't expect five-star accommodations in a warehouse."

"Frankly, it's pretty much what I'd expected," Russell said.

Ava nodded and sipped her glass of water, which tasted like vegetation, soil, and bugs. The days of drinking filtered, clean water and organic foods seemed to be in the past. She pursed her lips. *It won't stay in the past. It's our only future.*

"Is there a doctor in this place?" Russell asked.

"I have no idea," Ava said. "Those in charge don't offer much information. You'll have to ask, and maybe you'll get an answer."

Russell laid a hand on his father's arm. "It's just my father has a weak heart and has some allergies that cause him bad sinus headaches and postnasal drip." He patted Walter's arm. "He's nearly out of his heart meds, so that's why we're needing to get him to a doctor here as soon as possible."

Before Ava could respond, a policeman approached their table. Recognizing him from downtown, she smiled. "Holland. I didn't realize you were going to be here."

"Half my shift is now spent here," he said. "The other half back at the station. Are you settling in all right?"

Mary pushed her tray to the side. "It's lonely."

Holland patted her shoulder. "There are lots of people here you can get to know."

She shook her head. "They're not my son."

Ava reached for one of her hands and squeezed it. "I miss my daughter and grandson too."

"How old is your grandson?" Mary asked.

"He's eighteen." She clenched her jaw. The thought of him possibly being drafted haunted her.

"Was he sent to war like my son?" Mary asked.

She scowled. "I don't know, but I plan to find out."

"You don't know?"

"I was in the county jail for the past few weeks."

"Why?" Russell asked.

"Protesting the war."

"Oh, right." Russell wiped his mouth with a napkin. "Can't have that, can we?"

"Nope."

Walter sneezed, and it reminded Ava about Russell's question before Holland had arrived. She turned toward the officer. "Is there a doctor here?"

"Not here but on call if we need him."

Russell muttered, "Well, it's better than nothing."

Walter grunted in response.

"Do you need a doctor?" Holland asked.

"Yes." Walter coughed.

"I'll go to the office and see what I can do."

It's a start, and he's my best bet here. "Thanks," Ava said.

Holland nodded then walked off.

Mary rose and picked up her full tray of food. "I'm not feeling well. I'm going to go back to my room and rest."

Ava took the tray from her. "Rest well."

As Mary plodded out of the cafeteria, Ava frowned. *Poor woman.*

After setting the dish from Mary's tray by the large metal sinks, Ava left the kitchen and headed toward the administrative building. Holland would be there tomorrow afternoon. She'd try to contact him then. The worry gnawing at her needed to be resolved as soon as possible.

Twenty-Nine

Sergius lifted his dirt-filled shovel over the open earth where a pine box sat. He tilted the head of the shovel and let the soil sprinkle on top of the wood. Only an hour ago, he'd been met by Brody in the secret room, who told him about the deacon's murder. So stunned by the horrible news, he hadn't been able to respond at first. But he followed Brody and his daughter to the narthex where his brother and Olga had stood with somber expressions.

Sergius and Father Herman had carried the deacon inside the church while they searched for something to put him in.

After finding a row of simple pine coffins in a room next to the one with the church's art and relics, they were able to place the deacon in one.

Sergius surveyed the garden and frowned. His home country had become further saturated with the spirit of the evil one since Father Herman and he first arrived. The shocking murder of Deacon Michael struck his heart. He scooped up more dirt, then paused. What was going on in Russia and the rest of the world? He suspected every place was shrouded in this dark spiritual malaise.

Although the funeral service was usually done before the casket was lowered into the ground, a sense of urgency had prompted them to bury the deacon first. They finished filling the dug-out burial spot.

Pulling out his prayer rope, Sergius began an abbreviated funeral service with the portions he knew by heart. "Grant rest, O Lord, to the soul of your servant, Michael."

Father Herman chanted along and covered the verses he didn't remember.

The church's large back doors opened, and a man in a suit, followed by two others dressed similarly, walked toward him.

The first man stopped in front of them. "Hello. I'm Mayor Bryant." His eyes slid to the fresh mound next to Sergius. "It's terrible what's happened. However, due to the circumstances..."

"Circumstances?" Sergius asked.

"Yes. There are no other clergy available to lead the services in this church. Therefore, we are closing it." He held up two padlocks. "If you'll follow us, we will be locking the front and back doors."

The precious relics in the basement surfaced in Sergius's mind. How safe would they be without the deacon or him and his brother present?

A drone darted overhead, streaking toward downtown. Sergius flicked a glance at Father Herman, who gave him a slight nod, his gaze traveling to his hand halfway out of his cassock pocket. Sergius didn't know what his brother was trying to tell him and didn't have the chance to mull it over. The mayor and his associates gestured toward the back doors of the church.

The back doors locked, they walked silently toward the narthex and front doors. The coolness of the foyer gave Sergius relief after having perspired from the shoveling he'd done earlier.

On the icon stand, streaks of fresh blood ran down the face and robe of Saint John. Sergius crossed himself, believing this was due to Deacon Michael's death.

The two associates opened the front doors, and Sergius and Father Herman shuffled outside.

The mayor himself put the second padlock on the front doors, then turned and smiled at them. "Gentlemen, have a good rest of your day."

The three men strode to the parking lot and got into a black sedan.

When the car drove out of sight, Father Herman laid a hand on Sergius's shoulder. "Brother." He lifted his fisted hand from his pocket and opened it, palm up. A round metal chain with three keys sat in the center.

Sergius's brows knitted. "Where did you get those?"

Father Herman clasped the keys. "Deacon Michael. It's his set of keys for the church." He lowered his eyes. "He gave them to me minutes before he died."

Sergius's gaze fell on the deacon's grave, his mouth drooping. He then glanced at the doors. "What about the mayor's locks?"

Father Herman scratched his beard. "We'll need to find a way to remove them."

"And the hatch to the secret passageway in the garden only opens from the inside," Sergius added.

The sun dipped below the horizon where the silhouette of modest homes stood across the street. Sergius and his brother headed to their car.

"We'll have to figure something out as soon as possible."

"Can we get to our hotel outside of town?" Father Herman asked. "The wall…"

"Is one of those keys for the deacon's house?"

"If it is, how do we find his house?"

Olga came to Sergius's mind. "Maybe Olga knows where his home is."

"Okay. How do we reach her?"

"Maybe Wednesday when there's the *Molieben* service. She'd probably be there for it."

"That seems likely."

"In the meantime, we'll need to find a hotel inside the city for the night." Sergius opened the driver's door to the rental car, and he got in as Father Herman sat in the passenger seat. Gripping the steering wheel, Sergius closed his eyes. *Lord, please watch over your holy relics and open a gateway to get back into the church tomorrow.* He crossed himself, then started the engine.

A KNOCK SOUNDED ON STEPHANIE'S FRONT DOOR. HOBO came out of nowhere and rushed to the door, barking. She held his collar while opening the door, then moved aside for Logan to cross the threshold. She let go of Hobo, and the dog sniffed Logan. He petted Hobo's head before the dog settled on her mother's chair.

After closing the door, she clasped her hands together. "Thank God you got my message."

"Yeah, Possum passed it along. He's a good guy, and I trust him with my life."

She nodded, then bit her lip. "The Intrepid Intelligence Agency is onto me. Withers knows I hid the drone in my basement."

Logan's brow furrowed, and he put his hands on his hips. "How?"

"It's a long story. Long day..." She pressed a palm to her forehead. "Terrible day..." Tears gathered in her eyes. A lump settled in her throat. *Poor Pam.*

Logan guided her to the couch. She dropped onto the cushion while he sat next to her.

"What happened?"

She pushed away the tragic scene of Pam unconscious in her bedroom and focused on the break-in by Withers. "I'm positive Agent Withers came back to my house, broke in, and took the drone pieces away."

"How do you know this? Did he leave a trail?"

"Hobo was locked outside in the backyard, the doggie door closed off. It was open when I left the house this morning." Images of the drone hovering over her sent goose bumps down her arms. "They're going to throw me in jail."

Logan put an arm around her shoulders and gave her a squeeze. "That won't happen."

"How do you know?"

"I took the pieces from the box and put them in my pocket before I left the other day."

Her jaw dropped, and she shoved his arm off her. "Why didn't you tell me? I've been worried sick!"

He put his hands up. "I was planning on telling you, contacting you on the CB last night, but you'd already talked to Possum—"

"Can't you at least tell me his first name?"

"Luke."

She stood and waved her hands. "Where are the drone pieces now?"

"In a safe place, temporarily."

"You aren't going to tell me where it is? After I shared the whole downed drone incident?"

He gave her an apologetic shrug. "I figured the remnants would be safer with me."

"I have a right to know."

"You do." He pointed to the basement door. "Can we get some fresh batteries for that old radio you have down there?"

"Why?"

"I've got a hell of a lot to tell you and will do so while we work on the radio. There are a lot of people involved and invested in fighting against the rogues running our government. All of us need to work together and keep each other informed."

She folded her arms. "Yes, we do. So spill whatever info I need to know."

"Do you have batteries for the radio?"

She sighed, then rummaged in the kitchen junk drawer. Pulling out two C batteries, she held them up. "Satisfied?"

He took the batteries and strode toward the basement with her behind him. He flicked on the lights, and they descended quickly and headed to the radio.

While he changed out the batteries, Stephanie paced the concrete floor. "I'm waiting."

"We're gathering up an army of resisters and revolutionaries who still managed to keep their weapons. They're in each capital city for as many days as it takes for us to gain back our freedoms and rights. We started this project six months ago."

"An army? How many people are you working with?"

He snapped the back of the radio shut, then turned to face her. "Here in Fairview, we have around three hundred, but we've recruited more in the past few days, and I'm hoping you'll also be one of them."

"How are three hundred people going to make a difference even in our town?"

"There are thousands in other cities, and that includes DC."

"There were millions in Europe protesting lost liberties, and still they are in the midst of World War III."

Logan grimaced. "The war isn't going well for anyone."

Stephanie stopped pacing. "No projected winners?"

"No."

"How do you know these things?"

"The people I'm in contact with are in the inside. Law enforcement, military, State Department, Intel."

Stephanie froze. "Aren't they afraid of being found out? Arrested? Imprisoned?"

Logan shook his head. "They've got something more important to fight for—a secure life for their children and grandchildren."

Her mother's face flashed in her head before Jake replaced it. *Somehow I've got to help, join this resistance. Maybe safety in numbers is a real thing.*

Lost in her thoughts, she didn't see when Logan had turned on the radio. It crackled as he adjusted the knob until he stopped on a clear channel.

"Channel 97.6 still carries local independent news podcasts. It usually reports more accurately what's going on," Logan said.

"...and eleven more homes in town foreclosed in the past week, while B & B stocks took a five-hundred-point slide. On the war front, in the past twelve hours, our sources are reporting that allies are fighting each other in Turkey and the Middle East. It is unclear why this is happening. With five hundred million killed, this catastrophic war shows no winners. Some congresspeople in DC and state governments have begun to question the rationality of America's participation in the war. As new developments come, we will report them."

Logan switched off the radio.

Stephanie backed into the table and leaned on it to catch her bearings. "Five hundred million dead?" The number didn't compute in her spinning head.

Logan took her in his arms as tears welled in her eyes. "Nuclear weapons tend to do that to human beings, let alone any other life on the planet."

She squeezed her eyes shut against images of so many deaths that wanted to invade her mind. *What about Jake? Is he among the dead?* Stephanie gripped Logan's shirt and buried her face in his chest. *No! Stop thinking that way!*

"But the questioning of some government officials about this war looks like the tide may be turning in our favor," Logan said.

"Only if it means this war is done and our government officials come to their senses."

"A must."

"I need to know that my mother and son are all right."

"I know. Luke and I may be able to reach out to a few of our contacts."

Stephanie gazed up at Logan. "I would really be grateful."

He smoothed down her hair.

"I'll be going to church Wednesday evening. It'll be good for me to be there petitioning His Holy Mother."

Logan gestured toward the stairs. "We're planning a protest at Fairview City Hall Wednesday afternoon. Would you join us there at two?"

Stephanie chewed her inner cheek. *Lots of people are putting themselves out there to stop the madness. I can't sit by any longer and let everyone else do this.* She followed him up the steps and settled again on the sofa. "I'll be there. Now tell me where have you hidden the drone pieces?"

"In a tucked-away spot in my house, but I'd like to move them to a more secure location. I just don't know of one right now."

Stephanie sighed, exhaustion of the day's events hitting her. "I've got to get some rest. Please keep in touch."

"I'm on channel forty-four every night after eight. We can connect there tomorrow."

"Okay." Stephanie saw him to the door.

After Logan left, Stephanie picked up Hobo and climbed the stairs to her bedroom. *This war must end, and Jake needs to come home alive and well.*

Thirty

Ava sat with Mel on a bench next to the administrative building. A single halogen light at the entrance shed a faint glow on them. She found the quiet darkness a comfort. Stars dotted the ebony sky, taking her back to her childhood summers where she would lie on a blanket in the backyard and watch for comets and shooting stars. Her mother would often lie with her and point out constellations. Having grown up in a rural part of Virginia, light and noise pollution weren't a problem. She smiled at the memory—a much-needed recollection to boost her mood.

"Hey, there's Venus," Mel said, pointing at the sky.

Ava gazed at its brightness. "Yep."

Two blinking drones glided over them and disappeared into the blackness of the firmament.

"So much for enjoying the view," Ava mumbled.

Mel shrugged. "Gotta take what we can get."

A flicker of light glimmered by the side of the hotel. Ava strained her eyes to focus on the shadowed building. The darkness came to her in splotches. She couldn't make out anything and chalked up the flash to her imagination and being tired.

"Lights out in five minutes," the administrative building's speaker announced.

Ava pressed the tiny button on her watch, and its face lit up. Nearly ten p.m. At least it was a later bedtime than at the county jail.

"Best get inside," Mel said.

They entered the building and headed down a hall to their shared room. After changing into pajamas that had been provided for them, they climbed into their respective beds separated by a nightstand.

Mel switched off the lamp on the end table. "Night."

"Night." Ava turned on her side and stared at the wall. For the past decade, she'd spent every Saturday in downtown Fairview passing out food to the homeless. This community service wasn't too different from that. Again, there was a comfort in that familiarity. She could do this work at the cafeteria easily, but the months away from Stephanie and Jake bugged her.

Holland.

When she saw him tomorrow afternoon, she hoped he'd have some news on the whereabouts of her grandson.

Jake had to be home. Not in the middle of a damn war zone. Ava closed her eyes and drifted off with the starry sky in her thoughts.

BOOM!

The earsplitting noise shook the room. Ava shot up in bed, glanced at her watch. It glowed 2:17 a.m. Mel scrambled out of her bed the same time as Ava.

"What the hell was that?" Mel said, as she stuffed her feet into her sneakers.

"Don't know, but I'm about to find out." Ava pulled on her sneakers and ran out the door with Mel behind her.

Scarboro darted out of a room with another security guard behind him and sprinted toward the lobby before barreling through the front doors.

In the hallway, other doors opened, and Ava's fellow protestors flooded the space, running with Ava and Mel toward the lobby.

They pushed open the front doors, and a gust of heat swept over Ava. Jogging toward the hotel, she came face-to-face with billows of smoke the same color as the night. Roaring red and yellow flames engulfed the back half of the building.

The three women with Ava and Mel screamed. They stayed close to the administrative building's front doors. One of them, Renee, yelled, "I'm calling 911!" and ran back inside.

There were people still inside the hotel, and Ava wasn't going to sit around waiting for the first responders. She'd sure as hell help as best she could. Ava raced toward the front doors. A hand jerked her back. She looked up into Scarboro's scowling face.

"Are you crazy?" He pointed toward the admin building. "Get back there."

Huffing, Ava retreated with hands on hips. Little good she could do there. She folded her arms so tightly they ached in response.

Mel leaned against the doorframe. "I know it's killing you, but you gotta let the experts do the rescuing."

Ava clenched her teeth. "Damn right it's killing me! There are thirty-two people in that burning hotel!"

Ashes flew in the soupy breeze and coated Ava's skin. She scrubbed her face and coughed.

Renee came out the admin building. "The police and fire trucks are on the way!" Her pale face gleamed in the dark of night.

Someone burst out of the hotel's front doors. Mel gasped, and Ava jumped forward, but Mel held her back. Ava couldn't make out the figure until the person was inches away from her, bent forward, coughing.

"Mary?"

Ava led her to the bench she'd been sitting on only a few hours ago. Mary grimaced and put a palm against her forehead. Black splotches smattered her gray, ashy face.

"What happened? Did you see anybody else inside?"

Mary shook her head, her eyes squeezed shut.

Sirens blared. A police car, two fire trucks, and a couple of ambulances rolled up to the parking lot outside the chain-link fence. A police officer opened the gate to the fence, and the vehicles rumbled through. They stopped near the hotel. They got to work with their hoses and began spraying the powerful streams of water on the growing fire while three firefighters dashed inside the lobby doors.

Another figure stumbled out while the doors were still open and limped toward Ava and Mary. When the sooty person reached them, Ava recognized the man from the cafeteria—Russell.

He shook his head before collapsing on the bench next to Mary. "I couldn't save him. He's gone."

Ava put a hand on his shoulder. "Who?"

"My father."

"I'm so sorry."

He kept his head bowed, then let loose strangled sobs. Mary put an arm around him and leaned her head on his shoulder.

Three other figures scrambled out of the lobby doors, and the firefighters escorted them to the administrative building's entrance. Paramedics rushed to the group of people.

Ava dropped onto the end of the bench, wiping sweat from her brow. Taking in the hotel once more, she grimaced. The fire was finally out, leaving a charred back portion of the building.

As one of the firemen finished directing the three people to the lobby of the administrative building, Ava hurried over to him, curious to know what caused the explosion.

"Sir, can you tell me what happened?"

He removed one of his heavy gloves and wiped his blackened, soot-smudged face. "Our investigators will look into the possibility of a natural gas leak and anything else they may suspect caused the fire." He nodded toward the two policemen nearby. "Excuse me."

"Of course." Lightheaded, Ava sat again on the end of the bench as other firefighters continued to run into the building for survivors.

A possible natural gas leak. The flash by the rear of the hotel came back to her. That wasn't her imagination after all. She surveyed the area. *This place isn't safe.* Everything inside her urged her to collect the remaining homeless people, along with her protesting friends, and hightail it out of there. She scanned the chain-link fence. No barbed wire sat on top. One could easily climb over it, even someone her age. The cameras perched on every corner of the administrative building would make their escape more difficult. She would need some time to formulate a plan. In the meantime, the police needed to know what she witnessed before she went to bed no matter how vague.

When she approached the men, Scarboro was with them, his face in a scowl once more.

Before she could speak, he flicked his dark eyes her way and sniffed. "Didn't I tell you to wait over there?"

She narrowed her eyes at him. "I've got something to share with the policemen, and I'd like to do it alone."

One of the policemen held out a hand in a welcoming gesture, then pointed to one of the other benches unoccupied. "Please, ma'am, we can talk over there."

"Thank you." She followed him and sat down while he stood in front of her.

"What were you wanting to share with us?"

"It's not much, really, but I felt I needed to tell you anyway."

He nodded, then pulled out a small notebook and pen from his uniform front pocket.

"I saw some type of flickering light by the back of the hotel before I went inside to go to bed."

"What time was that?"

"A few minutes before ten."

"Did you see anything else?"

"No, sorry."

"Thank you for the information." He looked her over. "Do you need any medical assistance?"

She shook her head. "I'm fine, thanks."

The paramedics were examining Mary and Russell. The three others, whose clothes were singed and tattered and skin ashy, slumped on the bench next to them.

Her thoughts returned to the explosion. The proof wasn't there, but she found it hard to believe this was an accident. From all the years she'd spent feeding the poor and homeless people in town and witnessing the local government officials' contempt for them, it was certainly possible they sent them to this place to eliminate them. Ava fisted her hands. She'd bring up this disaster to Holland tomorrow.

Thirty-One

After four hours of sleep, Ava left her room and headed to the office in the administrative building. Marching down the hall, she checked her watch. There had to be someone in. It was nearly eight o'clock. She wanted news on the injured people who were taken to the hospital, and maybe there was more information on the gas leak.

She approached the closed office door and knocked. It opened a second later with Scarboro filling the space.

He scowled, looking her up and down. "Jenkins, you and the others will not be reporting for work today. The building is condemned and must be rebuilt."

Ava narrowed her eyes at the director. "How many people survived?"

His face reddened. "That is a police matter."

"I'm guessing most didn't."

Without looking at her, he raised his chin and smoothed out his uniform.

"Where are the survivors going to sleep after they return from the hospital?"

"That's not for you to worry about."

"What caused the gas leak?"

"Again, this is not your concern. We are working with law enforcement."

Behind the grumpy director, she spied Holland coming around the desk on the left side of the room.

Ignoring Scarboro's blustering, she focused on the man approaching them. "Holland, you're early."

Scarboro rolled his eyes and glanced at Holland. The director's mouth pinched before he opened it to talk. "Captain Holland is filling in for one of our guards who was injured by the accident last night."

Accident. Ava grunted. *That remains to be seen.* Her brows raised. "Ah, so the captain will be here with us until lights out?"

Scarboro grumbled, "Yes," then made a sweeping motion with his hands. "You're dismissed. I won't say it again."

Holland gave her a reassuring gaze. "I'll be doing the rounds in about an hour."

He knows something. Excitement stirred within her. After a nod toward Holland, she turned and hurried to her room.

WHEN A KNOCK CAME TO HER BEDROOM DOOR, AVA RUSHED toward it, but Mel beat her there.

Mel passed Holland as he entered the room. She turned toward Ava, said, "I'm going to see Renee. Be back in a few minutes," then shut the door.

Ava held out her hands. "What do you know? I've got so many questions."

"I may not have all the answers."

"Understood."

"We've got about five minutes. I'm making the rounds."

"Okay. How many died in that building explosion?"

"From the police reports, twenty-seven died, two were seriously injured, and three survivors are recovering."

Ava gaped. "Unbelievable. They nearly killed them all."

Holland studied Ava with a piercing stare. "You think Scarboro and the others in charge caused the explosion?"

"Our town's government has no use for homeless people."

"It has no use for those with homes either."

She smiled. "So we understand each other. I knew we would."

"Any other questions?"

"Please tell me you know something about my daughter and grandson."

He frowned.

"Come on! Don't give me that look. If you know, you've got to tell me."

"She's all right. Your grandson is overseas somewhere fighting in this war."

She froze, her body growing cold.

Her eyes met his as he said, "I'm sorry."

Swallowing back tears, she only nodded. Dread nearly stopped her from asking the painful question, but she let it come. "Is he alive?"

"There's no information on him other than what I've given you," he said. "Sorry, again."

Sudden fatigue spread through Ava's body. She sat on the edge of her bed. Holland's hand rested on her shoulder and gave it a slight squeeze.

Stephanie. I've got to break out of here, get home. She needs me. Ava looked up at Holland. "Can you get us out of here?"

He stood silent for a moment.

"Like I just told you, I don't believe that gas leak was an accident." *Would he risk his position to help them when so many police have gone along with the status quo?*

His eyes reflected compassion. "When do you want out?"

Stunned for a moment, she couldn't respond. "You'll help us?"

He gave her a quick nod. "I've got connections. Just need time to get ahold of them."

A rush of adrenaline coursed through her. "Great."

"Give me until seven tonight when I do my next sweep of the building. I should have info for you."

"Thank you."

He exited the room.

A smile, rare for her these days, spread her lips. *I'm going home!*

❧

Stephanie held Hobo's leash and stepped onto the porch. His bobtail wagged. She stroked his back. "Yes, I know you're way overdue for a walk. We're going now."

The mailbox next to her front door held a few envelopes that caught her attention. After yesterday's harrowing events, she hadn't had the chance to check the mail.

Before she could take another step, drones flew over the houses across from hers. Yells erupted from down the street. A group of three men were running in the opposite direction from her house. Gunshots went off. Hobo whimpered.

Stephanie snatched him up, then threw open the screen door. A cranking and screeching came from the street. An army tank followed by a police car rolled down the road, the latter vehicle's lights flashing and sirens blaring.

Scrambling inside, Stephanie set Hobo down and removed his leash. The dog trotted toward the living room. She slammed the door, bolting it shut. With a hand pressed to her chest, she moved on weak, wobbly legs to the couch where Hobo joined her. "Seems we're going to have to hold off on your daily walks until this madness ends." She stroked his head. "I'm so sorry, bud. You'll have to do your exercise and business in the backyard for now."

As the sound of the siren faded, she stood up. "Something needs to be done right now."

Hobo jumped off the couch and ran through the doggie door to the backyard.

Stephanie headed up the stairs, then stopped in the hallway. She pulled the rope to the attic, and the steps unfolded, straightening out in front of her. The gunshots reminded her of her father's guns that she hadn't had time to think about, let alone search for until now.

With her joining the resistance, she would certainly need a firearm as well. Hoping at least one of his guns might be in the attic, she climbed the steps and crouched as she walked across the wood floor to a group of her father's boxes. Knowing her father, it was possible that he'd stashed a gun in one of them. She tore through three of them filled with her father's clothes and shoes. She frowned. *No guns. Crap.*

There were two boxes left to go through on the left side of the stuffy space. After opening the next box, she dug through the clothing inside. One of her father's sweaters was bulky and crinkled as if paper was bundled inside it. She slid her hand into the sweater and pulled out a newspaper wrapped around something. Tearing off the paper, a gun dropped onto the clothes in the box. One of his pistols. Instead of excitement, dread streaked through her. Not one who liked guns, it took a great amount of effort to force herself to pick it up. She paused. "I've got to leave this here until tomorrow. It's in a safe place. I'll get it tomorrow. Where are the bullets?"

Digging again through the mounds of clothes, she found a box of bullets between two pairs of slacks. After making a mental note of where the items had been stashed, she placed them back in the box, then alighted the attic stairs. Folding and pushing the steps back up into the ceiling, she went downstairs.

Hobo greeted her near the entrance to the living room.

The mailbox flashed in her mind. She opened the front door and grabbed the few items from the metal holder.

A large envelope sat between two pieces of junk mail. She set the two ads on the kitchen counter, while keeping the large envelope in her hand. The return address read: DEPARTMENT OF THE ARMY.

She caught her breath. *Is it about Jake?* Her trembling fingers dropped the letter. It landed on the kitchen floor. Queasiness swam through her stomach as she reached for the envelope. Before touching it, she hesitated, fear paralyzing her. *What if it's bad news? What if my baby boy...* Just the thought brought tears to her eyes. *God, help me. Give me the strength.* Taking a deep breath and exhaling slowly, she reached for the letter again. *I need to know either way...*

Thirty-Two

As gray clouds gathered above, Brody opened the back gate to the church and led Lindy into the garden. The sweet scent of flowers clashed with the metallic-almond smells of recent bombs near the church. Four silver-and-black drones streaked through the pewter sky, their lights flashing, while rapid gunfire nearby punctured the air.

He looked up and around, cold fear filling his chest. He needed to get his daughter to a safe place. The church loomed in front of him. *I shouldn't have come back here. I've already caused enough trouble. But I don't have anywhere else to go. Maybe I should've taken that bus to the homeless hotel after all. At least we would've had a place to sleep and food to eat.* Brody ran a hand down his face as regret and guilt sat like an anvil on his shoulders.

A huge blast across the street shook him from his thoughts, his ears ringing. A fireball consumed a house. Screams echoed through the air.

Lindy clung to Brody's waist. "Daddy, I'm scared!"

He picked her up and rushed to the steps of the church's back door. "Wait here," he said, pointing to the eaved entrance.

Lindy held on to him tighter. "Don't leave me!"

Squatting in front of her, Brody gently cupped her wet face. "I'm not going to, honey." He stood, and she clung to him again.

He glanced toward the cemetery where a freshly dug grave and a small wooden cross sat. *The deacon.* Tears stung his eyes.

Light rain began to fall, pattering his head. A moment of silence came over him. Realizing his daughter wasn't going to let him go, and he couldn't blame her, he took her hand and approached the grave. Lindy's weeping added to his misery.

Brody wiped his running nose and bent in front of the mound. "I'm so sorry, Deacon. So sorry. It's my fault you're dead. Please forgive me."

Another explosion lit up the sky northeast of them. He couldn't stay there. Lindy was in danger. He picked her up and ran toward the church's door but spotted the padlock. His heart sank.

"Hey, loser!" an angry voice yelled from behind him.

Brody slowly turned his head in the direction of the menacing voice. Three men with hands fisted swaggered down the path toward him and his daughter. Lindy whimpered in his arms. He put her down but kept a protective arm around her shoulders.

As the three thugs came closer, he recognized them from downtown—the day the bus came to collect the homeless people to transport them to the hotel. He'd taken Lindy and run away toward the church. The creeps had stopped following him then. But they were back now. Back to confront him… get rid of him? The raindrops spattering on him felt ice cold.

He whispered to Lindy while giving a slight shoo of his hand. "Run, Lindy. Get away from here."

"No!" She hugged his leg.

A gruff laugh came from one of the men.

"Did you think we'd forget about you, worthless piece of scum?" said the tallest man with a stocky build.

The bald man next to him added, "We're gonna finish off the last of the trash in this stinkin' town."

The third man snorted, rubbing his snout-shaped nose, his beady eyes boring a hole through Brody.

Brody moved his daughter behind him. "This isn't the place for—"

"Sure it is," the first man said.

He felt for Lindy behind him. "My daughter is with me."

"That's your problem," the bald man said with a sneer.

Brody surveyed the area. Nobody was around to help. He bent and whispered in his daughter's ear, "Hide and seek, Lindy. Go hide in the flowers. I'll come find you."

She gazed up at him with questioning eyes and quivering lips.

"Go hide. Play the game with me." He gently pushed her toward the garden.

A smile settled on her lips. She ran through the misty rain to the bed of flowers.

"Good. We don't want her. Just you," one of the men said.

Brody glanced at the grave where the deacon lay and imagined his lifeless body deep in the ground next to the clergyman.

The three goons lunged forward, a fist hitting him in the eye, another near his throat, and another pounding his ribs. He swung his fists but missed, managed to push one of them off him, but they piled on him seconds later, throwing him to the ground. His head banged against the concrete. Searing pain penetrated his skull, his vision blurring. Something warm oozed from his pulsating scalp.

Groaning, he sputtered, "Lindy," but it only came out a whisper. He covered his head and curled into a ball as they continued to beat him. Something hard smashed his temple. Images of Lindy's smiling face faded as darkness overcame him.

With his brother behind him, Sergius crept toward the church's backyard gate, bolt cutters in one of his hands. Wiping the rain from his eyes, he entered through the opened gate after Father Herman. They headed toward the church as gunshots rang out in the distance.

"Things have gotten worse. It's not safe to be out here." Father

Herman glanced behind him, then back at the church doors. "We better get inside as soon as we can and check on the relics."

Sergius nodded, wiping off his beard.

Ten feet from the back door, through the sheets of rain, Sergius spotted a body on the ground and a young girl slumped over it.

"Dear God!" Sergius scurried up the stairs with his brother by his side.

Thunder rolled overhead as Sergius knelt next to the body and touched the sniffling girl's shoulder.

The girl raised her head, her face puffy, red, her eyes vacant.

Lindy. Lord, have mercy! He moved over and gathered her in his arms. "Dear child, we are here. There, there." He ran a hand down her hair several times, working to comfort her.

Father Herman put a palm to Brody's forehead and leaned his ear toward Brody's open, bloodied mouth.

Sergius continued to hold Lindy as Father Herman laid two fingers against Brody's neck, his brows knotted.

Sergius closed his eyes. *God help him.*

When he opened them, Father Herman frowned at him and shook his head, his eyes filled with sadness.

His brother waved a slow hand at him. "Take her into the church." He gazed down at Brody and crossed himself. "I'll bury him."

With the child gazing at nothing and silent in his arms, Sergius stood and carried her to the back doors. Another bomb went off down the street, followed by flashes and beams of bright lights from three drones in the gray firmament.

While Father Herman carried Brody toward the cemetery, Sergius set Lindy down next to him, then took the metal cutters and sliced through the padlock, breaking it apart. Pulling out the key chain from his cassock pocket, he slipped the key into the lock and opened the doors. He set the cutters on the floor in the narthex, then carried Lindy toward the elevators and the secure room.

The town's speakers squeaked on. "This is Mayor Bryant. As of now, the town is in lockdown due to enemy fire and attacks in the city.

The two checkpoint gates into and out of our town have been closed. Please stay indoors. We are in lockdown until further notice."

Sergius closed his eyes and crossed himself. *We are here for the time being. In His House. Thank you, Lord, we made it here and can be of help for little Lindy through Your leading us, granting us the empathy and nurturing she needs.*

After pressing the button for the elevator, Sergius studied Lindy. Her skin was pale, her face on the cusp of lifelessness. Sergius kissed her forehead, then gave her a blessing, saying, "Lord, protect her and embrace her in Your love and comfort," before entering the elevator.

Thirty-Three

The words of Mayor Bryant drummed in Stephanie's head as she leaned back against the sofa cushion. Hobo hopped onto her lap, and she stroked his head. "Trapped inside and outside my house."

The Army's unopened letter still lay on the coffee table.

"I've wasted enough time." Picking up the letter, she tore open the top of the envelope and pulled out a paper reminiscent of an old Western Union telegram.

Ms. Stephanie Jenkins,

Your son, Private Jake Jenkins, has been medically discharged and is returning home on Tuesday morning at 1100 hours. Further information will be provided on the day of arrival.

Captain Burt J. Foster,

Casualty Assistance Officer

Fort Belvoir, Virginia

Relief washed over her as she gripped the paper. "He's alive!" She hugged Hobo. "He's coming home!"

He's been medically discharged. Stephanie bit her quivering lip. *He's been injured badly enough to be discharged from the army.* Tears streamed down her face.

An explosion near her house shook the walls. Startled, she felt

Hobo's head burrow under her arm. She gave him reassuring pats, then went to the sliding glass doors and pushed the curtain aside. She could barely make out the backyard through the pouring rain. A bolt of lightning flashed, and rumbling thunder followed.

Closing the drapes, she gathered Hobo into her arms. "Great. Not only is the town a war zone, but now this thunderstorm too."

A clap of thunder echoed through the house.

The lights in the living room flickered.

I've got to grab a flashlight. Stephanie stepped toward the kitchen.

The lights went out. Total darkness engulfed her. Fear trickled down her back. Hobo barked while the muffled booms and thumps outside continued. He barked again.

She felt around for him, using his faint panting to guide her. "Hobo, come here, boy."

His warm body bumped into one of her hands. She picked him up and held him closely, thankful he was with her.

When her eyes adjusted to the darkened room, the hearth with the candles on the mantel were only a few feet away. Setting Hobo down, Stephanie stepped toward the fireplace and lit the two candles.

Once their warm glow filled the room, Stephanie exhaled.

Hobo curled on her mother's chair, seemingly calmer despite the continuing rumbles and blasts outside. Perhaps the dog had gotten used to frightening noises over the past couple of months.

She glanced at the letter once more. *Jake's coming home tomorrow.* A spark of excitement kindled inside her, while at the same time, dread slithered through her stomach. *How am I going to handle this?*

IN THE LOBBY OF THE ADMINISTRATIVE BUILDING, AVA stood with Mel, Renee, and two other fellow protestors.

Scarboro paced in front of them, his hands clasped together behind his back. He signaled a guard coming down one of the hallways, who carried a mop, broom, bucket, and a box of cleaning supplies. He set them down next to the women.

Scarboro pointed at the box. "You have things to do while the hotel is being renovated and the lockdown is in place."

"You want us to be maids?" Ava sneered at the man.

Soft snickers came from Mel and the others.

"Cleaning is a community service, Jenkins," Scarboro hissed, then pointed at each of the women. "Would you rather go back to jail?"

Ava folded her arms across her chest. "I'd rather go home."

"That isn't an option."

"It should be."

"You broke the law. You should be grateful you're only cleaning the rooms in this building."

Fresh explosions rattled the walls in the lobby. The trees outside lit up against the smoky, pewter sky. Blinking lights dashed across the clouds, heading east.

Scarboro glanced out the front door's windows. "You also ought to be grateful you're not out there."

"Speaking of the hotel," Mel said. "Where are the homeless people that survived the terrible explosion?"

The director didn't look Mel's way. "Soon we'll be moving to another facility that will accommodate everyone."

"Why do we need another building when there are only three poor homeless people alive here and five of us?" Renee asked. "This place has twenty rooms. Can't we just stay here and finish out our service?"

"I don't know about that, Renee." Ava shrugged. "Can you be sure this building won't face the same fate as the hotel's?"

Scarboro glared at Ava. "That was an accident."

"What's to say another 'accident' won't happen?"

Stepping in front of her, Scarboro pulled out his nightstick and pressed the butt of the baton against her cheek. "You and that mouth of yours should've stayed in jail."

The stick dug into her face, but she said nothing and kept glowering at him.

Holland appeared from one of the hallways and joined them. "Good evening, ladies."

She suppressed a smile.

Scarboro slid his nightstick back in the loop of his pants and turned toward the officer. "You managed to make it on time."

Holland said nothing, but Ava caught the slight roll of his eyes while Scarboro looked away.

Checking his watch, Scarboro said, "I'm off for the evening." He took a step toward the front doors, then swiveled on his heel and gestured toward the cameras in the corners of the lobby. "Don't forget you're being watched. We'll know if you're failing to do your community service."

Nobody answered him as he flashed a phony grin and passed through the doors.

"How could we forget?" Ava grumbled.

Holland gave Ava a conspiratorial smile.

"What is it?"

The women gathered around him.

"Everyone, get to cleaning." He pulled bottles from the container. "Ava, at eight thirty tonight, report to my office."

"But you didn't answer—" Mel began to say.

"Later. Chores come first." Holland gave a slight jerk of his head toward one of the cameras in the corner of the room, then headed down the hall to his office.

Ava rubbed her hands together and smiled. "He's got a plan for us."

"I hope it's a good one," Mel said.

AROUND EIGHT THAT EVENING, STEPHANIE MOVED THE dial to channel forty-nine, then spoke into the mouthpiece. "Logan's Run, are you there?"

"Who's asking for him?" a familiar voice said.

"Server Steph."

"Hey, Server Steph, this is Possum. He's not available right now."

She slumped in the car seat. "Oh."

"I can pass along your message if you want."

Leaning her forehead against the steering wheel, she let out a sigh. "Please just tell him to stop by sometime in the morning."

"Will do, but I'm not sure he'll be able to with the lockdown."

She tapped her forehead on the steering wheel. How could she have already forgotten about the lockdown? "I understand."

"Sorry. I'll pass along your message."

"Thanks."

"Over and out."

Stephanie turned off the CB, left the garage. Hobo met her in the kitchen.

She leaned her elbows on the counter and head against the palms of her hands. Her mind filled with images of her mother the last time she'd seen her at the jail. Flashes of her visit with Deborah, the lawyer, surfaced, when she'd found out her mother had been moved to a hotel for the homeless to do community service for the next few months. *I don't even know where they've taken her.* Her stomach knotted. *God, I hope she's okay.*

Ava knocked on the open door to the office where Holland stood behind his desk.

"Come in," he said.

She approached him. "What's the plan?"

Holland came around his desk. "I have access to the computers controlling the security cameras around the compound, which means I can turn them off when needed."

"Good."

"Round up your friends after you leave here. I'll reach out to the rest. We're leaving at twelve thirty."

Ava didn't move, stunned he had the escape plan figured out. "You work fast."

"We really don't have time to waste, with the war zone in town, the precarious situation in this place, and the impending protests tomorrow," Holland said. "We've got to bust out of here no matter what we'll face on the way to our homes."

The building shook from another blast nearby.

Ava lifted her chin, said, "I'm on it," and left his office.

After eleven, Ava slipped on her small backpack while Mel grabbed her tote.

"Let's start with Renee and Jenn, then move down the hallway," Ava said.

"Got it."

Exiting their room, they crossed to the door opposite theirs and quietly knocked on it. The door opened, and Renee appeared.

Ava gripped the straps of her backpack. "We're leaving at twelve thirty. Get your stuff together."

Renee blanched. "Ava, is it safe to do that? What about the guards? The cameras? Scarboro?"

A boom outside shook the walls. Ava and her friends instinctively covered their heads.

"It's not safe here," Mel said.

"It's not safe out there either!" Jenn and Renee said in near unison.

"I'm not going out there and get myself killed," Jenn said.

"Me neither," Renee added, then motioned them with a shoo of her hands. "None of us are leaving tonight with the lockdowns and craziness going on outside."

Ava planted her hands on her hips. "What? None?"

"Yeah, we already talked this over with Carol about an hour ago and decided we're waiting this out."

Ava released a frustrated sigh. "I can't believe you guys."

"Hey, it's their choice," Mel said, then jerked a thumb behind her. "We need to check on Mary and the others."

Giving her longtime friends one last look of disappointment, Ava followed Mel out the door and moved down the hallway to the other two rooms. The one on the left, Mary and another homeless woman had moved to, and Russell in the room on their right.

After Ava spoke with the three, Mary and Russell joined her and Mel in their room. An hour later, Ava paced the carpet. Her friends in the room across from hers flashed in her head. She paused and turned toward Mel. "There's still time to change their minds. Should we try again?"

"They've had plenty of time to show up here," Mel said. "They haven't."

"I hate this… that we can't do anything to convince them."

"You can't control other people," Mel said.

Ava flapped a hand. "Yeah, I know. It just stinks."

"They're afraid to leave," Mary said.

Ava swung around to face her. Mary had been quiet the past hour, keeping to herself. Somehow it was a relief to Ava that Mary had spoken up. "Yes, that's what they said. Even with the hotel blown to bits a couple of days ago."

"Yeah, that part gets me," Mel said.

Mary sat on Mel's bed. "There's more familiarity in this place than whatever is out there."

Russell had been standing by Ava's bed, watching them with a furrowed brow. "I'm going to stay with them so they're not alone. Maybe by then they'll want to leave, and Holland can guide us out of here tomorrow night."

"Are you sure you want to stay here?" Mary asked.

Russell crossed to the door. "Yeah."

"That may work," Ava said. "Gives you time to convince them."

With a salute, Russell left the room.

Fifteen minutes later, Ava walked down the hallway with Mel and Mary to Holland's office.

He glanced at them from a computer on his desk. "Where are the rest of them?"

"They aren't coming," Mel said.

Ava leaned her hip on the edge of the desk. "Russell is staying and trying to change their minds and hoping you can guide them out of here tomorrow night."

"I wasn't planning on doing this again."

"Can you make an exception for them?" Ava asked.

"Don't know. I'll have to see how it goes tonight."

"That's fair," Ava said.

He focused on the computer and typed for the next couple of

minutes, then looked her way. "Okay, the security cameras are off." Rising from his chair, he said, "Ready?"

An explosion chased by machine gun-type fire echoed in the distance.

Ava paused. In a few minutes, she would be out in that chaotic violence. Still, with all the noise, darkness, and confusion, this could be a good cover for her and her friends. "Yes."

Holland strode to the door. "Let's go."

Everyone filed out of his office.

The scent of rain in the cool air brushed over Ava as she and the others crept along the side of the building. Stopping at the corner, she spied the two blue towers on either side of the compound shining harsh spotlights on sections of the admin structure. Thankful they were in a spot shielded by the night shadows, she exhaled quiet relief.

In front of her, Holland pointed toward the forest beyond the chain-link fence. "That's where we need to go."

Two patches of light flooded the asphalt between the edge of the building and the fence.

A drone flashed in the sky. It ejected a yellow bolt that pulverized a solid structure about a half mile away. In the moonlight, clouds of smoke ascended into the firmament. Another blast sputtered out sparks of fire farther north. Gunshots popped closer by.

Between the bombings was an eerie silence. The dichotomy of the explosions and the quiet of the lockdown was hard for Ava to digest. She'd never encountered anything so terrifying in all her life.

Holland gave a sharp flick of his hand, and she and the others moved after him in the shadow of the night, their shoes scuffling on the pavement. He jerked to a stop outside one of the spotlights about ten feet in diameter gleaming in front of them. Gesturing for them to go around, Holland led them forward.

Three drones sped overhead, shooting lasers, leaving fire and smoke near downtown.

The gate stood twelve feet ahead of them. Holland picked up the pace, and Ava hurried after him, keeping in the darkness, with Mel and Mary right behind her.

Holland raised the bar on the gate and pushed it open. Ava and the others rushed through.

A bomb thundered nearby. Ava covered her head while she ran after Holland into the dense forest that blocked out the moonlight. A few feet in, Holland stopped. Ava bumped into him. Mel and Mary halted before colliding with Ava.

Their puffing and panting broke the stillness surrounding them.

Ava could make out Holland's arm moving, then a pinpoint of light came on, directed at a small map in his hand. She came alongside him.

He tapped the map. "We're five miles from downtown. The street on the other side of the forest is Elm. It goes into town. Elm then intersects with two streets—Bowling and Ranch."

Ranch. Ava spotted it on the map and pointed. "Ranch also intersects with Lilac Road. Where my house is."

Holland brought the map closer to his face, using his finger to follow the road. "Yes. It's about two miles from us."

"Pretty close by—"

An ear-piercing explosion shook the trees and vibrated the ground beneath Ava's feet. A whoosh of warm, dusty air hit them like a wave. They crouched on the ground. Ava gritted her teeth. *What the hell is happening?*

Thirty-Five

"Oh my God." Mary's voice stabbed the dense air.

"The admin building," Mel muttered in a tone of disbelief.

Light blazed in the direction of the compound. Shafts of the light penetrated through the tree line behind them.

Ava rose and stepped toward the opening in the forest, facing the compound. Holland and the others flanked her.

When Ava attempted to move outside the forest, Holland grabbed her arm. "Stay here. Out of sight." He folded the map and shoved it into his pocket. "We can see well enough from here."

Towering orange flames engulfed the crumbled building with black smoke billowing upward.

Ava swallowed hard. "Renee, Jenn…"

"They're gone." Mel squeezed Ava's hand. "All of them."

"We've got to help. Some may have survived." Ava reached forward, but Mel held her back.

"We can't go back," Holland said. "We'll end up the same way."

Ava ground her teeth. "We sure as hell should try!"

"No," Holland said, his voice stern.

"Murderers!" Ava shouted at the burning compound.

Mary crossed herself. "May they rest in peace."

Mel's arm rested around Ava's shoulders.

"We've got to leave here before they kill us too!" Mary sucked on her bottom lip.

Gesturing for Ava and the others to calm down, Holland said, "They think we're dead. It's our best protection."

No one answered as the crackling and creaking of the burning building filled the moment of silence in the darkness.

Holland swung around and headed deeper into the forest. Mary scrambled after him.

Mel linked arms with Ava. "Let's go."

With a frustrated sigh, Ava strode with her best friend into the ever-increasing denseness of the forest.

Under an eave in a shadowy alley behind a strip mall, Ava congregated with her fellow escapees. Ranch Road met the end of the alley.

"You going to be okay from here?" Holland asked her.

"Yep." She peered down Ranch Road. "The intersection for my street is only a block away."

Gunshots went off in the distance.

"Be careful." Holland pivoted and headed down the alley with Mary in the opposite direction.

Mel hugged Ava. "I'll see you later, my friend."

"You better believe it." Ava squeezed her tightly. "Stay safe."

Mel strode after Holland and Mary.

Ava jogged to the intersection and continued down dimly lit, deserted Lilac Road just as a police car rounded the corner at the other end of the street.

"Crap." She picked up the pace, racing through a neighbor's yard, and crawling into a set of bushes.

A blast near downtown lit up the night sky that was partially blocked by the hedge's branches.

She kept tucked inside the bush, barely allowing herself to breathe. The police car rolled slowly by. The windows were open, and white beams poured over the yards and street. A shaft of light brightened the bush she hid in. She retreated farther until her back pressed against the side of the house. The streaks of light settled on the branches and ground three inches from her. With sweat streaming down her neck and armpits, she held her breath. Closing her eyes, she prayed, "Lord, help me."

The patrol car moved down the street at a continued slow pace, then turned at the intersection.

Exhaling, Ava wiped her damp forehead. "Thank you, Lord."

After surveying the street and homes three times, she crawled out of the bush and crept toward her home—the next building ahead of her.

Three drones flew overhead, their searchlights flashing through the street and over the roofs.

Ava cut the corner and fled down the grassy space between the two homes. She opened the back gate to her house, then closed it behind her.

More drones passed overhead with their searchlights, just as an explosion went off nearby, making the ground vibrate below her.

She rushed toward the back door, grabbed the handle, and yanked down.

Nothing happened.

Ugh! Locked, of course! Pulling out her house key, she slid it into the lock. It didn't turn.

"Damn!" Letting out ragged breaths, she smacked her forehead. Then a smile came to her lips. *She changed the locks. That's my girl.*

Gunfire popped down the street. She turned toward the sound. *Resisters out during lockdown. God, protect them.* Ava crossed herself, then shoved the key in her pocket.

After scanning the backyard twice, she was satisfied no one was around. She held up her knuckles, then licked her lips. "Not too loud."

She rapped three times, then waited.

Faint barking came from inside. She grinned. *Hobo, my boy! How I've missed you.*

But she didn't hear the door unlock. *Where are you, Stephanie?* Ava stayed close to the sliding door, inches from its glass, under the shadow of the patio eave. She leaned her forehead against it. *Come on, daughter. Where else could you be in this godforsaken lockdown?*

Thirty-Six

Stephanie let go of the string to the attic, and the folded stairs disappeared into the ceiling. With her father's loaded pistol in her hand, she headed downstairs where Hobo was barking by the back door.

She crept closer to the door. The new lock was holding, but if it didn't, she'd be ready for intruders this time. Gripping the gun, her hand shook. Without any experience using it, how much protection would it really be? She clenched her teeth. *It'll have to do.*

Two knocks on the glass door made her freeze.

What murderer or burglar knocks? "None," she told herself. *Maybe it's Logan.*

She pulled back the curtain just enough to peek outside to the lit back patio and found herself face-to-face with her mother. Her jaw dropped as her mother smiled wide and gestured to be let in.

Hobo jumped up and down, smacking his front paws against the glass.

Ava grinned at him and waved.

Stephanie set down the gun, unlocked the door, and slid it open for her mother to enter. She was in her mother's arms a second later.

"Mom, I can't believe you're home!"

"Yes! Thank God!" Ava locked the door, then pointed to the firearm on the floor. "Good. I'm glad you found one of your father's guns." She bent to pet Hobo, and he covered her cheeks with kisses.

After her mother had given ample attention to Hobo, he plopped on the couch, curling up, appearing content. He must have missed Ava almost as much as she had.

Stephanie placed a comforting hand on Ava's back and led her to her chair.

Ava settled into it, leaning back with closed eyes and a sigh. "I think it'll be hard to get back up." Letting out a chuckle, she looked up at Stephanie and yawned.

Stephanie could barely believe her mother was sitting there, back in her chair, in their home. She leaned over and gave her another embrace. "I've missed you and was so worried about you."

Her mother patted her back. "Sorry. It couldn't be helped."

Stephanie frowned and sat in her father's recliner. "Where have you been all this time?"

"At a compound with homeless people and my protesting organizers. We were serving meals to them in the hotel cafeteria before it was blown up."

Stephanie slid to the edge of the seat. "What?"

Ava's jaw tightened. "Yes. Those monsters wanted us all dead. Done in a way they couldn't be blamed."

"My God, Mother! How'd you get out of there?"

"Holland."

"Holland? Is he the blond policeman we'd see downtown sometimes when we fed the poor?"

"Yes. He's part of the resistance."

Stephanie arched her brows. *So there are some cops going against the State.*

"It was a good thing he got us out tonight. Otherwise, we would've been burned to ashes in the explosion."

Stephanie's stomach somersaulted. She left her seat and knelt in front of her mother. "Mom! You're scaring me."

"It's over now." Her mother's brows met. "It's so sad the others didn't want to escape with Mel, Mary, and me."

Stephanie took her mother's hand in hers. "What happened to them? Were they...?"

"Yes. Those beasts murdered my friends and the last of the homeless people who'd survived the hotel explosion."

Squeezing her mother's hand, Stephanie bowed her head. "You all have been through so much."

Ava clasped Stephanie's hand in return. "It's over now, hon. And I'm tired."

"Oh, of course." Stephanie stood. "Do you want help up to your bedroom?"

"Nah. I'll manage."

"There's just one other thing I need to tell you." Stephanie bit her lip. "It's about Jake."

Ava rose slowly with a wave of her hand. "Yes, I know. Holland told me he's fighting in this horrible war. I'll drill him tomorrow to find out where he's located."

"Mom, he's coming home tomorrow morning... er, this morning." Stephanie wrung her hands. "He's been medically discharged."

"Christ."

"But your timing couldn't be better. I was so worried about what to do and what to expect when I see him." Stephanie covered her face as tears welled in her eyes and her throat closed.

Ava gathered her in her arms. "You're not alone now. I'm here, and I'll be right beside you when he's back home."

Stephanie cried on Ava's shoulder, clinging to her, taking in her mother's presence with weeping gratitude.

Stephanie had barely slept, waking every couple of hours from nightmares of the war and Jake in the middle of it. No matter how many times she tried to blot out the images and thoughts, they crept back when she drifted to sleep.

Around seven o'clock, she gave up and got out of bed. She dressed, then paced her bedroom floor. Hobo sat on the bed, watching her with his head cocked to the side.

Three hours before he's supposed to show up. What am I going to do with all that time? Pausing, she listened for any noise from her mother's room. *Maybe she's awake.* Stephanie tiptoed to the room across the hall with Hobo on her heels. *I hope she's awake.*

The room was draped in shadows, and silence answered her thoughts.

Of course she's still sleeping. All that horror she went through yesterday. Mom needs the rest. Stephanie went downstairs to the kitchen and made herself a latte with Jake's espresso machine he'd gotten for Christmas last year. A nice, warm, sweet latte was what she needed since she wasn't sure she could stomach any food.

Hobo bounced out the doggie door. She pushed aside the curtains veiling the sliding glass door, letting in sunrays. The blue sky held a few puffy clouds. Finally the rain had passed.

Two silver drones streamed through those clouds. *They never take a break.*

The protest this afternoon flashed in her mind. She'd nearly forgotten. Maybe after she met with Deacon Michael and he anointed Jake, she could… *No. The protest will go on without me. Jake's first and always first in my life.*

Her father's gun sat on the end table between her parents' chairs in the den.

Sitting on the couch, she reminded herself aloud, "Don't forget that when you go to town later. You'll need it."

"Yes, you will." Her mother appeared at the bottom of the stairs and approached her. She sat in her chair. "What are your plans in town?"

"There's a protest in front of city hall at two. Logan will be there with around two hundred people." She gestured a no go with her hands. "But I won't be with them."

Ava drummed her fingers on the table. "Good, because, dear,

protests are illegal. Remember, your mother spent weeks in jail and was forced to do community service at a death trap outside of town?"

Stephanie pursed her lips. "Yes, it felt like forever."

"So how are they going to pull off the protest?"

"I don't know, but they'll find a way."

Ava rubbed her chin. "Logan. Why is that name familiar?"

"He's my old boyfriend from high school."

"No kidding. It's been ages since I've seen that kid."

"He's not a kid anymore, Mom."

"Of course not, but how did you two reconnect after all this time?"

Stephanie leaned back in her chair and couldn't help but laugh. "Dad's CB radio."

Her mother leaned forward. "No."

"Yes."

"That ancient radio has come back to life. Amazing." Ava chuckled. "Reminds me of my talks with your dad on that thing when we were kids."

Stephanie shrugged. "Ever since the government ordered the internet companies to cut off Wi-Fi service for our computers and phones, I had to find another way to keep in contact with what was going on. Dad comes through again."

Joy swirled in her heart. She relished the conversation with her mother after all this time.

Ava went to the espresso machine and made herself a cappuccino. Turning to face Stephanie, she said, "I'm taking this heavenly java upstairs. The bathtub is calling me, and I'm going to enjoy lounging in it with bubbles and all."

Stephanie glanced at the wall clock. "You've got plenty of time for it." It wasn't even seven thirty yet. *Ugh.*

"Yep. Later, hon." Her mother headed up the stairs.

Stephanie picked up the letter from the army and read it again. Her stomach knotted. She went to the closet. An old jigsaw puzzle would keep her busy until Jake arrived. God willing, things wouldn't be as bad as her nightmares.

Thirty-Seven

Stephanie and her mother sat in silence in the den. The late-morning sun spread a few shafts of white light through the glass door and onto the carpet and coffee table. In the distance, gunfire popped every so often.

The clock on the wall read 10:56. Stephanie rolled her head and shoulders, trying to release the tension in her muscles. Jake would arrive soon. She rubbed her churning belly. *Don't expect the images in your head to be his fate. There's no way to know what Jake's wounds are. Just be prepared for anything.*

Her mother wore reading glasses and worked on a crossword puzzle, seemingly unaffected by Jake's upcoming return.

"Mom, aren't you worried about Jake?"

Her mother gazed at her over her glasses. "Worried? Maybe a little. Angry, one hundred percent." She removed her eyewear and gave Stephanie a piercing stare. "He never should've been called up to fight in this damn war in the first place."

Stephanie sat up, wiping her damp palms on her jeans. "That's right. He should've stayed home since he had declared himself as a conscientious objector."

"Which our government erased so they could produce more cannon fodder."

"I hate that expression."

"Hate it all you want. It's still the truth." Her mother harrumphed and went back to her puzzle.

The doorbell rang, and Stephanie froze, her muscles tight as cable cords.

Her mother leaned forward as if to get up. "Do you want me to get it?"

Stephanie forced herself to rise from the sofa. "No, I will." She walked with hesitant steps to the entryway, then pulled open the door.

"Good afternoon, Ms. Jenkins," one of the two army officers said.

They stood on the porch with their hats in their hands. Between them sat a young man in a wheelchair with both legs in casts from the knees down. He was dressed in civilian clothes, and his sandy-blond hair was cropped close, military-style. His head bowed, he stared at his hands resting in his lap.

A wave of recognition rolled through her, and tears came quickly, dripping down her face. Any thoughts of addressing the men flanking Jake was forgotten. She bent and wrapped her arms around his shoulders, hugging him, sniffling. The faint but familiar smell of his lemon-scented soap and the feel of his breath on her neck caused more tears to stream from her eyes. "Jake. Oh, Jake, I'm so glad you're home."

He hadn't put his arms around her or responded. Her heart sank into the pit of her stomach.

"Ma'am, I'm Officer Dugan, and this is Chaplain Kanelos." The words floated by her, as if they were far away.

A hand touched her shoulder. "May we come inside?"

She absorbed the words, then let go of Jake. "Oh, sorry. Come in."

The men pushed Jake into the foyer, and Stephanie led them to the living room. Hobo sprang through the doggie door, barking. He sniffed the men, then ran to Jake and jumped in his lap. Hobo welcomed him with wet kisses on his cheeks and hands.

Her mother approached Jake, kissed, and hugged him. "Welcome home, Grandson. I've missed you so much."

Jake didn't respond to Hobo or his grandmother, and Stephanie's heart broke a little more. She'd been certain he'd light up seeing his buddy, Hobo. But nothing. No reaction.

The officers retreated to the foyer.

As her mother squatted in front of Jake and spoke quietly to him, Stephanie came alongside Officer Dugan. "Wh-what's wrong with my son?"

Dugan gave her a sympathetic stare. "An IED… er, improvised explosive device, hit close to his tent at the army post in Iraq, and it shattered bones in his legs and feet. However, he has recovered from the concussion."

Jake sat in silence, as if the life inside him had left his body.

She swallowed hard. "Why isn't he talking to us? Even looking at us?"

Chaplain Kanelos, who wore a small gold cross on both his lapels, frowned. "He quit talking to anyone after the incident. We don't know why. But he was diagnosed with PTSD."

Officer Dugan nodded. "These are the reasons he was medically discharged."

Her mother approached the men, hands on hips and a snarl on her lips. "You've destroyed my grandson."

Stephanie's mind raced with horrible images she believed he might have witnessed. Angry heat mixed with her agony. "Thanks to the army drafting him, my son will suffer the rest of his life!"

Her mother spat out, "How many other young men and women's lives have you ruined?"

Officer Dugan held up his hands. "I understand your frustrations and anger."

"No, you don't," Ava snapped. "Do you have a kid stuck over in that hell?"

"Well, no—"

"See?" Ava retorted.

Chaplain Kanelos clasped his hands in a gesture for a truce. "There are good therapists for people suffering from PTSD, which the VA will pay for."

"That should be a given," Ava grumbled.

A sliver of hope stirred Stephanie's heart. "How can we get him set up for this therapy?"

"We've already set it up with the VA. He starts next Monday."

Hobo nudged his head under one of Jake's hands.

"We're very sorry your son has suffered these injuries," Dugan said.

"I'd like to say a prayer if you don't mind," said Officer Kanelos.

Ava came alongside Stephanie, putting an arm around her shoulders. "Go ahead."

Stephanie worked to stay in the bubble of peace the prayers brought and vowed she'd help Jake every hour, every day until he healed. Although the protest was this afternoon and the lockdowns were in effect, she'd have her mother take her and Jake straight to church and have Deacon Michael anoint him with holy oil. So many healings had happened to people from the oil. Why shouldn't it happen for her beautiful son?

Thirty-Eight

A block down from the church, Stephanie's mother parked the car under one of the large oak trees lining the street. Its canopy of branches and leaves sheltered and hid the Subaru from any possible passing drones.

Stephanie opened a section of her purse, slid her hand inside, and clutched the pistol. She swallowed her fear and felt a sense of security with the firearm.

"Be careful," her mother said.

"I will."

The partly cloudy sky shed faint rays of sunlight on the area. Patches of grass in the median were a deep green due to yesterday's drenching rain.

Surveying the empty road, Stephanie quietly opened the passenger car door and went to the back of the vehicle, pulling out Jake's folded wheelchair.

After she helped him out of the back seat and settled him in the chair, she bent to look at her mother in the car. "Please pick us up in an hour if you can. If something comes up, we'll stay in the church until you're able to come get us."

Ava gave her a thumbs-up. "Got it."

With one more sweep of the street and sky, Stephanie moved carefully and pushed Jake toward the back of the church as quickly as she could.

Two black drones streaked across the sky. She froze under one of the oaks buttressing the sidewalks around the church. The flying machines had already disappeared. She exhaled, then pushed Jake toward the back gate.

Out of nowhere, two young men appeared from behind a bush, knives in their hands. Her heartbeat thumped against her ribs as they approached her and Jake at a fast pace.

"Skipping lockdown, are we, pretty one?" one of them said, his grin showing bright teeth against his filthy complexion.

The streets remained deserted, and her son was helpless. "What do you want?" she asked, but she had a good idea why they were there.

The other man, who was tanned and had large brown eyes, held out his hand that didn't hold a knife. "Hand over your wallet."

She swallowed the nonexistent saliva in her dry mouth and nodded. Taking hold of her purse to unzip the middle section, she, instead, opened the partition where the gun lay.

Before she could shove her hand inside, the first man stepped closer to Jake and held up his knife. "Slowly."

His proximity to her vulnerable son sparked a raging fire inside her. She stuck her hand inside her purse, slowly as directed. Grasping the gun, she whipped her hand out of the bag and pointed it at the man, then the other one who moved forward.

"Stay away from my son!"

The two men paused and held up their hands. "Hey, no problem." Their eyes exchanged something conspiratorial that had Stephanie pointing the gun back and forth from one to the other.

They smiled at each other, then her. "She don't know how to use it," the first man said and pointed at her shaking hand.

"Yeah, she's bluffing," the other said.

The first man sauntered a foot closer to Jake.

Stephanie held the gun with both hands, aiming it at the first man's torso. "Take another step, and I'll shoot."

Both men laughed before the first one lifted his hand to touch Jake's head.

Stephanie clenched her teeth and pulled the trigger. The *bang* pierced her eardrums.

The bullet penetrated the man's stomach, leaving a crimson stain.

Shock locked her in place as she stared at the gun in her trembling hand.

Jake groaned, the first sound from him since he'd returned home. His arms lifted to cover his head. His body shook like a mini earthquake was inside him.

The gunfire. Oh no! She put her free hand on Jake's shoulder. "I'm sorry, son!"

The shot man bent forward, then stumbled backward, dropping his knife on the ground. His eyes wide, his mouth gaping, he said, "She shot me."

As if to avenge her harming his partner, the other man sprang toward her.

Her shock vanished, replaced with protective instinct. She pointed the firearm at the other man. "I'll do it again if you don't leave us alone!"

He backed up and grabbed his friend's arm. "Let's get out of here."

The wounded man limped after his partner down the street and turned the corner, out of sight.

She leaned against the gate, feeling weak, as her heartbeat continued to pound against her rib cage. Glancing up to thank God, the same drones circled back, going the opposite direction.

Placing the pistol in her purse, she pushed Jake's chair back under the nearby tree.

The drones streamed toward the east, oblivious of them. Stephanie wiped her damp forehead, then gazed at her unresponsive son.

A laugh erupted from her as she imagined what Jake would've said before he'd been injured. *"Shit, Mom, you've got skills. A real markswoman.*" The laugh turned into giggles. She bent, holding her belly.

The blare of a siren in the distance snapped her back into her surroundings, and she grasped the handles of the wheelchair. Scanning the empty street, she nodded. "Time to get inside."

Thirty-Nine

Safely reaching the back steps to the church, Stephanie rolled Jake up the side ramp to the cracked-open door. A broken padlock hung from a chain on one of the handles.

Where did that come from?

The door opened fully with Father Sergius filling the space.

Where's Deacon Michael?

Behind him, Olga's wrinkled, solemn face pressed between the frame and the monk's arm.

"Olga!" The sight of the elderly woman brought tears of joy to Stephanie.

Father Sergius moved aside as Stephanie approached Olga, giving her a hug and kiss on the cheek.

Stephanie looked at the monk. "It's good to see you too, Father."

He gave her a small smile and stroked his beard. "And you. Thank God you're all right." His attention turned to her son in the wheelchair. "Hello. We haven't met."

Jake's head was up slightly, his eyes staring at nothing.

Her throat closed. Swallowing back tears, she laid a hand on his shoulder. "This is my son, Jake. He just returned from the war this morning."

The monk squatted in front of Jake. "God bless you."

Her son continued to stare past the monk, then blink.

Stephanie gently squeezed his shoulder and kissed his cheek. "I'd like to get him anointed by the deacon."

A blast shot flames up from a house across from the church. Black smoke rose in the tepid air.

Stephanie gripped the handles on the wheelchair. "Hurry! Inside!"

Father Sergius ushered them into the church after Olga and closed the door behind them.

Stephanie remembered the padlock. "Is there a reason there's a new lock on the door?"

Father Sergius's face drooped, along with Olga's.

Olga took Stephanie's hand in hers. "You haven't been here in a while. The cat is trapped in the attic."

Stephanie looked to the monk for help.

Father Sergius gestured her and the others down a hallway toward the front of the building. "Come. I will explain to you once we're in a safer area."

"Safer?" A chill trickled down her spine. "Has the church been targeted?"

The monk continued walking ahead while she pushed Jake, and Olga hobbled alongside her.

They reached the ancient elevator and entered. He pushed the Up button. Stephanie wrinkled her brow. *We're going to the balcony?*

On the top floor, they stood before the room with the painting of the Russian church she recalled seeing a few weeks ago. That encounter seemed like years ago.

The monk took the flashlight on the end table.

Stephanie followed Father Sergius while she pushed Jake through the secret passageways, the elevator to the basement, and more hallways to rooms, ending in front of one of them.

With the flashlight's beam on the door, Father Sergius put in a code, and the door opened to a dimly lit room and with a metal safe in the center. To her right, the other monk sat on a folding chair with a young girl, who looked familiar to Stephanie. The girl's blank stare and expressionless face eerily mirrored her son's.

"What's happened to her?" she found herself saying out loud. She covered her mouth. "I'm sorry. It's just..."

Olga's shaky hand clasped her forearm. "You've missed so much. Although I have to say, I just found out about the lost laundry shirt. Never to be found."

The elderly woman's convoluted statements only added to Stephanie's frustration and feelings of impending calamity.

"Hello, Stephanie," Father Herman said, rising. He turned his attention to his fellow monk. "How are things up there?"

"Better than it has been," Father Sergius said.

A faint floral and sweet scent that reminded her of holy relics drifted in the shadowed room only lit by two candles on top of the safe.

Stephanie sniffed. "I'm smelling... Are relics here?" Before the monks could answer, realization came back to her. She gaped. "Did you finally find the relics you were looking for?"

Father Herman opened the safe and pointed to the piece of the Cross and the half-burned yellow letter. "Indeed."

"That's wonderful!" Stephanie smiled and clasped her hands tightly as if in prayer. "What prophecy did you find in the saint's letter?"

The monk carefully opened the folded letter and read the only clear passage on it. "The blood will not stop running without repentance. He will come to our aid only when our hearts soften and warm like the comforting blaze of a fire in the hearth and love expands as wide as the earth's firmament."

The words sounded familiar to Stephanie. And the voice that had first uttered them. In the choir loft. Olga by the elevator. Before her daughter took her home. As if she'd been woken from a dream, Stephanie pivoted to face the elderly woman, who was now lowering herself onto a folding chair next to the one the girl sat in.

How had the woman remembered the saint's writings? Did she recall those words from her grandparents when she was a child? It was as if she'd memorized them. Perhaps she had. But she rarely recalled or retained anything. At least not in the past decade when she had become more confused and odder than she'd been when Stephanie first met her. "Olga, you told me these exact words when we were in the choir loft. You remembered a part of the saint's prophetic writings."

Olga's face pinched, her lips puckering. "I don't know what you're talking about. You must be mistaken. Delicates don't mix with whites in the wash." She tsked, then turned her attention to the little girl and brushed hair from the side of her angelic face.

The old woman gave an answer Stephanie was used to. And she knew the woman wouldn't return to the memory of what she'd said that day, so Stephanie let it go, but she'd never forget. She stepped toward them and bent in front of the girl. "What's your name, sweetheart?"

The girl didn't respond, but her blank stare moved to lock with Stephanie's gaze.

Olga continued to pet the girl. "This is Lindy."

Lindy. An image of a man and young girl sitting on the church steps flashed in her mind. "Oh, yes."

The monks and Olga gave her somber stares.

Stephanie scanned the room. Something wasn't right. "Where's Deacon Michael? Shouldn't he be here with us?"

Father Sergius, face drooping again, approached her. "Deacon Michael died two days ago."

Her breath caught in her throat. She stepped back. "What?"

"One of the men in a group of ruffians shot at the deacon and Olga, but the deacon shielded her. He died shortly after," Father Herman said.

Stephanie slouched, covering her mouth. "Oh my God. Poor Deacon."

"And..." Father Sergius leaned near her ear and whispered, "Lindy's father was killed yesterday." He crossed himself. "May their memories be eternal."

Stephanie's stare fell on the little girl. "Oh no. No wonder..."

The monk gave a nod.

Father Herman closed the safe, then approached the door and opened it. He turned. "Are you coming?"

"Yes," Father Sergius said. He laid a hand on Stephanie's shoulder. "We need to go check on things upstairs and outside. We will be back soon."

She could only nod as she continued to digest what the monks had told her. In the quiet room with two traumatized children and an elderly woman, who often left the present for a distorted realm, Stephanie faced one of the walls and let the tears fall.

Forty

Outside the church, voices chanted something indiscernible. Sergius peeked out the front door. Around a hundred people with flags and posters were marching down the street toward city hall, and their numbers continued to grow with people on the sidewalks joining them.

"What is happening out there?" Father Herman's voice came from behind.

"Looks like some type of protest."

"How are they doing that during the lockdown?"

"I don't know." Sergius looked back at his brother. "I'm going outside."

Father Herman touched his arm. "We must watch over the church."

They went onto the porch, Father Herman shutting the door behind him. Sergius set up the padlock so it didn't look damaged, then headed toward the end of the porch where the steps met them.

Down the street near city hall, a couple of blocks away, military tanks and police cars were parked on either side of the road. About fifty National Guard and law enforcement stood in two lines in front of the steps to city hall. Strings of them were on both sides of the street, overseeing the crowd. The guards people wore military fatigues while the police wore bulky blue uniforms with helmets and shields that reminded Sergius of the storm troopers in the *Star Wars* movies of many years ago.

Every few minutes, drones slid across the cloudy sky, their lights blinking.

"God help those people. They're right out in the open where they could get hurt," Father Herman said.

"I'm not sure what they can accomplish protesting."

"And during a lockdown."

Sergius crossed himself. "God, watch over them."

The chants morphed into angry shouts in unison, with the mob pushing toward the steps of city hall. A wave of people pressed against the military and police that led to shoving and yanking.

The town speaker hummed on. "People of Fairview, this is your mayor. We are still in lockdown. Go home, or we will arrest all of you and put you in jail indefinitely."

"No more! We're tired of the corruption, the lies, the police state!" someone screamed from the middle of the crowd.

Dozens of arms rose with something in their hands among the sea of people that seemed to have increased in numbers. Shots rang, followed by a blast that echoed down the street. Pillars of smoke rose in the steel-colored sky.

Sergius squinted and retreated toward the door. "The people have weapons?"

Father Herman scratched his beard. "I thought guns had been banned."

"Looks like some kept theirs."

"Lord, this doesn't bode well."

"No, not at all."

"Fairview police, arrest these lawbreakers." The mayor's gravelly voice sounded more like grumblings over the speaker.

"Come out here, you coward, and face us!" someone in the crowd shrieked.

"Quit hiding behind your PA system!" another person screamed.

More gunfire went off, followed by a collective chorus of battle cries.

The mob swarmed the police and guards. The officers beat the protestors with batons. The thump of a released canister of tear gas hitting the ground delivered smoke, smothering a portion of the crowd. Rounds of fitful coughs spat from the scrambling people.

More shootings rang out while people tumbled into one another. The drones returned, blasting lasers below, slicing people, their blood spilling on those next to them.

Sergius closed his eyes, grimacing. "Lord, have mercy. Please stop this madness."

Hand-to-hand combat ensued in front of Sergius and his brother. Stepping backward, Sergius grabbed Father Herman's arm and pulled him toward the church doors.

Knives glinted in the glare of the overcast sky. More blood spilled from a nearby policeman, who'd been stabbed in the neck by a protestor.

Another deadly bolt from a drone pulverized a handful of people on the right side of the street, leaving charred body parts. Sergius looked away with his hand over his mouth, as bile rose to his throat.

Down the street opposite city hall, a fresh horde of people ran toward the macabre scene.

Moments later, Sergius witnessed a group of police officers beating their fellow law enforcement members, as well as those in the National Guard. The swarm of people joining the protestors was growing in front of Sergius's eyes.

More drones struck the crowds, while shots continued to go off. Another canister of tear gas smoked a knot of people near the steps of the hall.

Sergius exchanged a sobering stare with his brother. Taking a breath the same time as Father Herman, Sergius began to chant with him, "Let God arise. Let His enemies be scattered..."

Remnants of ragged bodies and severed limbs littered the areas between those still standing in the streets near city hall.

With a queasy stomach, Sergius looked away and locked eyes with his brother. They chanted, once again, in unison, "As smoke is driven away, so drive them away…"

Crossing himself three times, Sergius joined his brother amid the chaos, saying, "As wax melts before the fire—"

An explosion blew up the street in front of the church. The ground shook. A wave of hot air swept over them. Chunks of debris flew in every direction. Sergius and his brother dove for the door of the church.

Stephanie paced the floor in the secret room. "Poor Deacon Michael."

"He was a good man," Olga said.

"There are no clergy to keep the services going. They seem even more important now than ever before."

"Without prayer and the liturgy, the world would collapse," Olga muttered.

"My church is closed."

Olga said nothing with her arm around a dazed Lindy.

"No one to anoint my son..." Stephanie laid a hand on Jake's shoulder, then shifted her gaze to Lindy. "Or poor little Lindy. We no longer have our church."

Olga gave her a piercing stare through her cataract-laden eyes. "Another priest will come."

"How? The government isn't going to allow it."

"Another priest will come."

The elderly woman's tone reflected lucidity. But how could she know?

Stephanie folded her arms tightly. "What's going on up there? We can't hear anything down here."

"Be grateful you can't." Olga rubbed her nose, her eyes drooping.

Stephanie sat on the floor next to Jake's chair and leaned her back against the wall, knees to her chest, hand on her forehead. "Where can we go to get Jake anointed?"

"Lily is late getting home from school." Olga clasped her hands in her lap and lifted her chin. "She probably missed the bus again."

Stephanie's shoulders slumped. She leaned her head on her forearms with her eyes closed as helplessness weakened her body.

The door opened, and Father Sergius entered with Father Herman behind him. Gray ash and smoke splotches covered their cassocks.

Stephanie sprang up and approached them. "Are you okay?"

Sergius nodded with a frown. His brother's expression was nearly identical.

"What's going on up there?"

"Battles...," Father Herman murmured.

She froze. "Battles? What kind of battles?"

Father Sergius held up a hand. "We need a moment of silence and prayer." His gaze traveled to Lindy and Jake. "For all of us."

"Okay." Stephanie pressed her hands together.

Father Herman opened the safe and set the sweet-smelling relics on top of the metal box.

Olga leaned on her cane, rose, and hobbled toward the relics. Stephanie rolled Jake closer to her and the safe, with the monks on either side of it. In a circle, they bowed their heads.

"Lord, Jesus Christ, have mercy on us," Father Sergius said.

"Lord, Jesus Christ, have mercy on us," Father Herman repeated.

Together, the monks said, "Lord, Jesus Christ, have mercy on us."

With just the light of the candles, for a moment, Stephanie felt like she'd been transported to the nave of the church. The aura surrounding them mimicked a Vespers.

The slight scent of beeswax mixed with the floral sweetness of the relics.

The aroma grew stronger, filling the space. The monks prostrated, lowering onto their knees, foreheads touching the floor, then back on their feet, repeating the movements.

Over the relics, an unearthly soft blue light appeared, then spread throughout the room, brightening everyone in its bluish-white glow. A warm comfort embraced Stephanie, filling her with an incomprehensible joy. Tears welled in her eyes, and she found herself smiling. The peace settling around and within her matched the joy she was experiencing.

The light slowly diminished, leaving them with the glowing candles.

Olga beamed in her childlike way that always comforted Stephanie. Lindy stood next to Olga. Her eyes, no longer vacant, she stared at the Cross of Christ.

Clasping her hands as in prayer, Stephanie gazed at her son. His eyes sparkled, focused on the Cross. His face was as illuminated as the unworldly light she'd witnessed a moment ago.

She fell to her knees next to him as tears streamed down her cheeks. "Jake! Jake!" She gathered him into her arms and hugged him tightly.

"Mom, that light was intense."

She chuckled, her heart soaring, hearing his voice again. Letting him go, she gazed at his face.

Jake's brows came together as if in thought. "It felt like when I was a kid and sick and you'd cuddle me in your arms. It felt real nice."

Stephanie squeezed his hand. "It did. So much."

Olga bent and kissed the relics. "Glory to God."

The monks, still on their knees, kissed the relics, then crossed themselves.

"Glory to God," Father Sergius said.

"Glory forever," Father Herman replied.

Lindy stepped in front of the piece of the Cross. "I saw my daddy."

"Where?" Stephanie asked.

She lifted her eyes to Stephanie. "He hugged me and said he'd always love me and that I'd be okay." Tears glistened in her eyes. "I miss him so much."

Stephanie embraced Lindy. "He's always with you even if you can't see him."

Olga sat in her chair and gestured for Lindy to sit with her. Lindy took the seat next to the elderly woman and leaned against her plump body.

"My child, it's all right to miss your daddy and cry," Olga said. "You will stay with me and my daughter. We'll take care of you."

Lindy wrapped her arms around Olga's waist and buried her face in her chest. "You make me feel okay, Miss Olga."

Olga patted her back. "God takes care of us."

As Father Herman returned the relics to the safe, Father Sergius went to the door. "We're going up to find out what's going on."

Jake rose from his wheelchair. "Mom, I wanna go too."

Gaping at Jake standing, Stephanie pointed to his legs. "Are you okay to be on your feet?"

He looked down at his feet. "Yeah. I'm fine, Mom."

Crouching in front of her son's shins, she laid hands on his casts, then glanced back at the relics. Realization tingled through her. The Cross had done more than give Jake back his voice. Tears poured from her eyes once more. She grinned and hugged her son. "Thank you, God!"

With peace lingering in the quietness of the space, everyone left the room and headed to the narthex.

Father Sergius opened the front doors while Olga hunched over the icon of Saint John. The streams of blood that had run down the painted wood the past few weeks were gone.

Olga made the sign of the cross and gazed at the ceiling. "Thank you, Lord, for Your mercy."

Stephanie came alongside Olga and kissed the icon after her. "Thank God." She touched the saint's robe.

The monks stepped onto the front porch. Stephanie and Jake filed out after them. The pungent smell of burned flesh and smoke hung in the air.

Stephanie grimaced, feeling sick to her stomach. Icy fear added to her malaise. Logan had been out protesting. *Is he okay?*

Down the sparsely populated street, charred cars with pillars of smoke rising from their hollowed-out bodies littered the road. Beyond them, a crowd pressed against the steps and doors to city hall. Their faint, indiscernible shouts carried down to where Stephanie and the others stood. She squinted, focusing on the mass of people, hoping somehow she could locate Logan.

She felt the urge to run to city hall but checked on Jake and the others first. There was a sense of security with all of them together by the church. It satisfied her concerns. "I'll be back in a few minutes. I promise."

"'Kay, Mom. Be careful," Jake said.

Stephanie sprinted down the street and reached the back of the crowd. A dozen National Guard stood on either side of the stairs. On tiptoes, she scanned the occupied steps and area in front of city hall's doors flanked by four policemen. Twenty soldiers, along with eleven policemen lined the front of city hall's large windows on either side of the double doors. On the porch in front of the building, a few cops were holding some citizens, including a police officer already in handcuffs. His hair was striking—a platinum blond color. The man looked familiar. *Holland?* The man her mother had talked about. And he was arrested. His cover must have been blown somehow.

People pressed against her from both sides.

For space, Stephanie pushed her shoulder into a woman's arm, glancing at her face. She looked close to her mother's age. "Sorry," Stephanie muttered, then focused on the woman. Maybe she'd been in the streets during the whole protest and had information on Logan.

Stephanie leaned toward her. "What's going on?"

The woman eyed her. "What?"

"I'm sorry. I just got here. Could you tell me what's happened?"

"Stephanie."

Logan's voice. Stephanie whipped her head around while standing on tiptoes. *Where is he?* "Logan?"

He appeared out of a cluster of people on her left. She reached for him as he approached and pulled her into a fierce embrace. Joy swelled inside her. "You're okay!"

"Yeah." He let her go.

"What's going on?"

"We're waiting for the mayor. He announced he'd come out and talk to us since everything is under control." A hint of mystery flashed in his brown eyes.

"Under control?"

He gave her a slow nod. "Yes. The protest is over, and the police have done their job, arresting some of us."

She touched his arm. "But you're not."

"No, and I don't plan to be."

He seemed to be speaking in some type of cryptic manner like he'd done on the CB radio the first time she'd heard him on there, which now seemed like a lifetime ago. She shook her head in confusion.

"Wait and see," he said.

The doors opened. Mayor Bryant, holding a megaphone, walked out with two men flanking him. He smiled at the guards, soldiers, and law enforcement. Stopping in the center of the patio, he said, "I'm pleased you've taken care of the rioting."

The policemen on his left rushed him, taking the mouthpiece from his hand. The mayor yelped before shrieking, "What are you doing?"

One officer cuffed him while a few others did the same to his bodyguards.

The cop holding the cuffed blond officer released him.

Logan raced up the steps through a narrow path the crowd parted for him, and he took the megaphone handed to him. A man with auburn hair and a mustache and the blond cop came alongside him, one raising his fist in the air, the other planting his hands on his hips.

"You and your cronies are done, Bryant. We've got proof that the state government used our military's drones on us citizens. That you murdered twenty-nine homeless people by bombing their new shelter and two more in the bombed administrative building, along with three protest organizers working there."

The mayor's face lost all color. His jaw dropped. He struggled against the two cops on either side of him. They gripped him tighter. He stopped moving, his gaze lowering to the ground.

"We have plenty of contacts inside yours and the feds' circles. We and our fellow resisters in each state, who've protested today.

President Harden will be resigning soon. His corrupt business dealings with Lithuanian drug lords and the profits he and his administration and others in congress got from weapons sales and the use of illegal chemical weapons used in the worst war in human history will send him and his fellow criminals to jail for life."

People hooted and whistled, and someone yelled, "Yeah! Where they belong!"

Logan held up a hand, and the crowd grew silent. "We won't forget the killing of millions of our men and women for greed. Thankfully for us, an hour ago, our sources within the Pentagon said a cease-fire had been implemented last night our time and an armistice has been produced and will be signed within twenty-four hours. No more bloodshed. The terror is over."

A chorus of cheers rang out, and the people next to Stephanie jumped up and down.

Stephanie cried, "Thank God!"

While Logan was busy with his group of resisters and the mayor, Stephanie waved at him and jogged back to her son and the others.

"What's going on, Mom?" Jake asked.

She kissed his cheek, then hugged him. "The war's over! The rotten criminals in our government have been held accountable. A lot of change is on the way."

"Indeed, Stephanie. Our repentant prayers have reached our Lord. His Light and Peace are upon us," Olga said, then touched Stephanie's cheek. "And soon Father Alexander will arrive to preside over the church services."

The monks crossed themselves.

"Thank God for all these things," Father Sergius said.

Father Herman beamed.

"That's a lot of awesome news," Jake said.

"Yes. Lots of awesomeness." Stephanie chuckled and draped an arm around her son's shoulders.

Lily's Volkswagen Bug pulled up to the curb ahead of Ava's Subaru.

Lily emerged from her car, gasped at the leftover carnage in the street, then rushed Olga and Lindy into her car. They drove off.

Her mother's old Subaru sat at the curb, and Ava hurried out of the car toward them. She embraced Jake, kissing his cheeks. "Holy God, Grandson! You're walking!"

"Yeah, Gran. I've been doing it since I was one."

Stephanie and her mother laughed.

Ava grabbed one of Jake's cheeks. "Yes, you have. Now you and your mom get in the car. We're going home."

Forty-Two

Stephanie stopped by the café to share the good news with her friend and boss, Abby. As she walked in, Abby was talking with a woman with long black hair and a teenaged boy next to her. The woman looped her arm around the young man's and beamed.

Abby spotted Stephanie and waved her over. "It's good to see you! Feels like years since we've seen each other. How's Jake?"

She grinned. "He's doing great."

"We'll be able to open back up next week, thank goodness," Abby said, then looked to the woman and young man. "Oh! Meet Mary and her son, Noah. He'd been drafted into the horrible war, but he's back and doing well."

"Yes, my son came home safe and sound." Mary beamed.

Stephanie shook the woman's hand. "That's wonderful. Nice to meet you."

"Mary will be working with us."

"Great," Stephanie said.

While Mary and her son were talking, Abby leaned over and whispered in Stephanie's ear. "She was on the street, homeless, for I don't know how long."

Stephanie recalled what her mother had said about the homeless hotel and all that had happened. Mary must have been one of the few survivors. And her son came home safe. Both Jake and Noah came home. If only Laura had come home too. She made a mental note to visit Pam's grave.

Taking Abby's hand in hers, she said, "Abby, you're an angel."

"I try." Abby batted her eyelashes.

"And the war's over. The crooks are going to jail. Amazing times we live in."

"Amazing is right!"

AROUND SIX THIRTY THAT EVENING, SOMEONE KNOCKED on Stephanie's front door. Hobo raced to the foyer, barking.

She rushed to the door and found Logan on the porch. Hobo sniffed him, then jumped on his legs, a smile on his face, tongue hanging out.

"I'm so glad you came by!" She wrapped her arms around Logan.

He held her tightly against him. "Me too."

After Stephanie let him go, Logan bent and petted Hobo.

She took his arm and guided him to the den, as Hobo trotted next to them.

Her mother, who was sitting in her chair, gazed up from her novel. "Wait a minute. Is that Logan?"

He nodded. "Sure is, Ms. Jenkins."

Ava sat up and removed her reading glasses. "You haven't changed much, young man."

Grinning, he tilted his head. "A little."

Sitting on the couch, Jake gave him a puzzled expression. "Mom, have I ever met him? Like maybe when I was a kid, because I don't remember this dude."

Stephanie chuckled. "No, you wouldn't, honey. He was my boyfriend in our last year of high school."

Sizing up Logan, Jake leaned back against the couch cushion. "Wow. That's a long time ago."

Stephanie shoved her son's arm. "Not *that* long ago."

Everyone laughed.

"Tell me, Logan. What's the situation with our local and federal governments," Ava asked.

"For our federal government's administration, a temporary one will be in place with people from every political party until the next general election in eight months. Officials in the interim administration and those left in Congress, who weren't arrested for any crimes, had to push the election back to give ample time for new candidates to campaign and for our country's systems to be reformed for voting in the elections."

"Local elections for a new governor and mayor and other officials will take place in six months. There's a lot of work that must be done to rebuild our government structures and systems, and it'll be done by the people, for the people." He gave a thumbs-up. "These elections will be the first honest and free ones in decades."

"That's what I like to hear." Ava clapped her hands. "Bravo! And if you need any help, let me know." She winked at him.

With a wide grin, Logan said, "I'll keep that in mind." He checked his watch. "I've got to get going."

Stephanie walked him to the door and opened it. He stood on the porch and stared at the ground as if he was nervous.

Her stomach churned. "What is it?"

"Sorry. I'm still not good at this type of stuff." He glanced at her, then looked away, letting out a chuckle. "I haven't had any practice all these years."

Practice? What was he getting at? It had been too many years for her to read him like she used to.

Her anxiousness and curiosity grew. "What type of stuff? And practice of what?"

"Well, it's just." He shoved his hands in his jean pockets, a smile tugging at a corner of his mouth.

"Just what, Logan?" She fidgeted from one foot to the other. The man was driving her crazy and reminded her of his eighteen-year-old self, unable to commit to their relationship then. *Ohhh... Maybe that was it...* "Logan, just tell me."

"Okay, okay." He licked his lips and squinted at her. "Would you be willing to give us another try?"

Her heartbeat sped up; knees nearly buckled. "I think I can do that."

He exhaled. "How about dinner next Friday at our old hangout?"

"Luigi's?"

"You got it, and I'll pick you up."

"What time?"

"Six."

She leaned toward him and kissed his cheek. "See you then."

He turned so that her lips landed on his. Their kiss deepened, and her heart felt so light she thought she'd float away. When his lips parted from hers, he leaned his forehead against hers and rubbed his nose with hers. Sweet memories of their affectionate act from when they were teens resurfaced. Cozy warmth flooded her mind and heart. She laughed with tears in her eyes.

"See you next Friday," he said.

Logan was in his car a second later, driving down the street.

Stephanie leaned against the wood siding and sighed. "I'm going on a brand-new romantic adventure. No, a continued romantic adventure in a brand-new world."

Forty-Three

Sergius stood with his fellow monk in front of the glass case of relics at Saint Innocent's newly renovated monastery. The enclosure of treasures now included the piece of the Holy Cross and Saint Dimitri's prophetic letter.

Thank you, Lord. With a smile, Sergius crossed himself, along with Father Herman. They'd returned the relics safely. A sense of joy uplifted Sergius as he and his brother walked to the front doors.

They headed to the saint's grave. "Father Dimitri, your letter is back where it belongs," Sergius said.

Father Herman bent and touched the cross on his grave. "Saint Dimitri, pray for us."

When they turned to trod down the path toward the vegetable garden, an elderly father in an old cassock and *kamilavka* approached a bench next to the tomb. He sat and clasped his hands in his lap.

At first glance, the man didn't look familiar to Sergius, and his cheeks warmed. Didn't he know all the priests in the monastery? He glanced at his brother, who wore a confused expression. He didn't seem to know the elder either. Nevertheless, he needed to greet the old priest with reverence.

Sergius bowed with his hands cupped. "Father, bless."

The priest raised his hand and gave Sergius his blessing. Sergius kissed his hand. Father Herman and the priest did the same exchange. Before Sergius said anything else, the elder gazed at him with soft brown eyes and a small smile. There was something familiar about the man's face, but Sergius couldn't place him.

"Countries will rebuild, and it will take a while. Afterward, there will be peace for a few decades. God gives us this time through His mercy. The thirst for Christ by the multitude of souls will be so great that on every street corner, someone will be saying His name or asking about Him. The poor will become rich, along with their wealthy neighbors. And the Good News will spread to all the corners of the world. You have but one life on this earth to dedicate yourself to Christ and grow closer to Him. Use this time wisely and help rebuild His ministry and churches."

The elder rose, turned, and shuffled down a path toward the rose garden.

As if glued to the spot where he stood, it took a moment for Sergius to digest what the holy elder had said.

Father Herman stroked his beard. "The elder just gave us a prophetic homily."

Sergius could only nod as he took a few steps back to Saint Dimitri's grave. Squatting in front of the tomb that held a small black-and-white photo of the saint below the cross, Sergius placed a hand on the stone. "Father Dimitri, a priest just came…"

Sergius studied the faded picture of the saint whose eyes and face matched the elder's he'd just seen. Tears welled in his eyes, and he kissed the picture. "Glory to God."

THE END

Acknowledgments

I thank God for granting me the gift of writing. I'm thankful to my supportive family, especially my son, Nicholas, who has been a sounding board for my reading a chapter or portion of one. He has helped with excellent suggestions on the scenes, characters, and plot-line. My editor, D.A. Sarac, is a lifeline in making sure my novel is shined and polished. My critique partners for this novel, Paul, Scott, Tammy, Maven, Michelle, and Kim have been vital in the sharpening and polishing of my novel. Without these supportive people, my book would not be the finished product it is today. Thank you all!

About the Author

Dorothy Robey writes predominantly under her pen name, Dorothea Anna. She writes primarily women's fiction with usually a splash of suspense, humor, and Greek Orthodox traditions. However, she's published books in political satire and dystopian genres. Dorothy lives with her family in beautiful Colorado.

Website: https://dotluvs2write.com

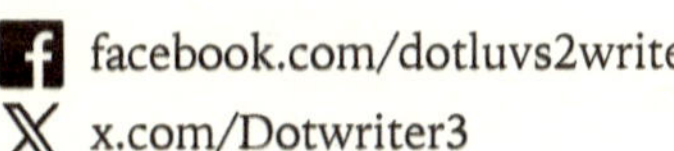

facebook.com/dotluvs2write

x.com/Dotwriter3

Passage of Promise

What She Didn't Know

Behind the Stone House

The Rocky Retreat

Painted with Good Intentions